CW01464743

Prologue - **The Serpent's Dt**

"The river keeps what the sea cannot."

New Orleans, 1853.

The summer heat clung to the city like a fever. It filled the streets with the stink of fish and horse piss, of rotting cane and sweet decay. Beneath the galleries, in shadowed courtyards where lanterns burned blue, the drums had been beating for hours. Artemis Danger sat cross-legged on the worn brick floor, her white skirt clinging with sweat.

Around her, chalk veves had been drawn in careful lines: a crossroads of salt, ash, and powdered bone. She had seen these patterns before, but tonight they wavered as if they lived, their edges curling like smoke.

Mère Éloise leaned close, eyes glittering in the firelight. "You carry more than your own soul, girl. The sea did not spit you back for nothing."

Artemis wanted to answer, but her tongue was heavy. Her heartbeat thundered in her ears like surf.

Another priestess sprinkled rum and honey, whispering in Kreyòl: *Serpan, reveye. Serpan, pale.* The snake, wake. The snake, speak.

The room grew thick with shadows. From the farthest corner came the dry rasp of scales against stone. Artemis's vision blurred. She smelled river-mud, copper, and blood. Then her body convulsed. Her teeth rattled. Her hands clawed the air as if she were drowning again.

The women's voices rose, urgent now.

And in that writhing dark, Artemis saw it: a carved idol, serpent-headed, its eyes inset with shards of green stone. Bound around it was rope made not of hemp but of braided hair. She felt it watching her, hungering for her breath.

A voice spoke through her own throat, low and sibilant:

"The river keeps what the sea cannot. My body is broken, lost in the green hell. Bring me home, or be broken in turn."

Her back arched until she thought her spine might split. Then silence fell.

When Artemis woke, she lay in Mère Éloise's lap, trembling like a child. The veves around her had smeared into black stains. Her lips tasted of iron.

"You see now," said the priestess softly, stroking her damp hair. "Your life is not your own. You were spared for a reason. The idol waits, deep in the serpent's country. If it is not returned to the hands that know how to keep it, death will hunt you. Death, and worse."

Artemis tried to rise, but her body was weak, her blood pounding as if some hidden poison crept through her veins.

"I can't—" she began.

"You must," Éloise cut her short. "Or the curse will eat you bone by bone. And if you will not go for yourself, then go for us. There are men who would wield that serpent's power for chains and whips. We cannot allow it."

Through the open shutters, the night air pulsed with music: fiddles from the dance halls, a trumpet's cry. Life went on in New Orleans, careless and bright. But Artemis lay shivering, bound to a fate older and darker than the city's stones.

And so, before the week was done, she found herself pledged to a journey no woman in her right mind would take — from the Mississippi's mouth to Caracas, across mountains and jungles, into the very heart of the Amazon.

The serpent had called her. And the serpent would not be denied.

Table Of Content

Chapter I — Ash in the Veves

"A bargain struck in shadow binds deeper than blood."

She woke with ash in her mouth.

The courtyard was a ruin of last night's work: chalk veves smeared to gray mud by sweat and feet, spilled rum drying sticky on the bricks, candle stubs guttered into waxy tears. A bluebottle fly droned in the window-shade. Artemis lay still and counted—in, one... two... three... out, one... two... three—until the tremor in her hands eased enough to push herself upright.

Her white skirt had gone a gutter-water slate. She brushed at it and only made the stains larger. The smudged sigils on the ground looked like the map of some country that had decided to swallow itself.

Mère Éloise stood in the doorway with a basin and a folded cloth. "You'll wash. Then you'll eat. After that, you'll listen."

Artemis nodded, throat raw as singed rope. The water was cool on her face, cool in the dry cup of her mouth. She counted again—seven gulps, exactly—and forced the last swallow past the iron taste lingering on her tongue. When she lowered the basin, the world steadied by a hair. Her heartbeat no longer sounded like surf inside her skull, only an impatient fist at the door.

Outside, the city stretched and yawned. Somewhere along the river the long horn of a steamboat called, and the sound made her stomach go slick with wanting: to be on water without drowning, to be carried without being taken.

Éloise crossed to the veves with her bare feet and a slow patience that made Artemis feel like a child. The priestess knelt and dipped the cloth in rum, cleaning a line with careful strokes until the crossroads reappeared, a ghost within the smear. "The ash settles," she said, as if to herself. "But the pattern is still there."

"What came through—" Artemis began. Her voice failed.

"We heard." Éloise did not look up. "And we believed before we heard."

They were alone. The other women had gone home to children and men, or to the work that kept them fed—the laundry tubs, the kitchens, the beds. The House felt too quiet without their breath and laughter, like a drum left cooling by the fire. Sun came in through the shutter-lattice and drew bands across Éloise's shoulders, the muscles moving beneath her skin like ropes shifting on a deck.

"What is it," Artemis said, "that wants me?"

Éloise wrung the cloth. Rum pattered on the bricks. "Not a god you know by church-name, not one who loves to be called in public. An old guardian carried over when our mothers were carried over. It traveled hidden, wrapped in hair and prayer. It was stolen by men who prayed another way and taken upriver where green swallows sky. It has been vexed ever since. To be bound and carried is an insult that stones remember." She glanced at Artemis then, and the glance was not unkind. "You were marked by water. You came to us soaked in its anger. The thing that speaks for the guardian knows you will walk where others refuse."

"I barely walked from the sea," Artemis said. "I crawled."

"Crawling is an honest verb." Éloise made a small smile. "You live. That's what it wanted. Living women can be made to fetch."

Artemis stared at the fractured sigils. In the corner of the room, where shadow pooled deepest, she thought she heard again the faint dry rasp of scales against stone. It might have been memory. It might have been roaches. She pressed her tongue hard to the roof of her mouth and tasted ash and blood. "If I don't go?"

"You'll sour from the inside." Éloise's eyes sharpened, not cruel but bracing. "There are signs. They will come in countable ways, because spirits do love their numbers. First the dreams. Then the nosebleeds. Then the hands will shake and you'll drop what you love. Then the seizures. Then the fever that burns without sweat. I could be wrong in the order. But not in the end."

Artemis flexed her fingers. They obeyed, though a twitch ran along the thumb like a fish under skin. "Last night—"

"You did well for a woman with weight tied to her." Éloise folded the cloth and set it aside. "And it is not only you." She wiped her palms on her skirt and stood, taller somehow now that instruction had become a blade. "There is a man from Caracas buying in the markets, asking shameful questions with clean hands. He wants our history as if it were a bolt of cloth. He has coin enough and men enough to make fools of the hungry. If he finds what you were called to find, he will sell it to men who know how to make chains fit the living and the dead."

"Who is he?"

"Some Hidalguito with waxed hair and a cane like a snake. They give themselves new names when old ones rot. He called himself Don Iñigo. He paid a boy to bring him to our door. He did not come in." Éloise's mouth flattened. "He spoke to the boy across the street instead and asked why girls in white came to this house at night. He asked other questions too that don't belong in any honest mouth."

Artemis tasted bile. "He's still here?"

"Not for long. There's a brigantine loading rice and flour at the wharf, bound for La Guaira. We heard his man curse the swell yesterday. He will take that ship." Éloise brushed the veve's center with her fingertips as if soothing an animal. "You will take another. The same sea. Different teeth."

A clock chimed somewhere—a neighbor's parlor, one of those dignified timepieces that kept respectable hours while the street kept its own. Artemis counted the strokes without meaning to. Seven. She let the number lodge behind her teeth.

"I have no money for ships," she said.

"You have favors. And you have a face that looks like it knows how to keep a secret." Éloise crooked a finger and led her inside, past the curtained bed, past the table where a bowl of limes perfumed the air with their green bitterness, to a trunk under the window. From within it she drew a small oilskin packet tied with twine. "This was left for you."

Artemis recognized it before Éloise set it in her hands. The old waterproof skin, the twine knotted in an impatient sailor's hand. The leather smelled of salt and smoke and long pockets. She untied it. Within lay the cards—a deck cut down to only a handful, the rest long lost to ship and storm. The Queen of Cups lay on top, her face serene and stupidly kind, her chalice overflowing with what might be water, might be blood. Underneath, the Tower split with lightning, people falling headfirst into the dark. Artemis had carried these through her wreck, through her hunger, through the House. She had not opened them since the night she crawled ashore and lay on her face on the levee stones and swore to listen only to bodies, not to symbols.

"Take them," Éloise said. "A thing you keep and refuse to use still works on you—but crooked. Better to look it in the face."

Artemis shuffled the cards and drew two without prayer. Queen of Cups. The Tower. The same pair she'd seen when she still had a ship under her feet. She made a low sound that could have been a laugh if you slapped a coat on it. "Well then."

"Water and ruin," Éloise said. "A woman who holds both." She went to the shelf and took down a small spoon carved from pale bone. Its bowl was shallow, smooth as river stone. "And this."

Artemis took it as one takes a child, with reluctant care. "What is it?"

"A spoon," Éloise said, smiling for true now. "And a compass. Hold it over a basin and drip water through salt. If it turns, the thing you want is near. If it doesn't, the thing you want is hiding." She closed Artemis's fingers over it. "It belongs to the House. When you come back, you bring it home."

"When I come back," Artemis repeated. The words felt like a plank thrown out over empty air. She put the spoon in her pocket beside the knife that had been a sailor's and then hers, the familiar balky weight of it a comfort against the bone.

"Go see Baptiste," Éloise said. "On the river. He owes me two days and one apology. He knows which captains can be trusted, and which will sell your name for a bottle. He will send you to the right wharf and put the right lie in your mouth."

"What lie?"

"That you are going south for love." Éloise's mouth wrinkled in pleasure at her own joke. "Men will believe more quickly in love than in curses."

The House of Veils opened timidly to the street, as if the door were a mouth that had been slapped too often for speaking. Artemis stepped into the day and the day stepped into her: heat like a hand on the back of the neck, scent of chicory and frying dough and the river's wet iron. Down on the banquette a boy drove a lopsided mule with a cart of melons, calling *pastèk* as if the word itself were sweet. A pair of girls in yellow kerchiefs laughed into their hands and did not bother to hide that they were laughing at a passing man's hat.

Artemis turned toward the levee, keeping to the shade and counting her steps to keep her breath in order.

Thirteen to the corner. Twenty-one to the alley with the sagging gallery where laundry dripped like white tongues. Thirty-four to the back gate of the yard where the cane man sharpened his knife against his own teeth. She stopped counting when the river's voice drowned the numbers: the creak of lines, the slap of the water's palm against stone, the calls of men whose lives were rope and distance.

Baptiste Roux kept an office that barely contained itself. It was more of a long shed leaned up against a wharf-pile, tar-scented, its door hung open so the river could lean in. He sat behind a desk scabbed over with old wax drippings and letter-seals, his shirt unbuttoned to his breastbone, his hair tied with a bit of red string. He had a face like a coin that had traveled so much its king was unrecognizable.

"Éloise's girl," he said without surprise, as if the river had sent him a note beforehand. "I heard the drums last night. You break anything important?"

"Only myself," Artemis said. "She said you owe her two days and an apology."

"The apology, yes. The two days, maybe. What do you need?"

"Passage." She took the oilskin packet from her pocket and set it on the desk. No need to open it; the smell alone told a story. "South and east. To Caracas, or La Guaira."

Baptiste's eyes narrowed. "Bad harbor and worse mountains. You planning to go to church when you get there? Or to jail?"

"Love," Artemis said, and lifted her chin. "The kind that eats."

Baptiste laughed so hard he had to grab the desk. "God's balls. Éloise told you to say that, didn't she."

"She did."

"Well, it's a better lie than most. A captain won't look too hard at a woman running toward a man. Toward a woman, that gets talk you don't want. Toward money, that gets interest you don't want." He sobered. "You'll take the *San Ignacio*. Jory Black's got her for this run— he'll drink, but he won't gamble his ship, and he can make weather talk to him if it comes to that. He's at Wharf Nine today, loading. He owes me three dollars and a bottle of rye. You tell him if he gives you any grief I'll tell his wife what he does with his afternoons."

"Does he have a wife?"

"I'll tell one of them." Baptiste leaned back until his chair sighed. "Who else you taking?"

Artemis felt the numbers come back, a habit as old as fear. "I don't know yet. Seven, Éloise said." She did not add that the number had weighed on her since she woke: seven gulps, seven bell-strokes, now seven bodies to stand between her and the green that wanted her bones. "I thought to ask Tamsin. She can shoot and sew, and she's got a back like a dock-post."

"And a mouth like a saw." Baptiste grinned without disliking. "You'll want a man who can read jungle as if it were written in French. Not me. I've had vines around my ankles but only as a joke. There's a fellow off a Venezuelan brig calls himself Isidro. He tells lies with the grace of a saint and the detail of a ledger. If half of them are true, he's walked with jaguars." He scratched a name on a scrap and slid it across. "And you'll need a man who can lift things without anyone seeing his hands. Jonah Bell. He used to steal for a living until he learned there was better coin in making people believe he might. He's been wanting to leave this city ever since he discovered he can't." Baptiste's mouth angled. "You'll want someone who knows missionaries, because missionaries are a road all by themselves. Sister Séverine will know who took ship upriver last year and never came back, and who pretends not to mind."

Artemis tucked the names away. "And you?"

"I owe Éloise," he said, softer, like a man remembering a night he almost drowned. "But I've got a wife sick with the child and a boy with a cough that sounds like a door hinge. I'll get you to your wharf and I'll see you sign with a captain who won't sell your hair as a charm. After that, I'll drink to your health and to your foolishness." He stood, came around the desk, and took her hand in both of his. His palms were callused and smelled of hemp. "You're walking into green teeth. You know that."

"I do."

"You'll bring me a story when you come back."

"When I come back." The plank again, out over air. She let the words lie on it like weight. "I'll bring you a story with teeth."

Baptiste's grin creased one cheek deeper than the other. "Wharf Nine, then. If you meet a boy selling oranges with a cough, give him a copper and tell him his father says to stop pretending he doesn't like syrup."

The *San Ignacio* sat low in the water and looked like a woman who'd gotten through her marriages by learning when to bite. She was two-masted, rigging neat as braids, her hull tar-shiny, her carved saint on the prow worn soft by hands and weather. Men moved along her decks with that half-skip step of people who knew that to be careless was to be dead and yet had let carelessness touch them often enough to call it by a nickname.

Jory Black stood with his boots at the edge of his gangplank, watching rice sacks walk themselves aboard on men's backs. He was long and dry as a cane stalk left in the sun, scar white across one cheekbone. His hat had been a handsome hat once and now was a hat that held shade. He looked Artemis over in one slow pass that did not feel like a hand and did not feel like charity either.

"You Roux's errand?" he asked.

"He says you owe him," Artemis said. "Three dollars and a bottle of rye."

"I owe him five and a beating." Jory Black's mouth showed the smallest white of tooth. "What do you want, and how much can you pay?"

"La Guaira." Artemis kept her shoulders squared. "I can pay thirty before the gangway lifts and thirty more if I walk off your deck alive at the other end." The number hurt. It was almost everything the House could spare from the blue bowl under Éloise's table, coins given by women who ironed other women's dresses and washed other women's sheets, by men who didn't say where they got theirs but came to the courtyard anyway when the fever took their brothers.

"And what do you carry?" Jory's eyes flicked to her pockets out of practice, not suspicion.

"A spoon," Artemis said. "And a knife. And a lie for customs." She held his gaze. "Love."

He snorted. "The dirtiest kind. Any baggage?"

"Only what my hands can hold." She lifted the oilskin packet. "And this."

Jory tilted his head. "Cards?"

"Memories." She tucked them back.

"You sleep where I tell you and you don't wander at night," Jory said. The lazy humor left him. "Men get strange on water and they get stranger when the moon bites them. If anyone puts hands on you you call the man with the short leg 'Hob.' He'll put a rope around them. If you put a knife in someone, holler first so we can throw him over neat. I don't like stains." He held out his hand. "Deal?"

Artemis took it. His grip was dry and firm and smelled of tar. "Deal."

"You get the rest of your seven on board, do it quick. We don't sit so long we start to rot." He looked past her then, toward the street, where the world broke and came back together as people moved through it. "What's your name?"

"Artemis."

"Artemis who?"

She waited a heartbeat, two, three. "Artemis Danger."

"Jesus Mary." He barked a laugh. "Then you're suited to my deck." He pointed with his chin. "Hob will show you your berth. If you need to piss, you piss where he tells you. You go over the side when you're meant to, the sea won't mistake you for something it's allowed to keep."

She followed Hob—short leg, yes, but a stride like an oxcart—down into the dimness where the ship smelled of pitch and old bread and the ghost of pepper. Hammocks hung in rows like a field of tired smiles. She chose one with her back to a bulkhead and a view of the ladder and set the oilskin under it, the knife under the oilskin, her hand over both. Counting quieted her again: knots in the hammock line, thirteen; slats in the ladder, eight; the breath of the man two pallets down, long-short-long, long-short-long.

When she came back on deck, the sky had put on a wider blue and the sun was standing there as if to say, *You will answer to me today.* She stepped to the rail and let the river wind blow her hair off her neck. Across the wharf a slender figure in a gray dress leaned a hip against a stack of barrels and raised one gloved hand in a lazy salute.

"Tamsin," Artemis called, and the name lifted something inside her that had been dragging one ankle. She went light-footed across the gangway, ignoring Hob's grunt, and in three steps she had the woman by both hands.

Tamsin Reed looked like a Sunday in a city that kept Saturdays late. Her hair was a tidy riot under a hat that might have come from a dead lady's trunk, and her eyes were the color of pewter taken from a cold church. She squeezed Artemis's fingers bruisingly hard. "You look like you've been prayed over with bad grammar," she said.

"I was," Artemis said, and wanted to laugh and didn't. "Will you come with me?"

"To Caracas?" Tamsin's eyebrows climbed. "I've never even pretended to speak Spanish. Besides, there's a man at the tailor's who thinks I'm in love with him and I'd hate to disappoint him by being alive."

"The House needs me to go," Artemis said, and then, naked in the mouth, "I need me to go."

Tamsin's face changed. Something sly and bright slid aside to let seriousness stand. "And if you don't?"

"I rot," Artemis said simply. "And men with clean hands get what doesn't belong to them."

Tamsin looked down at her gloved hands and tugged the fingers, one by one, as if warming them. "All right," she said. "But you're paying me if we don't die, and if we do die I'm going to haunt you. I've been practicing walking through doors." She lifted her skirts just enough to show the hem, quilted with little hidden pockets. "Bullets. Needles. A bit of sugar so I can be friendly when I'm not. And a rosary, in case God feels like pretending to listen."

"I have a spoon," Artemis said.

"Of course you do." Tamsin kissed her cheek quick as a pickpocket. "Find me a bunk that doesn't drip and a man who doesn't snore. I'll fetch my trunk like a lady even if it goes overboard like a rock."

By afternoon, the seven began to take shape, as if the number had been written somewhere and men and women were only ink creeping along to meet it. Jonah Bell arrived with a jacket that had too many pockets and a smile that promised nothing and kept that promise. He touched the brim of a hat that had never belonged to him and said, "I heard there were snakes where we're going. I thought I'd bring one of my own," and produced out of nowhere a coil of rope that looked like it had opinions.

Isidro, who might or might not have been born Isidro, came with a scar that began in one eyebrow and ended somewhere a shirt hid. He spoke English the way a knife speaks French: without affection, but well enough to be understood. "You pay me half now," he said to Artemis. "You pay me the other half when I show you a tree old enough to be your grandmother."

"Éloise will hold the other half," Artemis said. "If I don't come back, you won't need it anymore."

He considered that and, to her surprise, laughed. "You are honest like a bad priest."

Sister Séverine did not come, but she sent a man with a letter of introduction to a Jesuit in Bolívar who had once mapped rivers until the rivers learned his name and took him for a joke. "Don't trust the map," the letter said in a clean, tight hand. "Trust the man holding it only if his shoes look like he knows mud."

By the time the sun had a red ring, the *San Ignacio* was heavy with food and water and men and the noise of last errands. Jory Black walked his deck like a farmer at dusk, touching lines and wood with the brief certainty of a man who has to say goodnight to everything to promise he'll see it again. Baptiste came to the gangway and waved her up with two fingers.

"Here," he said, and passed her a small packet: a square of linen with something hard sewn into the hem. "For luck."

"Is it real luck?" Artemis asked, dry.

"It's a coin with a hole in it," he said. "Which is as true a picture of luck as any. It's been in my pocket through three storms and a fever. It might be tired. But it's likely to try again."

She put it in with the spoon and the knife and felt a comfortable argument begin in her pocket.

"Bring me a story," Baptiste said. "Bring Éloise her spoon. Try to bring yourself."

Artemis looked along the wharf, past shoulders and hats, past the low carry of women's baskets, to the far side where a man stood in a good coat despite the heat, his cane polished, his hair waxed. He watched the ship with an interest that didn't belong to cargo. He had a delicate mouth like someone who bit their nails. She felt more than saw his gaze drop to her, then lift, then slide away with studied carelessness.

"Don Iñigo?" she asked without moving her lips.

Baptiste didn't look. "Or his cousin. Or his mirror. Leave him on the wharf."

She closed her hand until her nails bit. She counted the bite-marks: five. "We will."

The bell rang—three slow strokes, then two—and men began to move with that quickening focus that turns talk into work. Hob lifted the gangway as if it were a sheet and folded it into the ship. Tamsin stood beside Artemis at the rail and held her gloved hand as if they were girls playacting a promenade. Jonah whistled something rude about saints. Isidro spat into the water and made a sign against the eye. Jory Black called commands like a man telling a story he'd told a hundred times and still liked the ending.

The *San Ignacio* eased herself away from the wharf like a woman sidling out of a room where she'd overstayed her welcome. The river took her weight and said nothing about it. The city slid by: galleries with their lacework iron, shutters thrown wide, music bleeding out of doors, an old woman throwing a pan of water into the street and watching it shatter into sunlight. The smell of chicory thinned and the smell of tide thickened. Artemis held the rail until splinters printed her palm.

As the current took them, a drop fell warm on her upper lip. She licked it and tasted copper.

"Damn," Tamsin said softly.

"It's only the first," Artemis said, and wiped her nose with the heel of her hand. She kept her eyes on the last thin line of the city as it flattened into horizon. "One—dreams. Two—nosebleeds. Three—hands drop what they love. Four—seizures. Five—fever. Six—death." She counted them not like a sentence but like steps to a door. "Seven—return."

Tamsin squeezed her fingers until they hurt. "All right," she said. "We'll walk them."

Artemis looked down at the water. It looked back, as water does. She felt the spoon and the coin and the knife argue in her pocket, felt the cards like a small patient weight at her hip, felt the city unhook itself from her bones and drift.

"River," she whispered. "We have business."

The wind came upriver, smelling of salt as if it had been held too long in a man's hand. The sails took it. The lines answered. The ship leaned. And New Orleans turned her face away, as if to say *go, then,* as if to say *come back different or don't come back at all.*

Chapter II — The Gathering of Seven

"Every expedition begins as a prayer or a wager."

By morning the ship smelled of tar, sweat, and flour-dust from the sacks stacked like coffins along the hold. The *San Ignacio* tugged against her moorings like a dog eager for release, but Jory Black held her still: "We sail when I say, not when she says."

That gave Artemis hours. Hours to find the rest of her seven.

Tamsin Reed was already aboard, sprawled across her hammock like a woman trying on sin for size. She had found a bottle of rough rum and was christening it with slow gulps. "If I'm to die in a jungle," she said, "I'll die with a warm mouth and a full tongue."

"You'll die with your tongue chewed by ants if you're not careful," Artemis said, hanging her small sack beneath her own hammock.

"Better ants than men." Tamsin tipped the bottle toward her. "To the seven."

"We are not seven yet."

"Then find them, darling. I'll hold the bottle till you do."

The wharf was a blur of shouts, barrels rolled like dice, gulls shrieking overhead. Artemis moved through it with the oilskin packet hidden under her arm and Éloise's bone spoon biting her thigh through the pocket.

She found Jonah Bell first.

He was leaning against a stack of molasses barrels, flipping a coin across his knuckles. His jacket was patched, his boots were good, and his smile was dangerous only if you believed in it.

"You've been looking for me," he said, before she'd spoken.

"Have I?"

"You walk like a woman counting debts. I can smell when one of those debts has my name on it." He snapped the coin into his palm, then let it vanish, then produced it behind her ear with an exaggerated flourish.

Artemis didn't smile. "You steal?"

"I take. When it needs taking."

"You fight?"

"When the taking goes wrong."

"You'll come south?"

Jonah weighed the coin, then flicked it into her palm. "If the stakes are high."

"They are."

"Then I'll play."

Next was Isidro. He stood at the edge of the fish market, one boot on the stone curb, one in the gutter, slicing a mango with a knife too sharp for fruit. His skin was the color of worn mahogany, his hair tied back in a rag, his eyes dark as river mud.

"You are the Irish girl," he said, without looking.

"And you are the liar," she answered.

He grinned, showing a single gold tooth. "Then we are well matched." He offered her a slice of mango, sweet and dripping. She bit it, juice staining her fingers.

"Do you know the Amazon?"

"I know rivers that kill slower. I know snakes that eat faster. I know how to bury a body so the ants find it before the men do."

"Will you guide me?"

He licked juice from his blade. "Half payment now. Half when we reach a place men call unkind names."

"Éloise holds the half."

His laughter was like gravel. "Then I will walk. For her, and maybe for you."

By afternoon, the dockside sun pressed hot as a branding iron. Artemis found her fifth: a woman hunched at a carpenter's stall, sharpening a blade. She looked up when Artemis cast a shadow across the bench.

"Your name?" Artemis asked.

"Clara," said the woman, voice blunt as the knife's edge. "I stitch sails. I stitch wounds. I know how to tie a man so he sleeps or screams, depending on what you want."

Artemis met her gaze. "I want you alive beside me when the fever comes."

Clara nodded once. "Then I'll pack my needles."

Six was found by accident: a boy no older than fifteen, caught with his hand in the rope coils on deck. Hob had him by the collar, ready to throw him headfirst onto the wharf.

"Please!" the boy gasped. "I can cook! I can patch sails! I can—"

"You can steal," Hob snarled.

Artemis stepped forward. "What's your name?"

"Otis," he stammered. "I only wanted aboard. Caracas is my mother's home. She's dying there. I swear I'll work, not steal."

Jonah smirked. "A thief begging to be a cook. That's a new trick."

Artemis studied the boy's thin wrists, the bruise-yellow beneath his eyes. She thought of her own hunger once, gnawing her belly hollow. "Let him stay," she said.

Hob growled, but Jory Black appeared, wiping his hands on a rag. "If he slows us, we'll feed him to the sea. But if he earns his keep, he's cheaper than another barrel of salt pork."

And so the boy became their sixth.

The seventh came at dusk.

As the ship prepared to cast off, a figure appeared at the end of the wharf: tall, cloaked despite the heat. She moved with the calm of someone who had walked through darker rooms and survived them.

"Danger," she called softly.

Artemis froze. The voice was familiar, though she had never thought to hear it again. Sister Séverine stood in the red light of sunset, veil drawn, eyes black as candle soot.

"You will need me," she said simply.

Artemis found her throat tight. "Why?"

Séverine touched the cross at her breast. "Because faith alone will not save you. And because not all doors in the jungle open to knives. Some must be opened with prayers, or with blood."

The priestess climbed aboard without waiting for permission. Jory Black looked her over once and shrugged. "Every voyage needs a soul to bury the rest."

And so they were seven.

That night, when the river wind turned cool and the ship's lanterns swung like tired stars, Artemis stood at the bow with Tamsin at her side. Behind them lay New Orleans, a city of masks and drums. Ahead lay only the dark seam of the horizon.

"Seven," Tamsin whispered, pressing her glove against Artemis's hand. "A holy number."

"Or a cursed one," Artemis murmured.

The river answered by carrying them out.

The Seven of the Serpent Voyage

Fire & Serpents — Character Roster

Artemis Danger

- **Origin:** Ireland → New Orleans survivor of wreck & famine.
- **Role:** Reluctant leader, cursed to seek the serpent idol.
- **Skills:** Survivor's instinct, stubborn endurance, sailor's knife, ritual-marked spirit.
- **Traits:** Quiet, haunted, but increasingly decisive.
- **Flaw/Arc:** Burden of fatalism; must choose between survival and sacrifice.

Tamsin Reed (Ally / Closest Friend)

- **Origin:** English seamstress & sometime gunslinger in New Orleans.
- **Role:** Confidante, sharpshooter, keeper of humor.
- **Skills:** Marksmanship, sewing/patching, sarcasm as armor.
- **Traits:** Witty, irreverent, loyal beneath the brashness.
- **Flaw/Arc:** Masks fear with bravado; will be tested when tragedy strips levity away.

Jonah Bell (Trickster / Rogue)

- **Origin:** American, former thief turned gambler.
- **Role:** Scout, opportunist, untrustworthy ally.
- **Skills:** Sleight of hand, thievery, bluffing, light-footed survival.
- **Traits:** Charming, glib, calculating.
- **Flaw/Arc:** His self-serving instincts may doom or save the group.
- **Foreshadow:** A likely betrayer, but one whose betrayal might cut both ways.

Isidro (Guide / Outsider)

- **Origin:** Venezuelan sailor, scarred and myth-thick with stories.
- **Role:** Jungle guide, lore-holder, pragmatic killer.
- **Skills:** Tracking, knife-work, uncanny jungle knowledge.
- **Traits:** Sardonic, half-believer in spirits, mercenary by need.
- **Flaw/Arc:** Cynicism hides old wounds; loyalty must be earned.

Clara Dupré (Surgeon / Anchor)

- **Origin:** Free woman of color from New Orleans, worked docks and sails.
- **Role:** Medic, stitcher of sails and wounds alike.
- **Skills:** Needlework, ropework, practical medicine, restraint.
- **Traits:** Blunt, stoic, no-nonsense; rarely laughs.
- **Flaw/Arc:** Duty weighs heavy; will face impossible choices of who to save.

Otis (Stowaway / Innocent)

- **Origin:** Creole boy, 15, runaway desperate to reach Caracas.
- **Role:** Cook's helper, cabin-boy, reluctant mascot of the group.
- **Skills:** Quick hands, endurance, surprising cunning under pressure.
- **Traits:** Naïve, hopeful, eager to prove himself.
- **Flaw/Arc:** Youth in a merciless world; his fate will sharpen the group's grief.

Sister Séverine (Faith / Darkness)

- **Origin:** French nun turned Vodou-touched mystic.
- **Role:** Spiritual ballast, interpreter of omens, dangerous faith-bearer.
- **Skills:** Ritual, prayer, uncanny insight into the "doors" of the jungle.
- **Traits:** Severe, enigmatic, unsettling calm.
- **Flaw/Arc:** Her faith is double-edged — salvation for some, damnation for others.

Chapter III — Departure on Calm Seas

The *San Ignacio* slid downriver on a tide of sunlight and song. Sails swelled, gulls wheeled, and the Mississippi carried them toward the open gulf like a mother eager to be rid of quarrelsome children.

Artemis stood at the rail, breathing air that smelled more of salt than soil now. The city had vanished behind them, only its memory clinging in her lungs. Ahead lay the blue seam of horizon, clean and cruel.

For the first time in months, she was not in a skirt.

Éloise had pressed them all to prepare as if for a war, not a picnic, and so Artemis now wore plain sailor's trousers belted with rope, a linen shirt rolled at the elbows, and her boots greased for wet. The skirt and petticoat she had once thought a kind of armor lay stuffed deep in her sack. She touched her hip where the sailor's knife rode, where the bone spoon knocked against the coin Baptiste had given her.

Tamsin Reed leaned against the mast, already at ease in her own pair of men's breeches, the fabric hugging her long legs as if she had been born to them. A pistol rested tucked into her waistband, gleaming like a sly promise. She tilted her hat back with one finger and grinned.

"Well then," Tamsin drawled, "it seems we've dressed ourselves into trouble."

"Trouble?" Artemis asked.

"Oh, men can stomach many things on a voyage — rats, salt beef, even ghosts. But women in trousers? That is blasphemy of the highest order."

Jonah Bell sauntered past at that moment, balancing a crate on one shoulder. "Not blasphemy," he said. "Temptation. And temptation belongs on any good voyage." He winked at Tamsin. "Though if you shoot me for saying it, I'll fall in love before I fall overboard."

Tamsin pulled her pistol half an inch free of her waistband. "Try me."

The crew roared with laughter. Even Jory Black, stone-faced captain, let a corner of his mouth tilt upward before he barked at the men to haul line faster.

Clara Dupré emerged from below decks with a small satchel slung over her shoulder, her own trousers patched at the knee, her dark hair braided tight. She carried herself like a woman who expected the sea to test her patience. She eyed the others, then Artemis.

"You've never marched a mile in this heat," Clara said bluntly. "When you reach the jungle, it won't matter what prayers you've said or what spirits claim you. It will matter if your boots hold."

Artemis nodded. "Then I'll see that they do."

Clara's gaze softened for a heartbeat, almost approval, before she vanished back below to check her needles and bottles once more.

By late afternoon, the group gathered at the mess table —
a rough plank set with dented tin cups and a pot of rice
and beans that smelled better than it tasted. Hob
slammed the pot down and muttered about "cargo of
mouths."

Otis, the boy, was already at work stirring and serving,
desperate to prove himself. His trousers were too big,
cinched by twine at the waist, but his eyes burned with
determination.

"I can cook," he said brightly, "and clean, and—"

"And die quicker than the rest," Jonah interrupted,
snatching a bowl.

Artemis cut him a look. "Leave him."

The boy flushed, but he ladled out another portion with
chin lifted. Artemis saw the ghosts of herself in him —
the hunger, the desperation to belong somewhere,
anywhere.

Isidro arrived last, leaning in the doorway with a slow
smile. He had already stripped off his coat, left in only
shirt and trousers, knife gleaming at his belt. He looked
over the group as if appraising livestock.

"So this is the pack," he said. "One nun, two women
who dress like men, one thief who smiles too much, one
boy who won't live to see twenty, one healer who looks
like she'll sew us into sacks, and you." His eyes fell on
Artemis. "The cursed one."

Sister Séverine, seated with hands folded neatly on the
table, spoke before Artemis could. "A curse is only a

mark. Marks can be read as scripture, or as warning. Which way do you prefer to read, señor?"

Isidro chuckled. "As maps. And maps, Sister, often lie."

They ate in uneasy truce, the ship rocking them like a cradle. Above deck, the sunset bled red across the gulf, so bright it looked as though the horizon itself were on fire.

Artemis set her spoon down, aware of the eyes on her. Though she had not asked for it, she was the gravity pulling them together, the reason they sat at one table instead of seven.

She met them each in turn.

"Tamsin. Jonah. Isidro. Clara. Otis. Sister Séverine." Her voice was low but steady. "We are seven now. And we are seven because we must be. The journey will kill some of us. It may kill all of us. But if we do not go, worse will come. You've each heard whispers of what waits. You've each chosen to come anyway."

Silence settled. Only the slap of the waves against the hull answered her.

At last, Tamsin raised her cup. "Then let's drink — not to survival, but to spite."

Jonah laughed, and Clara shook her head, but one by one the cups rose. Even Sister Séverine lifted hers, though she murmured a prayer beneath her breath.

Artemis lifted hers last. "To spite, then."

They drank.

And above them, unseen, the first star blinked open —
watching, indifferent, as the calm sea carried them
toward the teeth hidden in its dark.

Chapter IV — Whispers in the Hull

"Ships carry more than men; they carry what men fear."

The Gulf spread smooth as hammered brass, the sails billowed white, and the wind sang steady in the rigging. By all accounts, the voyage should have been charmed.

Yet by the third night, men stopped whistling on watch.

Artemis learned it in fragments. A deckhand swore he heard chains dragging below. Another spat three times into the sea and refused to sleep in his hammock. Even Hob, who laughed at nothing but rope, kept his short leg braced as if ready for a fight he couldn't name.

The first time Artemis heard it, she thought it was memory: the groan of timbers under storm, the sea clawing a hull apart. But the *San Ignacio* was steady, her planks tight. The sound came again as she lay half-asleep — not groaning, but murmuring. Voices rising from the dark belly of the ship. Not in English. Not in Spanish. Not even in the French she had half-learned in New Orleans.

She lay stiff in her hammock, listening. Words indistinct, but the cadence was human — a prayer, or a curse.

Across from her, Tamsin rolled over and muttered, "If that's Otis talking in his sleep, I'm cutting his tongue."

"It isn't him," Artemis whispered.

They both turned their heads. The boy's hammock rocked with even breathing, mouth slack. The whispers came from deeper down, below the cargo.

Jonah Bell's voice came soft from the shadows. "I went down there last watch. Nothing but rice and flour. And the smell of brine where no brine should be."

"Did you stay long?" Séverine's question was calm, too calm.

Jonah chuckled without humor. "Long enough to know I won't again."

Isidro spat over the side. "Ships rot in ways men cannot mend. I've seen it — a boat that leaked blood instead of water. A canoe that sang with children's voices until dawn." He glanced at Artemis. "Sometimes it is the passenger who carries the rot."

Clara looked up sharply. "You'll not put that on her."

Isidro lifted his hands in mock surrender. "I only say what rivers say."

Artemis kept her gaze fixed on the black water. She could not deny it: the voices pulled at her, like a rope tied to the marrow of her bones. She felt them coil in her blood the same way Éloise's veves had burned.

That night she dreamed of water dripping, drop by drop, onto stone. When she woke, her nose bled again, a single dark streak across her lips.

On the fourth day, Hob went missing for an hour. When they found him, he stood barefoot in the hold, his lantern guttered, his short leg planted square in spilled rice. He stared at the wall as though it held scripture.

"What did you hear?" Jory Black demanded, hauling him up by the collar.

"Calling," Hob said hoarsely. "Not to me. Past me." His eyes rolled, and he spat grain from his mouth as if he'd been chewing it raw.

From that night on, Jory ordered the hatch barred at sundown. No man was to set foot in the hold after dark.

Still, the whispers rose — muffled now, but thicker, like many throats pressed against wood.

On the fifth night, Artemis went to the rail for air. The sea was moonlit glass, innocent. Yet when she leaned over, she saw shapes below — long and sinuous, gliding just beneath the surface. Too large for eels. Too graceful for dolphins. Their scales caught the moon like shards of silver.

Tamsin joined her, yawning. "Counting fish?"

"Serpents," Artemis whispered.

Tamsin squinted. "All I see is water."

But Artemis's skin crawled with certainty: the river's children had followed her into the gulf. And they were waiting.

Chapter V — The First Missing Man

"A silence at roll-call is louder than a scream."

The fourth sunset bled itself thin and the fifth dawn came on like a fever breaking—colorless, clammy, grudging. The *San Ignacio* moved with the pride of a cat that has hidden its limp. Wind steady. Sea kind. No reason at all for men to be chewing their lips to blood.

Jory Black rang the bell and made them form up, every soul from fo'c'sle to galley: two lines of faces turned toward the captain's scar and the way it flashed when he said a name.

"Hob." "Aye."
"Roux." "Aye."
"Bell." "Aye."
"Reed." "Aye."
"Dupré." "Aye."
"Isidro." Two fingers.
"Otis." "Here."
"Séverine." "Present."

"Raimundo Galvez."

Silence took the deck.

Not the expectant silence of a man late from the head, but the silence a church knows when a coffin is too small. The wind went soft around the sails, as if it didn't want to be heard asking questions.

"Mundo," Jory said, quieter. "Report."

Hob cleared his throat, then turned the clearing into a cough. "He took dogwatch, Cap. I swapped him for a spell—said his left ear was humming. After, he went aft to look at the yawl lashings. I told him leave it for daylight."

"Who saw him last?"

A Veracruz hand lifted his cap. "At the pump, señor. Cap on crooked."

"Search," Jory said, and the word went through the crew like a winch turning.

They searched. Not the polite riffling of hammocks men do when they expect to find a snoring fool, but a hungry search, the kind that lifts boards and insults salt sacks and asks rope if it has learned speech.

Artemis moved with them, sleeves rolled, trousers stained at the knee from kneeling to peer beneath the spare boat. She counted without wanting to—steps between hatch and scupper (nine), knots in the stern line (thirteen), the smears of something dark along the rail (two, spaced like fingertips). When she pressed her palm to the wood, it came away tacky and brown.

"Blood," Clara said, mouth tightening. "New enough to make me angry."

Caught in the scupper grating was Mundo's cap, the cheap felt soaked to black. Inside, as if tucked by a mother's hand, lay three long hairs braided together—black, black, and white.

Séverine's fingers hovered over the cap and withdrew. "Braided," she murmured. "Hair."

"Bar the hold," she told Hob.

"It is already barred," he said.

"Bar it again," she answered softly. "In case the bar was listening."

Jory shook water out of the cap and hung it on a belaying pin. The gesture had the shape of a promise: *you will return for this or you will not return at all.* He faced them.

"Until I'm satisfied, nobody walks alone. Night watches are doubled. Knives stay on belts, not under pillows. Any man goes below after sundown goes in irons till Caracas. We sail clean."

Men avoided shadows without looking like they were avoiding shadows. The whisper at the edges of hearing went on like a pot left barely to simmer.

Artemis went to the rail and breathed, slow to the count of seven. In her pocket, Éloise's bone spoon lay quiet as a small secret. She took it out anyway and, because she could not stop herself, asked Tamsin for a pinch of salt from her hidden hem.

"You and your kitchen witchery," Tamsin said, but she gave it over.

Artemis bled a mouthful of sea into a tin cup, salted it, and held the spoon above. For a heartbeat, nothing. Then, with the smallest stubborn motion, it turned—a quarter circle, like a fish trying the line.

Tamsin watched, humor gone. "Does it do that often?"

"No."

"Do we trust it?"

"I don't know," Artemis said. "But it trusts something."

Séverine had come without footsteps. "There are doors on ships," she said. "Not only the kind men hinge. When the dead want walking room, they borrow the nearest corridor."

"And when serpents want swimming room?" Isidro asked from the other side of the rail, appearing like a bad decision. "They borrow the nearest river."

"We are not in a river," Tamsin snapped.

Isidro's smile lifted one corner. "She is," he said, nodding at Artemis. "She carries it."

Clara set the tin away. "Ritual can wait for land. For now, we keep men fed, awake, and sober."

Sober lasted until sundown.

After dark, the bar thudded into its iron shoes and the hatch-cover went heavy, and still the sound seeped up— low, layered, many mouths speaking just out of understanding. Jonah made a show of complaining about the rice, then ate two bowls without tasting. Otis washed the pot three times as if scrubbing could keep something clean inside him.

Artemis tried to sleep. The hammock rocked an old lullaby. She counted slats, knots, breaths. Sleep bit once and then spat her out.

When the first bell of the middle watch struck, she slid to the ladder. Tamsin pressed her pistol into Artemis's palm. "If you're going to be foolish," she whispered, "be armed."

Séverine stood at the hatch like a sentinel, lips moving without sound. She did not try to stop them. Her eyes cut once to the spoon, then back to prayers that had no words.

The bar was cold under Artemis's fingers. Not just night-cold. A cellar cool that did not belong on a ship that spent its sweat all day. She put her ear to the wood. A breath came through that wasn't theirs. The words under it were as far from language as bone is from marrow, yet meaning clung to them like damp: *Open.*

"No," she said aloud, and her voice shook.

Something rasped on the other side—a sound like braid on wood. She jerked back, heart counting too quick.

From above, a shout cracked the night. "Man at stern!"

The deck exploded into feet and curses. Men crowded the taffrail, peering into a wake that glowed with churn and cold fire. Hob had the stern-lantern, his jaw locked.

"What did you see?" Jory barked.

"A hand," Hob said. "Swear by the rope that made me. A hand holding the yawl's line like it was climbing."

"And now?"

"Gone."

They leaned together, the whole ship leaning, as if peering could pull a man back up by the sight of him. The sea looked back without interest. A shape slid under the wake—long, sinuous, silvered—and was gone before anyone could admit to seeing it.

"Back to posts," Jory said, not trusting himself to shout. "Nobody sleeps."

Dawn found them raw-eyed. Jory rang the bell because habit is a kind of prayer. Names answered. Mundo's did not. He took the cap down, tipped it into the sea, and watched the cheap felt turn once and sink.

He looked at Artemis. Not accusing. Not pleading. Measuring. "You're a kind of compass," he said. "I don't know what points you. If it points us to Caracas without losing more men, use it."

"It doesn't point toward safety," she said. "Only toward what we're hunting."

"What's the difference?" Jonah said lightly. No one laughed.

All that day the ship felt watched from below. Lines twitched at the wrong moment. Clara stitched a split knuckle and did not scold, which was omen enough. Otis broke a plate and began to cry without sound. Tamsin set him to measuring beans with soldierly ferocity.

Near sundown, Isidro came with a string bag of dried fish and an old story. "In my mother's town there was a well that talked. Folks said it had swallowed a priest who would not drown, and now he prayed at the bottom until the water learned the words. People threw hair in to bargain. The well liked hair. Always hair." He nodded at Artemis's pocket as if he could see the braided strands she'd refused to touch. "Sometimes a thing will ask for the part of you that most refuses to be given."

"What does it want now?" she asked.

"Proof," he said. "Or promise. Or fear. They smell alike."

That night, the whispers did not rise from below.

They rose from the hammocks.

One by one, men stirred, frowned, turned their faces toward the planks as if a lover had called their names from under the floor. Artemis lay very still, counting: one breath, two, three. When the voice came, it used her name as if it knew how to spend it.

"Artemis."

Tamsin's hand clamped her wrist in the dark. "Don't."

"I'm not."

The voice came again, very gentle. Not the serpent's hiss from Éloise's courtyard, not the hold's many-mouth murmur. A man's voice. Warm with relief. "Help me."

Her throat closed. "Mundo?"

"Here," it said, from everywhere and the plank beneath her spine and the cup with the salt in it and the space between her teeth. "Here. Open."

Séverine's voice cut across it like a wire. "No."

Lanterns flared. Séverine stood with veil thrown back, rosary coiled around her fist like chain. "No," she said again, as if scolding a child or her own soul. "You will not be door in my hearing."

Men cursed her. One made the sign of horns. She did not look at them. She looked only at Artemis, and in that look was tenderness like a blade.

"Count," Séverine said.

Artemis did. One, two, three—up to seven. At seven, the voice thinned. It tried her name again and found it too heavy. It trailed off into the planks. The silence after was not relief; it was something told *no* that had listened—for now.

Morning showed them a ship that had slept little and lied less. Jory called them because men need bells to believe time exists. Names again; one absent, again.

Artemis pressed her fingers to the wet rail where the cap had gone under. The sea slid past, unconcerned. She thought of braids, of hair spun into rope around a serpent idol, of men with clean hands and expensive canes waiting in a Venezuelan harbor with names like knives. She thought of how easy it is to be subtracted.

Jory set his jaw. "We make for La Guaira and keep counting. And we do not open what wants opened." He swept them with a look that made no promises. "If this ship carries more than men, we'll make it carry us, too."

Artemis leaned a second into Tamsin's shoulder, the way a tired person leans against a wall to learn what holds. Clara stood near the hatch with her kit and her mouth, both closed. Isidro watched the water with a patient hatred that disguised itself as respect. Jonah dropped his coin twice; each time he picked it up slower.

In her pocket, the spoon lay quiet again, a little colder than before.

The day stretched. The wind held. The *San Ignacio* made her neat way over the breathing skin of the gulf. When dusk came, it came quick, bruising the horizon purple and then letting black spill everywhere.

Artemis lit a lamp by her hammock and did not sleep. She counted the flame's small tongues, the way it flinched each time the ship shouldered a wave. She waited for the voices.

None came.

The quiet that found them was not relief. It was the kind of quiet that comes when a thing that wanted in has found another door.

She lay awake until the first pale of dawn. When she shut her eyes at last, she saw a cap turning in water, and a hand that was not a man's hand sliding along the yawl's line, and three hairs braided, black, black, white, tied to a pin.

"Seven," she whispered into the thinning dark. "We will keep seven."

The ship said nothing back.

Chapter VI — Night of the Screams

"Walls do not keep out the things that feed in darkness."

The wind had a fever. It came hot from the east all afternoon, then went slack at sundown like a man dropping to his knees. The sails luffed and snapped; the rigging hummed in a way that suggested teeth. Jory Black ordered canvas reefed and lanterns trimmed. "No wandering," he said without shouting. "No drinks. No stories that make boys look at doors."

They barred the hold as they had each night, iron settling into iron with a sound like judgment. Sister Séverine paced the hatch, bareheaded, veil tied at her throat with sailor's twine, salt dusted from a horn into a thin white line around the cover. She whispered the Miserere under her breath and, in the breaks, something that belonged to the courtyards of New Orleans: the names of saints that never saw Rome.

Clara divided the deck as if it were a hospital ward: lamp here, water there, a basket of clean rags, needles boiled, tourniquets rolled tight and ready. "We don't wait to stop bleeding," she told Hob. "We break its fingers."

Tamsin checked her pistol, replaced the cap, checked it again. "If something boards us without a ticket," she said to Artemis, "I'll punch its hole."

"Don't miss," Artemis said. Her hands tried to be steady and failed. She breathed to the count of seven until they obeyed enough to tie her hair back with a strip of linen. Her fingers came away smudged with the rusty shadow that never quite left her nostrils now.

Isidro sharpened his knife on a bit of sail-needle as if he meant to shave God.

Jonah flipped his coin. It hit his palm wrong and skittered to the deck, spun to the rail, and would have gone over if Otis hadn't thrown himself flat and slapped it. He looked up beaming, coin in hand, until he saw Jonah's face—too pale for the heat. "Keep it," Jonah said, voice thin. "Buy yourself luck."

"Luck is our cheapest cargo," Isidro muttered.

Night came hard and quick. The sea went from iron to black glass. The sky put out its last coals and left the deck to its small domestic fires: a lantern by the hatch, one by the galley, one lashed to the stern. The *San Ignacio* seemed smaller, as if the dark had tightened its belt.

The first scream came from forward, thin and far, like a boy's voice on a cold street.

Every head turned. Every hand found wood or rope. The scream stopped so cleanly it left a ringing where it had been.

Jory Black didn't move for a heartbeat. Then: "Pairs," he said, and the deck was all boots and curses and the white of eyes. Artemis went with Tamsin; Clara with Hob; Jonah with Isidro; Séverine alone, which made sense the way knives make sense.

They found a boot by the hawsehole, toes pointing nowhere. It was still warm. The sock inside had the shape of a foot without the courtesy of flesh. Clara lifted it very gently, as if tenderness could persuade it back.

"Raimundo's cousin," Hob said hoarsely. "Andrés. He had a scar here." He touched his own cheek, then dropped his hand, as if memory were a kind of blasphemy.

"Blood?" Jory asked.

"Not enough," Clara answered, and her mouth tightened.

The second scream came from aft. The sound of running was a single animal; men arrived at the taffrail shoulder to shoulder. The stern-lantern shivered on its hook. In its light they saw the yawl's line jerking as if it had caught a fish that did not understand boats.

"Don't," Jory snapped when two men reached for it. "We cut." Hob's knife flashed; the line parted; the yawl fell back, then dropped—the little boat swallowed by dark so sudden it might as well have been a trapdoor. The wake frothed once, twice, then smoothed like a hand over a grave.

"Something's playing," Isidro said. He spat and made a sign that owed a debt to more gods than he was willing to admit.

"Back from the rails," Séverine said quietly. "If you must listen, listen from the middle of the deck."

A third scream rose. Not a single voice. A chord. A man howling from deep old hurt, another pleading in a mother's language, a third cutting off into a gargle that made the belly want to loose itself. It came not from fore or aft but from below, where no man was supposed to be.

All eyes went to the hatch.

The iron bar quivered.

"Hold," Jory said, and set his palm on it. The cold reached up into his bones. He swore, a sailor's prayer with no saint allowed in it. "Hob. Rope."

They lashed the bar as if the wood wanted out. The hatch boomed once, a big animal bumping, the kind you feel in your knees. Salt leapt from Séverine's ring into the air and fell like hail. The voices under their feet braided together into something that wasn't voices, wasn't air, was a pressure with speech in it: *Open.*

"No," said Séverine, palm flat to the wood. "No. Non."

Artemis tasted copper. She wanted to put her ear down. Every part of her wanted it—teeth, marrow, the tender meat behind the eyes. She'd been notched, she understood that now, like a key. And the lock below was the right shape to want her.

She took the bone spoon out with hands that weren't steady and weren't entirely hers. "Salt," she said. Tamsin, watching, bit the tip off the paper twist she kept in her pocket and shook out a little coned hill into Artemis's palm. Artemis wet it with a splash of sea from the cup left by the rail and held the spoon over, her lips moving with nothing—no word she knew, no psalm, just counting.

One. Two. Three. Four. Five. Six. Seven.

The spoon trembled, as if with old fever. It did not turn. It tilted, as if considering.

"It's listening," Tamsin whispered.

"To what?"

"To you," said Séverine without looking up. "And to itself, through you."

"Captain," Jonah said carefully. "There's another way down."

Jory's head snapped. "Where."

Jonah's hand lifted, then drifted toward the hatch again as if pulled by string. He shook himself like a horse at flies. "The pump well. The grating's loose."

"Otis." Clara's voice cracked like a stitching-knot. "Stay by the galley. If you move, I sew your trouser cuffs to the deck."

"Yes, ma'am," he breathed, and pressed his back to the stove so hard it must have burned. His eyes glittered like a little animal's in brushfire.

They went as three: Jory, Isidro, Jonah. Artemis started and Séverine touched her elbow. "No," she said, and Artemis stayed. When someone says *no* in that voice, it is the oldest word in the world.

At the pump well they found what Jonah had not found before: the grating shifted as if a hand beneath had tested it. Slime slicked the wood. Something pale lay caught in the lattice like kelp.

Clara arrived behind them with the lamp. She set it down and did not speak for a breath. Not kelp. Hair. A thick, roped braid of it, black shot with white, caught and jammed so tight Jonah had to saw with his knife to free it. The freed length slid away with such suddenness the lamp flame jumped. The pump mouth burped a little pink water and then, like a man embarrassed at his own fluids, ran clear.

Clara's face did not change. She took the grating up a finger's width, squinted down. "If I tell you it's nothing, I'm lying. If I tell you it's old, I'm lying. It's fresh and it's wrong. Put that back."

They heaved the grating home and nailed it with whatever nails could be trusted.

The night had begun to be too long. Men's mouths dried out of words. A bottle appeared and then disappeared under Séverine's stare. Tamsin hummed tunelessly through her teeth—the sound a dog makes when it refuses a growl.

Artemis gripped the rail. Her palms were slick. Her knife hilt slipped. She cursed and tightened her hand, but the next breath it went—slid right out, clattered to the deck, skittered two feet toward the hatch. She dropped without thinking and grabbed it. The movement pulled her cheek against the planks. The voice reached her like warm breath through lattice.

Child.

Her grip spasmed. Not from fear. From recognition. Not her mother's voice. Not any voice she possessed a right to love. But it wore that shape briefly, the way a thief wears a gentleman's coat to get a door opened.

Tamsin hauled her up by the belt. "If you plan to kiss the floor, tell me first. I'll lay a clean cloth down."

"I'm fine," Artemis said. She wasn't. She moved her hand—one, two, three times. The fingers obeyed; the tendons fluttered. Éloise's counting had been right. *Hands drop what they love.* She looked at the knife and knew that when the time came, she would drop it again.

The fourth scream was not like the others. It rose slow, like a rope being pulled through a wet pulley, and when it broke it broke into laughter.

Men can live with fear. Laughter in the wrong place makes them want to kill. Hob went white and then stone. Jory said, very gently, "Lanterns down."

"Down?" Jonah breathed.

"Down," Jory said again, and kicked his own with his boot. One by one, lights blinked out. The darkness came in at a full walk and then a run. The ship was sound and heat and the thin, mean gleam off a bit of moon on a brass buckle.

They waited in the new dark. The laughter walked the planks like something shod.

A whisper at Artemis's ear: *Open, and I'll give you rest.* The whisper moved to the other ear. *Open, and I'll give you him you miss.* To her mouth, like a kiss. *Open, and I'll give you a boat that doesn't break.*

"Non," Séverine said, louder now, not to the hatch but to the air. "Non. Non." Each no was a bell. Each no was a fist.

Something rushed the bar. The deck took the blow in its joints. The whole ship cried out the way a horse does when something bites what it cannot see.

Tamsin fired.

The pistol spat white, lit five faces in a ghastly gallery, punched a hole in night wider than the ball it spent. The smell of powder slapped every nose. The flash showed the hatch alive with a sheen like fish skin, showed—God knows it showed—a suggestion of a coil where no coil could be, then was gone. The ball clanged off iron and went into wood.

Silence. Not the relief kind. The kind you get right after a man hits you and right before he hits you again.

Otis sobbed once and bit it off. Clara put her palm flat on his chest and breathed him like a bellows until he matched her count.

"Again," Jory whispered. "Lanterns up."

They burned back the dark and found nothing but the bar, the salt, the nails in the pump, the smear by the hawsehole, the yawl gone.

"Hold watches," Jory said, and rubbed his scar until it shone. "We stand until dawn. Then we run this ship until her planks smoke. Ten days, we said. We keep ten."

No one sat. Sitting would have felt like kneeling. They leaned on rails, on each other, on habits. Someone sang something very softly and then stopped, ashamed. Séverine walked the deck in a slow figure eight that might have been a prayer if geometry could save. Isidro sharpened the same inch of blade to keep his hands from shaking. Jonah juggled nothing, then nothing fell.

The hour before dawn is a liar. It pretends to be empty. It is crowded with endings.

The last scream came from overhead.

Every head snapped back. A shadow moved along the yard like a blind cat. They saw bare feet, then nothing, then feet again, as if a man were learning to walk on air.

"Hob—" Jory started, and Hob was already climbing, short leg and all, body belling the shrouds. He went up with the mean grace of a man who has said *no* all his life and means to keep saying it. He reached the yard, flung himself like a hook, and came away with a bundle that wriggled.

They hauled together and brought both down. Hob landed with a grunt. The bundle was a sack tied with a woman's careful hands. He ripped it with his teeth. Hair spilled out—long lengths wrapped with twine, salted, braided, black-black-white murmuring like seaweed when a wave goes out.

"Who put that up there?" Jonah's voice was thin. "Who did that, and why over our heads?"

"To bait," Isidro said. He was not smiling.

The horizon bruised and paled. Dawn came not like salvation but like a clerk with a ledger. Jory rang the bell: empty sound, no metal in it. Names answered. He did not say the names of the ones he knew would not. When he counted, the number was small enough to live in one hand.

"Half," Hob said grimly, and no one corrected him. Men had gone without water makes noise; men had gone without light makes noise. This had been neither. It was subtraction.

No one untied the bar. No one un-nailed the pump. They did what sailors do when the sea teaches a new word: they learned to talk around it.

Jory set the *San Ignacio* on a hard point and drove her like a borrowed horse. Canvas strained. Block and tackle sang. The ship shuddered under the insistence and then gave herself to it, her keel speaking the language of speed.

"Ten days," Tamsin said, voice a scrape.

"Seven now," Artemis answered, because she could not stop counting even when numbers were knives. She wiped her nose; the blood was thin this morning. Maybe the thing below had taken its tithe and gone to sleep. Maybe it had learned patience.

Clara bound a forearm that had nothing to do with the night. Men get clumsy after terror; they give their fear something it can point to. She sewed and did not scold, and that frightened them more than screaming would have.

Séverine made the sign of the cross not in the air but on the planks, finger lingering on each point as if the ship might feel it. She looked up at Artemis and said, softly, "It wanted you."

"Everything that eats wants me," Artemis said. She tucked the bone spoon away. It lay against the coin and the knife and made no noise at all.

In the water alongside, something turned without showing its back.

By noon the sea had whitecaps like a field of rough sheep. By evening the coast would begin to suggest itself, a bruise on the rim of sight. Men kept to pairs without being told. No one pissed alone. Otis shadowed Clara so closely he might have been a pocket. Jonah stayed in the light. Isidro slept upright, knife flat on his thigh like a pet.

When darkness came again, their lanterns burned with a different smell—as if someone had mixed brine in the oil. The bar did not move. The hatch did not speak. The deck held.

Sleep came in found coins and was snatched away by memory. If there were voices, they hid under the creak and the wind.

At dawn, Jory rang again. The names that answered were the names that would carry them to land if the wind held.

Artemis stood at the rail in her trousers stiff with salt and felt the world tilt toward Venezuela, toward men with clean hands and canes, toward mountains with their own old appetites, toward rivers whose children did not need ships to find her. She lifted the spoon once more, salted water in a cup, held it above, counted. One through seven.

On six, it twitched.

On seven, it turned, slow and final, pointing her like a knife.

Tamsin came to stand shoulder to shoulder. "Toward?"

"Toward trouble," Artemis said.

"Good," Tamsin breathed. "I was worried we might be bored."

They watched the horizon bruise into land.

Chapter VII — Caracas at Last

"The dock is a salvation to some, a gallows to others."

Land rose like a bruise.

First a faint darking on the rim of sea, then the blue-black slab of mountains shouldering the sky, their ribs veined with ravines. La Guaira showed itself last, a chain of white houses hammered onto the narrow lip where rock meets water, cranes like thin saints with broken arms, gulls tacking on stained air.

Men cried out as if they'd come up from drowning. The *San Ignacio* answered the harbor with her bell and a tidy cock of sail, and Artemis felt the breath go out of her in a hard ache. The calm that had lied, the night screams, the cap turning over and under—none of that mattered to the dockhands waving their hats and the aduana men straightening their coats. On shore, life did what life does. It sold, shouted, sweated. It didn't ask where you had set your ghosts.

"Lines!" Jory Black barked, and the crew moved like men learning they had legs again. Hob flung the first hawser with a grunt; it caught the bollard as if it had been hungry for it. The hull kissed the fender piles with a sound like teeth knocked together. The harbor stink rose up—fish rot, tar, coffee sacks, piss, fruit gone too ripe—and the heat reached them in a wet palm.

"Everybody smiles," Jonah said, sunlight hard on his teeth. "Ports love smiles."

"They love paper more," Isidro replied. "And money most."

Artemis stood with her boots braced and watched land come on as if it might startle and run. Her trousers were stiff with dry salt, her shirt clung, and the bone spoon tapped her thigh with every breath—a small conscience. The Queen of Cups rode her hip in oilskin; the Tower lay behind as always like a house she might yet be asked to live in.

"Welcome to La Guaira," Tamsin said, shading her eyes. "God's doorstep and someone else's back door."

"Caracas is up," Isidro said, chin toward the wall of mountain. "A mean road with better views than saints deserve. You'll like it only when you get down again."

Sister Séverine crossed herself—not on her breast but toward the peak. "Ávila keeps the city," she said. "Mountains are stubborn guardians."

"So am I," Clara said, and shouldered her satchel.

They went down the gangplank into a heat that felt personal. Customhouse men waited under the corrugated tin with a bored grace, their pen nibs already wet. One had a little copper snake coiled on his cane as a handle; the sight turned Artemis's stomach before she could tell herself not to be superstitious.

"Papeles," he said without looking up. Jory handed over a packet. The man flicked through with the unhurried insult of authority. "Cargo?"

"Rice, flour, men who need washing," Jory said.

"Passengers?"

"Seven who think they're lucky."

The man's mouth turned. "Names."

Jory gave them: "Artemis Danger. Tamsin Reed. Jonah Bell. Clara Dupré. Isidro—only Isidro. Otis"—the boy swallowed and said his mother's surname and then changed it. "Sister Séverine."

"Motivo."

"Love," Tamsin said sweetly, in a Spanish that made itself understood by intention alone. "We run toward it."

The aduana clerk's pen hesitated long enough to be called a thought. He looked up, saw trousers on women and a nun whose veil was tied like a sailor's bandanna, and wrote something that was not what he had been told. He stamped the paper. "Bienvenidos. No líos." No trouble. He meant: no trouble I can see.

"Next," he said to the air.

They were free to go.

Free. The word had a new weight.

On the quay, the port showed its ivories. Bales of cacao, sacks of coffee, parrots nailed by their cords to market stalls where they shrieked heartbreak in green. Barefoot men rolled barrels with the intimacy of dancers. A woman in a white kerchief slapped arepas onto a hot stone and the smell—corn and fire and grease—walked across the water and took Artemis by the hair like a lover. Her belly remembered hunger in a hot rush.

"Eat," Clara said simply, and put a coin into the woman's hand. They burned their tongues on the first bites and breathed like fools. The woman smiled like a queen who has seen many men burn their tongues for her.

"Water," Séverine added. "And lime." She squeezed the fruits herself, a little domestic ferocity, and watched until each of them drank. "We pay Éloise's debt forward."

Something bumped the pilings underfoot. A dark shape turned in shadow.

Artemis flinched and nearly dropped her cup. Tamsin caught it but not her wrist. Crimson touched her upper lip; she wiped it on her sleeve and did not name it.

"Dock will play tricks," Isidro said. "It echoes last night to see if you are the same fool this morning."

"We are," Jonah said cheerfully, because that was cheaper than despair. "But with better shoes."

Jory Black joined them long enough to take payment and do the arithmetic of partings. Artemis put the last thirty into his palm and he measured it with his thumb as if he could feel counterfeit like temperature. He closed her fingers around one coin he'd pushed back.

"For luck?" she asked. It sounded like mockery in her own mouth, and she hadn't meant it to.

"For rope," he said. "If you run out, you can buy two feet with that. Tie yourself to something that won't drown. If there is such a thing between here and your river." His scar shone in the sun. "Leave the haunt on my deck, if you can."

"It may follow me where it pleases," she said. "We are badly acquainted."

He looked at her as if she were cargo whose weight he had misjudged but would not argue about now the crane had it. "Then go," he said. "And don't name my ship where mountains can hear you."

They stepped off the dock into the street's thin shade. La Guaira felt like a place hammered between the greater hungers of sea and cliff. Behind its whitewashed faces were rooms with no room in them. Laughter scraped. Coins ticked. A man with a cane paused at a corner and regarded them from under the brim of a hat waxed to a perfection that hinted at sins to match.

His cane head was silver. A serpent coiled for a strike.

"Don Iñigo," Isidro said without moving his lips.

"Or his cousin. Or his mirror," Tamsin answered, same trick.

He lifted the cane half an inch: salute, threat, suggestion itched into the same gesture. Then he turned with cat-slow grace and was swallowed by the market's colors.

"He'll go up," Isidro said. "He likes air cooler than other men breathe."

"So do the dead," Séverine murmured.

They found the mule road to Caracas with the help of a boy who swore he knew every stone by taste. It zigzagged into the mountain like a stitch, the ascent more a negotiation than a climb: mules that knew where to put their feet even when men did not, a precipice that threw down every careless thought. Heat changed its mind halfway—wet oven to a crisp that grated the nose. Sweat stung eyes, then dried, then stung again. The sea fell away behind them like a bad habit; the city above remained a rumor until, with insult of abruptness, the road tipped them onto a terrace of air and light and tiles and bells.

Caracas lay in its bowl like a saint's heart in a reliquary: ringed by green, veined with streets, voices braided with the clean-note peal that says noon to people who will not get to eat at noon. Orange trees flashed their fruit like coins in courtyards. Dogs slept with their ribs showing. Children ran and didn't bother to look both ways.

Artemis stumbled at the sight of so much living arranged as if it had never considered not. The mountain's cool hands had closed over her skull; for a breath she understood the luxury of thinking fever was only a word.

"Pretty," Tamsin said flatly. "Where do they keep the knives."

"In smiles," Jonah said. "And under coats." He touched his own where a pocket knew the shape of other men's lids.

"Padre," Séverine said, reading the letter again for the place name. "Church of Santa Rosalía, near the market of San Jacinto. He will have maps." She looked at Artemis. "He will also have opinions."

"Men like that do," Clara muttered.

They passed a plaza where women sold sugar in cones as yellow as candlelight. An old man clicked his castanets at a one-eyed dog. A boy in a rough shirt carried a cage with a finch that could sing freedom into a man's pocket if he taught it right. The plaza's shade felt earned.

Santa Rosalía kept her church small and blue, saints painted in colors that might have been fruit once. A pair of girls in black lace mantillas glanced up with eyes like knives and then down as the seven clumped in, dust falling from their cuffs into God's house.

Padre Tomás was thinner than the letter's hand had suggested. A man of angles: nose, collarbone, fingers stained with ink the way Isidro's were with oil. He had taken his shoes off. They lay like two old animals under the chair where he sat over his papers. He looked at them without getting up, expression arranged not unkindly.

"Sister Séverine," he said, as if he had talked to her every day of his life. "You grew Bruja in New Orleans and came home to me to make confession with mud on your hem."

"I grew hungry," she said. "And so did the dark. Hola, Padre."

He nodded at Artemis as one nods to a tool that will cut. "You are the Irish girl. The one who should have drowned."

"I didn't," she said.

"Good," he said. "The drowned are poor conversationalists." His fingers sorted papers. "You want Angostura."

"Ciudad Bolívar," Isidro said, the new name glossy in his mouth. "South-east. Orinoco."

Tomás smiled with three teeth. "Men change names as if it could change rivers. The river doesn't learn them."

He unrolled a map and held the corners with lead weights cut from the bottoms of saints' gowns. The paper had islands like scabs where sweat had fallen. Lines sketched like an apology. Names fought each other across it: Ocumare, San Sebastián, Calabozo, Valle de la Pascua, El Sombrero, Cabruta. The Orinoco lay like a black spine.

"The road," Tomás said, tapping where it hurt him to tap, "is not a road as you want it. The Llanos are water when they feel like it and knives when they don't. You will lose things faster than you thought you owned them. Men with governments and men without will ask for paper. You will show them your hands. If your hands are clean they will not trust you; if they are dirty they will want a share."

"Can we hire animals?" Clara said. "Mules?"

"You can hire anything across the Llanos," Tomás said. "Except mercy." He set his finger on the bend of the Orinoco. "This is Cabruta. Here you barter for a boat and a fever. If you don't die, you go to Angostura and lie to men with hats. If you live through those lies, you can take water east, or south toward the Casiquiare, or wherever devils hold parley this season."

"We go south," Séverine said. "Our devils are older than governors."

Tomás looked long at Artemis now that the map had been asked to do its parlor trick. "What rides you," he asked without softness.

"A debt," she said.

"To whom."

"To stone," she said. "And to women who kept me breathing."

He grunted the way men do when a woman says a true thing about survival. "Then leave fast," he said. "Before the city likes you, or hates you."

He found them a courtyard house with a roof like red scales and a landlord whose widower's grief had left him honest. "Cheaper than clean," Jonah judged. "But with fewer witnesses." They took two rooms around a square of shade that grew mint in broken pots and let sparrows bathe in the saucers. They slept on rush mats that hadn't been beaten and listened to a fountain that pretended to run all night.

"Supplies," Clara said, as soon as the packs lay down and breathed in their own sweat. "We go to the market and we buy as if we plan to be both wicked and noble." She ticked it on fingers: "Quina. Needles. Thread. Salt. Rope. Lantern oil. Wax. Hammocks. Netting that the mosquitoes cannot turn into lace. Lime. A pot that will not crack when you swear at it. A second pot for when the first does."

"Cartridges," Tamsin added. "Ball. A second pistol if the Virgin loves me."

"Fishhooks," Isidro said. "Machetes that don't bite your own hand."

"Bread," Otis whispered. "And a sweet. Please."

Artemis took the letter Tomás had written—three lines in a script that did not know how to lie. "For Father Almeida in Bolívar," Séverine said. "He will trade you names of pilots for your promise not to die."

"Promises are cheap," Jonah said, lighting a twist of tobacco into a mood he could carry in his cheek.

"Not this one," Séverine said, and tucked the letter into the Queen's oilskin like a psalm hidden in a soldier's boot.

They went to market and learned the human shape of the city: sellers who kept one price for widows and another for men whose boots were too clean; a butcher who used his cleaver like punctuation; a woman with three locks of hair tied around her wrist—black, black, white—who gave Artemis a look she had seen in mirrors, then turned away as if slapped. The quina bark cost more than Tamsin wanted it to and less than Clara expected. The netting was already bitten in one corner. The lime seller had fingers yellow with his own trade.

A man in a good coat tasted the air near them like a sommelier. He was too clean for real work and too polite to be harmless. "Señores," he said lightly. "Señoras. A word."

"Many words," Jonah said. "Pick your favorite."

"I represent a gentleman," the man went on as if men like Jonah were a local insect, annoying and harmless. "Don Iñigo de la Cuerda. He admires courage. He invests in it when it goes his direction."

"Tell him we have no direction," Isidro said. "We pin the tail on places as we walk."

"Tell him he can eat my direction," Tamsin added, less polite.

The man's smile did not move. "He proposes employment. A retrieval. An antiquity lost in the forest. A fair price for objects that cannot appreciate being worshiped by mud."

Séverine's mouth flattened. "We are not retrieving for other men's altars."

"Then at least take his favor." The man slipped a little packet toward Artemis, wrapped in paper the color of hospital walls. "For the road. A token."

"We don't take candy from snakes," Clara said, but Artemis took it—because you want to know what your enemy thinks you need—and did not open it in his sight. He bowed with the slow insolence of a man who believes his shadow will outrun you even on a bright day.

They turned their backs. In the alley leading back to their courtyard, a boy with a split lip tugged at Artemis's cuff. "Señorita," he whispered, eyes white in his brown face. "No vayas." Don't go.

"We're not good at that," Tamsin told him gently, and flicked a copper into his hand. He didn't look at it. He looked at their shadows and then ran.

Night fell without apology. In the courtyard, the fountain lied; mosquitoes made a ciborium of their bare ankles and took communion. Otis fell asleep with a sweet in his cheek and Dennis the one-eyed sparrow— who had followed them from the market—perched on the eave as if to stand a foolish watch.

Artemis sat on her mat with the packet from Iñigo's man in her lap. Tamsin watched without talking. Séverine rolled her rosary between finger and thumb as if measuring out light.

Artemis opened the paper.

Inside lay hair.

Three lengths, braided together. Black, black, white. Sewn with something like gut through the end so it could be tied to a limb, a line, a throat. It smelled of salt. It smelled of the pump-well and the bar and the queer bright arc to the pistol flash.

Beneath, a card. The Queen of Cups—no, not hers; another deck entirely, Spanish pattern, the cup fat as a jar for organs. Across it, written with a careful, greedy hand:

ABRE.

Open.

Tamsin took a breath that wanted to be a laugh and failed. "Subtle," she said. "He must have hired poets."

Clara's jaw had set. "We burn it," she said. "Hair goes to air."

Séverine did not move to stop her. "Hair remembers. Fire teaches forgetting." She looked at Artemis. "You choose."

Artemis took the braid by the gut thread, held it up. It swung with an elegance that made the stomach turn. She thought of the hold's voices and of the spoon's tremble and of men who had not learned the last of their names. "We burn it," she said, "and we don't breathe the smoke."

In the corner of the courtyard, over the kitchen's charcoal, they fed the braid to red. It went with a noise like a whisper being pulled through the eye of a needle. The smoke was sweet and wrong. They turned their faces and did not breathe.

Otis coughed in his sleep; Clara eased him and pressed a cup to his lips. He swallowed as if taught in infancy to obey cups.

Jonah rubbed the soot into his fingers as if to put prints on the night. "If he knows to send hair," he said, "he knows where we sleep."

"Only tonight," Isidro said. "Tomorrow we sleep where the road is too mean for people with shoes like him."

Artemis took the letter to Father Almeida and tucked it into the oilskin with the Queen that had followed her since salt broke her. She set the bone spoon on the rim of the water basin in the corner and spoke to it without moving her mouth. *Point us wrong if wrong is safer. Point us right if right is the only thing left.*

The spoon did nothing. Inaction could be mercy.

"Dawn," Clara said. "We leave at dawn."

"Without confession?" Jonah said, teasing habit.

Séverine lifted her eyes to the small blue saints who watched the courtyard from the tiles. "Confession without leaving is only gossip."

Sleep came in handfuls thrown at them by an ungenerous host. The fountain lied. Knives lay under palms. In the deepest part of night, Artemis woke with the absolute certainty that someone had stepped into the courtyard and turned to look at her. She did not move. She counted: one, two, three, four, five, six, seven.

The certainty slid away like a fish in warm water. She slept again and dreamed of a road that cooked the soles of her feet and of a river whose children showed their backs at last and those backs were armored with little green stones.

They rose in the violet hour when bells sound less like
bells and more like metal remembering it was ore.
Packs on shoulders. Netting rolled. Hammocks tied
with learned knots. Pistols checked, knives counted and
counted again because counting is a superstition that
keeps hands busy.

At the door, the widower who'd rented them rooms
handed Artemis a bundle wrapped in clean cloth. "Pan,"
he said. Bread. "Y papelón." Sugar. He did not look at
their coins when they tried to give them back. "Vayan
con cuidado." Go with care.

"Con cuidado," Artemis echoed, and meant it as a
promise to him because she could not promise it to
herself.

They went into a morning that tasted of coffee and dust
and the first whisper of heat. In the plaza, men with
papers pretended to forget who they worked for.
Women cut fruit with knives you could shave with and
never once cut themselves. Don Iñigo stood beneath a
jacaranda whose flowers had outlived their own color
and watched theirs leave the city as if he had a rope tied
to their belts and was amused to see how far it might
stretch.

He lifted his cane a fraction. Artemis did not nod. She
did not spit. She did not give him her mouth in any
fashion.

They took the road east, the map in Tomás's ink-stained
hand drawn in their heads now: Ocumare, San
Sebastián, Calabozo—the names like teeth, like rosary
beads, like bets. Ahead lay the llanos, then the brown
god of the Orinoco, then Angostura where hats made

lies look like law, then south into the green mouth that would chew them, then the serpent city, then the idol with hair-rope binding it like a patient body.

Behind them, the mountain watched. The sea breathed. The *San Ignacio* put her head out into open water again and pretended nothing had ever tried to come aboard.

"Count," Séverine said, as if the road were a rosary.

Artemis counted: one for each of them. One for Tamsin's grin and pistol. Two for Jonah's coin flipping a long thread through fate. Three for Isidro's blade that knew the shapes of meat. Four for Clara's hands that would stitch anger into order. Five for Otis's thin wrists and appetite. Six for Séverine, whose prayers had edges. Seven for herself, who had been thrown back by sea and would be eaten by land if she let it.

She did not count the dead. Not out loud. They had their own tallies.

Chapter VIII — Road to Bolívar

"Every mile inland is a mile further from mercy."

They left Caracas before the bells had the breath to argue about it. The road tilted them out of the cool bowl of the city and down into the first heat like a scolded child pushed from church to sun. Packs bit shoulders. Tamsin's pistol rode her hip with a lover's weight. The netting rolled tight as a priest's secret.

"Names," Sister Séverine said, not looking back at the mountain. "Say them."

"Ocumare," Isidro answered. "San Sebastián, La Victoria if we're foolish, Valle de la Pascua, El Sombrero, Calabozo. Then Cabruta and the brown father river. Angostura—call it Bolívar if you want a modern hat." His mouth slanted. "We will be bones by one of them, so choose your favorite."

"Bones travel light," Jonah said. "I prefer to remain extravagant."

The road began proper, a wound sewn through scrub and cane, then became what roads always become where the earth has better ideas: suggestion, rumor, habit. Mules stamped and breathed dust. Larks scissored the morning air. The first muleteer they hired had a laugh like a snapped twig and a rosary plaited into his hatband; the second had a scar at the mouth corner as if words had once been caught there and cut out.

Artemis tasted iron two miles from the city. She dabbed her upper lip with the back of her hand and looked at the color without letting anyone see. *One—dreams.*

Two—nosebleeds. Three—hands drop what they love.
She flexed her fingers around the walking stick Isidro
had pressed on her. "Use the earth's bone," he'd said.
"Your own will shatter later if it must."

They made Ocumare at noon and ate oranges under a
rag of shade that pretended to belong to a tree. A soldier
in a blue coat the wrong blue wandered past and tried to
look like a wall; his companion had a paper he wanted
stamped and a stamp he wanted paid to lift. Séverine let
him see her cross and not the steel under it. He blessed
himself and tried to bless the paper by association. The
stamp went down with a thud that said bribe more than
law.

"Your government is efficient," Tamsin told him with
the kindness of a knife.

He did not hear English and liked the tone. He smiled
like a man carving meat.

San Sebastián baked them like tiles. The street ran from
church to barracks and did not admit of any other story.
A woman with hair like a storm cloud sold quina bark
dear; Clara paid and counted change into the woman's
hand loud enough that the soldiers could hear arithmetic
and not temper. Otis squinted at a string of lizards hung
for sale by their tails.

"Eat?" he said, half-wondering, half-hopeful.

"We eat what doesn't eat us first," Clara answered.

"What's that leave?" Jonah asked.

"Sugar. Regret. Each other," Tamsin said. "Try the sugar first."

They marched. Sun climbed and clawed. The last green shoulder of the mountain gave its shade away as if to be rid of them, and the world spilled into the *llanos*—an anvil of grass hammered flat to the horizon, sky so large it bruised the eyes to look at it. Heat came up from below as well as down. Birds melted into blue.

"Water," Isidro said, pointing with his chin at a ribbon dark as a belt. "Tuy when it's in the mood. Don't believe it stands still. Rivers in this country never stand still. They pace."

They paced too. At the bank, Jonah pulled his coin and flipped it once, twice, thrice. The third time it skipped from his knuckle, arced, and vanished into water that looked knee-deep.

"Shit," he said mildly.

He had his boots off before Tamsin could smirk. "I'll fetch it."

"Don't," Isidro said. His knife lifted like a schoolmaster's finger. "You love your feet? Keep them."

The water around Jonah's ankles was liquor-clear. He could see the coin in a dimple of sand as neat as a saint's mouth. Something moved; the sand shivered; the coin slid and was gone as if pinched by an invisible child.

Otis leaned too far, curious; Clara hooked his belt and hauled him back with two fingers. "Fish," she said. "With teeth like a jealous wife's. If you must bleed, be generous on land."

They crossed with a line on a line—mules tethered one to the other, men to mules, men to each other, the world's dumb strength kindly so far. Halfway, a shape fanned from the shadows: broad head, yellow eyes, intention. Isidro flung a rock; the head sank without admitting to the insult. The line pulled the line. They came out into grass with exactly the same number of feet they had gone in with. Artemis counted them twice. The spoon in her pocket woke and went quiet again like a repaired clock.

By Valle de la Pascua, the road had learned to laugh at maps. There were flags of cracked earth that rang like crockery under boots, and pools where the mosquito swarmed his small blood-tax and sent larger collectors after. The muleteer with the rosary tipped his hat to a saint on a stick and muttered about *zorros del agua*, water foxes that took children too little to be called coins. He meant caimans. He meant hunger in a skin that smiled.

At El Sombrero, a man played cuatro in a shade like an argument and sang about a woman who left for the river and came back with pearls in her eyes. Jonah danced once around the stump and lifted a silver he swore had been in his pocket all day. "I make money by losing it," he told Tamsin. "It's a complicated strategy."

"So is drowning," she said. "You'll be a master by the time we reach the big river "

They bivouacked by a copse that had managed to persuade its limbs to hold hands, hung hammocks like patient tongues between branches. Mosquito netting unfurled with the sigh of a bride's veil and failed with equal theatricality where it met thorn. Séverine dusted the ground in a thin line of salt and murmured a psalm that had never been written. Otis fell asleep with a strip of sugar between his teeth and woke in panic until Clara taught him to spit sweetness and not swallow it.

The first night on the open plain they learned the bats. It began with a horse's soft unease, a foot stamping too soft to be threat, then a whickering nobody wanted to call frightened. Isidro's lantern showed them the dark leather shadows lifting from the ground where they had been kissing blood from sleeping animal skin. One bat rose with a little red flag of meat in its mouth. Isidro flicked his knife and cut it out of the air without triumph.

"Salt," he said. "On the wound. And a rag. They don't like to share."

Clara salted and bandaged and grunted when the horse's breath feathered her wrist. "We'll be crawling with worms if we don't keep our threads clean," she said, more prayer than prediction.

"Worms make good children," Jonah murmured, half-asleep.

"Tell that to yours," Tamsin said. "When you have them."

"My children will come out talking and run a faro table at baptism."

"Then their godfather is the devil."

"Already promised." He rolled over. His coin, lost, made him easier; his hands were empty for once. He slept without a trick on his fingers and therefore looked young for five breaths.

In the morning, soldiers. They had hats that did not fit their faces and rifles that fit their hands too well. Paper again. A stamp in a different blue. The scar-mouth muleteer smiled too much at the smallest soldier and got himself three extra questions for his trouble.

"What's in the packs," the officer asked Artemis in slow meat-spoon Spanish. "Guns?"

"Sugar and rope," she said. "Needles and quina. A nun if you shake it hard." She smiled in the angle men leave free for either threat or flirtation. "We prefer to keep our guns where our hands are."

"Your hands are trouble," he said, but as if he were bored of the taste. He stamped Séverine's letter again for the pleasure of a sound. "Cuidado en Calabozo," he added. "The road makes thieves there."

"The road made them here," Tamsin said after he wandered. "It carves faces until the eyes fit the lies."

Calabozo was a low sprawl wrapped thinly around a church that tried too hard. The bell sounded like a bucket kicked down a well. Children ran barefoot over stones that kept their heat like grudges. A woman with an infant sold *arepas* on a griddle and never burned her fingers; she watched them with the gaze of a saint who had been promised and promised until faith turned into arithmetic.

They bought rope. They bought a second pot. They bought more netting and pretended it had not already become lace. They bought a machete that had cut cane long enough to have a soul. Jonah flirted with a girl who sold *aguardiente* and got a bruise for his learning.

Isidro made a friend of a man with a hat wider than his honesty. The man called himself Falcón and had the whites of his eyes stained yellow as a lemon rind. "Cabruta in three days," he promised. "Less if you know which cattle belong to which men and how to step between their shadows." He smiled with his whole face and none of his teeth. "For a fee."

"Always a fee," Tamsin muttered.

"Three mules," Isidro said. "And your word you don't sell our names the second we turn our backs."

"My word weighs less than your gun," Falcón replied, and held out a palm. Isidro counted coins without flinching at the absence of change.

They went. The plain closed around them like a wide mouth. Vultures wrote their occupation across the higher air. Heat rubbed their skin until it complained. When clouds remembered themselves, they came bunched and black, and rain slashed the world into a thousand bright threads. The dry earth took it in gulps, then spat it back as steam and temper.

At a shallow ford the colour of tea, Falcón waded first, mule bell cocking like a question. Halfway, he stopped dead.

"What," Isidro said, already seeing it.

The water in front of Falcón wrinkled and went wrong. A head lifted, then another, then another—only eyes and nostrils, the smile you see in dreams that begin with knives. Caimans, driftwood until they are not. One slid across Falcón's thigh as polite as a clerk brushing past to his desk. He froze until the water put him down. "We wait," he said, voice thin. "They are counting."

"Who taught them," Tamsin murmured.

"The river did," Séverine said. "It has always known numbers."

They waited until the heads sank, eyes closing like coins placed by a careful hand. Isidro flung two haunches of salted fish as dowry downstream; the water took them, and the water was pleased. They crossed knee-deep, then thigh, then waist. The current took a fancy to Otis; Jonah caught him by the back of the belt and Tamsin took Jonah by the collar and for a wobbling breath it was a string of desperation like musicians linked on a stage. Clara braced them all and swore with pathologic precision.

When they came out, Artemis's fingers were white on the rope. She opened them one by one and the last refused. Séverine wrapped Artemis's hand in a strip of cloth without comment, the way a mother refuses to name a fever the first day it sits at a child's mouth.

The next miles laid themselves down one sting at a time. A thorn took Tamsin high on the calf; Clara cut and squeezed until the poison wept like sap. A viper, not far from the color of the dirt that had raised it, put its mouth on the heel of the scar-mouth muleteer and loved him in a way that stopped his breathing in five minutes. He did not thrash; he eased, eyes wide and interested like a man meeting a story that had been told to him all his life. They buried him in the thin shade of a tree that had never bothered to learn its name from men. Falcón said a prayer that sounded more like a receipt.

"If we were seven and we add two and subtract one," Jonah said too lightly, "what number protects us now?"

"None," Séverine answered. "Numbers do not love us. They only count us."

Night came, and with it a storm out of the east so sudden the sky had to borrow black from under the earth. Lightning walked its pet dog thunder; thunder obeyed. They hung the hammocks lower, then higher, then learned humility. Rain came sideways. Mosquitoes found the aperture between net and skin with a skill that belonged to saints or thieves. Tamsin wiped her pistol and wrapped it in oiled cloth and tucked it into her shirt as if willing a child to live through winter.

Artemis dreamed of the ship again: the bar across the hatch, the salt line, the spoon tilting like a listening ear. She woke with her heart at her tongue and the certainty that if she reached in the dark under her hammock she would find hair, braided three—black, black, white— tied to the rope with gut.

She reached anyway.

Her hands closed on rope and nothing else. She breathed to seven; on seven, the storm went from rage to sulk. She slept in corners until morning made everything cheap again.

By the second day with Falcón, the land learned to undulate. Grass hid water that did not look like water and holes that had been made by things that had no interest in their accommodation. A bull with a temperament like a colonel's stood in the road and forbade it to be a road. Isidro shouted the bull's father's sins; the bull considered; the bull allowed them passage and took a consolatory shit in their direction.

At noon, a dust-licked village that had never decided if it deserved a name. Little brown faces watched from doors. A woman carried a piglet like a baby. A boy with the solemnity of an undertaker sold them limes too green and bread too white.

"Cabruta tomorrow," Falcón said that night, counting his own fingers as if to be sure they were all present for the bargaining. "River after. Then hats and lies in Bolívar."

"What do we do with you after that," Jonah asked. "Hire you to guide us all the way to hell?"

"You can walk alone," Falcón said. "But hell keeps guides. It pays in what you cannot spend."

In the hours when men confess to selves they won't speak to in daylight, Jonah shook awake in a fizz of breath. "Something," he said. "Something just now walked past my face." He was not the kind of man to admit fear had its hand on his long throat. He did it now, briefly, then organized his mouth into a smile. "A dream with feet."

Séverine sat up on her mat and stared into the dark as if she'd seen the dark at a dinner party once and recognized its wife. "We are walking toward an old mouth," she said. "It's practicing our names."

In the morning, they found a line of ants crossing the path so dense it looked like a trickle of oil. Isidro bent and touched a finger into it and hissed. "Corredoras," he said. "Soldiers." He stepped over with respect. Otis imitated him with exaggerated care and earned a grin he pretended not to prize.

By noon—noon here meaning the hour when everything stops pretending it can work—they smelled the river before they saw it: vegetable rot, wet coin, a sweetness like bruised fruit, breath the colour of tea. The trees leaned inward to gossip about it. Falcón's hat tilted as if greeting a priest.

Cabruta was a congregation of huts and a memory of a fort. The men who owned the boats wore hats like laws and shirts that had known kinder soap. They looked at the seven and saw a number, not people.

"Hire a *curiara*," Falcón advised. "Not a *bongo*. Too many mouths on a bongo; they row you with hands that have already sold your load on shore."

Artemis's fingers itched in her pocket. The spoon made itself known as a small pressure like a child insisting. She took it out only far enough to feel air on its bowl. It wanted to turn. She kept it in her hand like a secret and let it quiver.

They bartered. A boat with a rib-scar, a pilot with two teeth and more dignity than men with twenty. Fishhooks, maize, salt, cash—the math of motion. When the paper-thin contract had more signatures than ink could bear, Falcón held out his hand for a last weigh of coin.

"Your word," Isidro said again, because men insist on their own superstitions.

Falcón touched his hat. "My word: I only sell you once." He grinned. "And I just did."

Tamsin laughed because it was either that or cut him. "Fair," she said. "At least he says it while we're still where murder costs extra."

They slept in huts with floors too clean to trust and woke to the breath of the river coming into their heads like a new law.

"Tomorrow," Séverine said, rolling her rosary until it clicked like beetle shells, "we change languages."

"From dust to water," Clara said. "And from far to near."

Artemis lay on her mat and listened to the Orinoco breathing. In the thin wall, a beetle scratched out a sermon. Men snored like old bellows. A dog gave its heart to the moon and took it back again. She counted: one, two, three, four, five, six, seven.

When she slept at last, the dream had green stones in it—little plates of jade set like armor on a great back moving through brown water toward a mouth framed in roots. Hands reached for her as if she'd been hung like bait in a doorway. Hair brushed her cheek—black, black, white. A voice that had learned its trickery on a ship said a new word it had not said to her yet: *South.*

She woke with her palm clenched and did not know if she had been holding breath or hair. The day came in the door like a dog who wants but doesn't know what it deserves. The river waited with the patience of a man who has owned the same chair all his life.

"Count," Séverine said.

"Seven," Artemis answered. "Still."

For now.

Chapter IX — Crossroads of Knives

"Trust is the rarest coin in the wilderness."

Dawn found Cabruta drowsing with one eye open. Fog clung in rags over the brown breadth of the Orinoco; the river breathed the way a sleeping animal does when it knows you are in the room. Roosters shouted at the wrong angles of light. Somewhere a woman beat laundry against a stone with a rhythm that announced she had survived other mornings and would survive this one.

They packed in the dim courtyard without speaking much. Trousers cinched, shirts rolled at the sleeve, boots greased, netting rolled in tight green sausage. Clara checked her kit with the quiet greed of a miser counting gold: needles, thread, quina, a lancet that looked like a small unsympathetic truth. Tamsin thumbed powder into a new paper cap, slid it into place, breathed once on the pistol mouth the way a gambler breathes on dice for luck she doesn't believe in. Sister Séverine wound her rosary around her wrist and knotted it, a cuff that could bruise if she wished. Isidro sharpened his machete until dawn could see its face in the blade.

Artemis palmed Éloise's bone spoon and the little coin Baptiste had pressed on her. Spoon cold. Coin warm. She let them argue against each other and said nothing.

By the river, a line of *curiaras* waited: long, narrow dugouts with ribs like the inside of a fish; paddles stacked like spare bones. Men in hats measured strangers with the same eyes they used to measure current. Falcón had kept his word and was there to sell them a pilot a second time.

"Tadeo," he said, introducing a narrow man with a mouth like a healed cut. "Knows the back-ways. Cheaper than dying."

"More expensive than breath," Tamsin murmured.

Tadeo showed them a grin the river could have carved. "You want Angostura? I take you above the mouths that bite. You want to see the crocodile's teeth? I take you there too." He spat neatly into the water, as if feeding a pet. "Your choice."

Sister Séverine's gaze flicked over his wrists, his boat, the charm tied to the bow: a bird's foot wrapped in red thread. She said nothing. Her silence had temperature.

They loaded: hammocks, netting, quina, pots, rope, a roll of mosquito cloth that was already learning to fail. Otis climbed in with the anxious dignity of a boy pretending not to be a boy. Jonah made jokes at the water and let his foot tap the gunwale exactly seven times before settling; superstition is a language even men who sneer at it speak when the grammar suits.

The *curiara* let go of dirt with a lover's reluctance and took them. The paddle stroke found its pace: draw, dip, push, breathe; draw, dip, push, breathe. Tadeo hugged the bank where roots laced like arthritic fingers. "The middle has appetites," he said. "The edge has manners."

Caimans watched them from the milk of the shallows, yellow eyes like cheap jewels. A log turned and revealed the idea of a tail. A swath of silver, piranha or their cousins, moved under the boat like a thought no one wanted to finish.

"Don't trail your hands," Clara said to Otis without looking. "If you must feed the river, feed it from a bowl."

They made the first bend, then two more. The sun got up and announced itself without apology. Mosquitoes came out of the idea of leaves and claimed tribute, a light constant siege. Sweat found their eyebrows and stung; the river-smell moved into their lungs and began to argue it had always lived there.

"See that cut?" Tadeo pointed with his chin toward a dark slit in the green ahead where the bank broke and a narrow channel slid away, slick as a knife's back. "Shortcut. Bring us above the reeds that hide the long ones."

Isidro's blade paused mid-stroke. "Back channels are where men set tables they don't invite you to."

"Or where saints lay out bread for those who trust," Tadeo said, teeth. "We save a day."

Jonah rolled a shoulder as if throwing a coin none of them could see. "A day is a fortune if it keeps the river from counting us wrong."

Artemis had been listening to the river with her skin. The spoon pressed itself against her thigh like a mouth wanting to whisper. She drew it, filled a tin cup with brown water, salted it from a twist Tamsin handed over without comment, and held the spoon above the cup.

One. Two. Three. Four. Five. Six. Seven.

On five, it trembled. On seven, it turned—not toward the broad honest brown lane, but toward the slit under the tangle, the shortcut with shadows like mouths.

Tamsin's jaw cocked. "I'll say now what I'll say later: I don't like that."

"It's what I have," Artemis said. "We asked. It answered."

Séverine's eyes were dark as spent coals. "Doors don't always open onto rooms. Sometimes they open onto falling."

Isidro spat into the river for the price of an omen. "We go," he said to Tadeo, as if the decision had been his all along. "But you turn us out at the first lie the water tells."

Tadeo's paddle eased, then bit. The *curiara* nosed into the slit.

Inside the side-channel, the world narrowed. Branches leaned until they touched each other and then learned to hold hands. Light went green and then darker than green. The river here spoke in whispers and in the small private clicks of things with joints. Leaves brushed Artemis's arms like uncombed hair. A monkey with a human's grandmother's face watched from a crook and condemned them to hell in a voice like a dry hinge.

"Pleasant," Tamsin said, because to name fear is to pretend to own it. Her pistol sat under her shirt and pressed a warm punctuation into her ribs.

The *curiara* slid like a needle through a seam. Once, a washer of metallic scales turned in place under the bow—so close Artemis could have touched with two fingers—then went away with the discretion of sin.

Isidro's ear tipped. "Hear that," he said softly.

"What," Jonah said, because he always pretended not to until he couldn't.

"Nothing but what the river should say," Isidro answered. "And it's saying it too clean."

They came to the crossroads of water: four cuttings meeting like thieves in a chit of shade. Tadeo eased the boat against a low bank hung with roots. "Here," he said. "Rest. We eat. Then the right-hand cut brings us behind the reed-bed that bites boats."

Artemis's skin crawled with the sense of being read. Her hands wanted to open and show their lines.

Séverine vaulted out with a grace that belonged to younger knees and years that were kind. She pinched a stripe of salt and drew it on the mud by her boot: a line. "We'll eat quick," she said. "And if you put your feet across this line you have a reason."

They ate bread that turned to paste and dried fish that remembered the sea more fondly than the living had done. Otis sipped from a cup and smacked a mosquito so gently it lived to try again. He wiped his lip. "Bleeding less," he said, proud as a man who has had a tooth pulled and kept the tooth.

Clara's mouth jerked toward a smile. "Keep that blood for your bones."

Tadeo stepped beyond Séverine's line without asking. For a piss, perhaps; for a look: who knows. The mud made a small private sound under his boot. Birds stopped. The air took a breath and held it.

Isidro didn't turn his head. His knife walked itself into his hand. "Visitors," he said.

They arrived like mosquitoes: not one and not two, but many enough to be called a fact. Men eased out of the green as if they belonged to the idea of it. Faces under hats. Machetes with personalities. A rifle or two whose histories were written in dents.

Falcón came last, hat canted, eyes the color of yellow fruit gone wrong. He smiled with his teeth this time, to prove he had them. "Friends," he said, and made the word into something like a price.

Tamsin's pistol came out and up with the economy of a woman adjusting a hatpin. "Oh," she said lightly. "I thought your business was only selling us once."

"It is," Falcón said. "To different owners."

Two of his men stepped down the bank, machetes low, not raised—this was not a threat; this was administration. Another man in a good coat with the wrong boots stood under a palm and tapped a cane into the root mat. Silver flashed at its head: a serpent in a loop.

"Señor Iñigo's compliments," the man in the good coat said, bored, as if reading a bad menu. "He asks for the thing that calls you. If you don't have it yet, he asks for the things that will get you there. Papers. Letters. Jewellery. Saints. Maps. And the spoon in your pocket."

Artemis felt the spoon weigh her. She could feel its interest, the way a needle in the hand can feel the gravity of skin.

"We have sugar," Jonah offered pleasantly, buying breath. "And a boy. He's small—eats little."

The good-coat man's smile did not move. "We don't take boys. They ruin discipline."

Clara stood square, hands low. "You take nothing," she said. "You go upstream and you drown in a puddle and your mothers think you ran away to a better place."

Falcón's grin widened. "I like her," he told the good-coat man. "But I like getting paid more."

Tadeo did not look ashamed. He chewed and looked at the green the way men look at a wall right before they wet it. "Shortcut," he said, to no one.

Artemis said nothing for the length of time it takes a hawk to return to its hand. Then: "How much for the privilege of you going away."

"A letter," said the good-coat man instantly. "The one from Tomás. Or the one for Almeida in Angostura. And something that smells like salt and women."

Séverine made a sound that could have been a laugh if someone had been born dead in the room when it was made. "Come take it," she said gently. "I set lines. They bite."

Tamsin's pistol breathed and the world jumped.

The ball took Falcón's hat and the inch of scalp that had spent the morning pretending to be skin. He fell back clumsy, surprised that a joke could turn into blood. The machetes came up with a sound like grass being taught an uglier word. The good-coat man stepped aside, immune to consequences by habit. His cane tapped in a little, polite rhythm.

The side-channel shook itself and became small sudden war.

Isidro met the first blade with a promise and kept it. His machete bit wrist; a hand flew and hit the water still opening its fingers like a thing told a story too late. The river took the hand and did not return it. Blood made a red that the brown loved; fish came silver and neat, their mouths a private economy. Otis cried out once and then bit it down and flung the spare pot at a face that had meant to be remembered; tin rang; a tooth went into the green and found a new religion.

Jonah ducked, rolled, came up under a man's arm, and showed him what pockets were really for: he took the man's knife and replaced it with a fist. The man swore and laughed and bled in three languages; Jonah bled in none.

Clara did not choose to be brave; she chose to be efficient. Her blade was shorter, more honest. She cut tendon above heel—one quick unkindness—and a man who had meant to be strong became a prayer for balance and fell, howling. She stepped back to avoid his dirt and did not spare him a name.

Séverine walked the bank, three paces left, three right, palm open. "Non," she said, not to the men, but to the place. She cast salt in a thin fan that hung in the green air the way breath hangs in winter. A man crossed her line and made the sound a dog makes when it steps on a coal; he forgot how to tell his own legs to be legs. He went to his knees and made the sign of the cross backward without knowing why.

Tadeo took his chance: he shoved the *curiara* off the roots and swung its nose toward the right-hand cut. Flee? Betray again? His paddle bit. The boat slid.

Artemis went to throw—what? the spoon?—and her hand opened. The knife that had been a sailor's and then hers slithered out obedient to whatever curse counted down in her bones. It hit a root, bounced, splashed, and hung in the water's skin mocking her with the absurdity of how close a hand can be to what it loves and still lose it.

Tamsin saw the look on Artemis's face and shot a man who was not yet a problem because she trusted Artemis to see the problem that mattered. "Leave the knife," she snapped, without looking away from her next target. "Buy another. Keep the hand."

The good-coat man smiled as if at a recital. "Señores," he began.

Isidro put his machete against the man's cane-hand and pressed just enough to open a thin pretty line. "Señor," he said. "This is the wrong jungle for manners."

The man did not flinch. He had been born into rooms where other men bled for him. He looked at the blood with academic interest. "It can be the right jungle for profit."

Séverine's line of salt hissed. "Go," she told him. "Your dead are following you; you are making them tired."

On the bank, Falcón learned to die slowly. His hat had fallen into a posture of apology; his hair stuck in the blood that made a cup of his ear. He laughed once, then twice, the sound of a man who has been paid and doesn't like the coin. "I said," he wheezed, "I only sell you once."

"You did," Tamsin said, re-priming with a good wife's efficiency. "And you sold at a loss."

He died before he learned to argue.

The good-coat man stepped back into the green the way a stage magician steps behind a plume of smoke. Two of his men dragged their wounded out with professional contempt; two more stayed to make the world smaller and didn't. A body rolled into the water without its owner's consent. Silver mouths spoke the only prayer they know.

"Boat," Isidro barked, blood on his forearm and no notion of who had put it there. "Now."

They slammed into the *curiara*—Otis scrambling, Clara shoving, Séverine cool as a clerk stamping NO over a petition. Artemis went last, palm flayed where the knife had humiliated her. Isidro heaved the bow around with a grunt, Tadeo throwing his pale weight into the paddle. The boat lunged like a dog freed to run.

Two bends and the green fell away, abruptly as a curtain. The side-channel spat them into the broader brown with an ungenteel burp. The river's middle shouldered them without interest. Behind, the mouth of the shortcut closed with the demure air of a sin that has learned to hide at confession.

They did not speak for longer than a minute knows how to hold. Breath had to be paid back. Hands shook because hands are treacherous animals with long memories for fear.

Clara braced her foot against a rib and bound Artemis's palm. "You'll not count with that for a week," she said, and in her voice was a tenderness she would have denied under torture. "So count with your head instead."

"It's loud," Artemis said, and found her laugh and let it hurt. "Everything is."

"Good," Tamsin said. She had blood on her cheekbone in a tidy fish's smile. "Alive things are loud."

Séverine unwound the rosary from her wrist and looked toward the green as if it were a church that had gotten bored of being holy. "That man has a theology," she said of the good-coat emissary. "It consists of the belief that the world exists to be counted in his ledger. He will follow. He will arrive before we think he can, because money runs faster than legs."

"Then we outrun money," Jonah said lightly. He was startlingly white under his tan; his hands found his pockets and found nothing they could amuse. "Two days to Angostura if the current forgives," he added— practical, because he needed something that could be counted that wasn't blood.

"Two days," Tadeo said, not looking at them. He had that new humility men find when the room reveals another door they didn't know they had been inside. "I will take you there and I will not take you anywhere else."

"Good," Isidro said. "Because beyond Angostura we don't go where men with hats go."

The river widened. Heat went from clever to blunt. Vultures stacked in the sky like notes on a staff and watched with professional disinterest. The current took them, kind enough so long as they didn't pretend to be smarter than water.

Midday, they made a low bank where men with lighter eyes than the locals sold *panela* and lies. No one spoke to them beyond praise of the weather. The world had learned they were the sort of problem that grows when you name it. A child with a swollen belly watched Tamsin rewrap her pistol and put her thumb to her mouth with the seriousness of a woman twice her size.

Afternoon flattened into a long brass plate. Shadows had to invent themselves. The boat moved, moved, moved. When voices came, they came from the bank high above—men the color of dust shouting down that the river had taken better than them and they had learned to be poor.

By the hour that earns the name gold whether it wants it or not, the hills gathered and the river decided to decorate itself with a city. Angostura—Ciudad Bolívar now, if you asked men with titles—rose white and yellow and dignified on a bluff. A bridge hadn't been invented there yet for this story; boats with opinions prowled the shore.

Tadeo nosed them into a dirt lip below steps that had taught too many calves humility. "Here," he said. A statement, not a gift.

Jonah paid him with the careful generosity of a man who understands the price of leaving a tongue attached to a mouth. Tadeo took the coins without courtesy and did the thing masks do when they are peeled: he blinked at his own face. "Forgive me," he said to no one. "I don't think I own that word."

Artemis looked up at the serried roofs of Angostura and saw hats and ledgers and Father Almeida and the river beyond into which men with clean boots did not go. The spoon at her hip lay with an exaggerated innocence.

Séverine touched her elbow. "Do not give papers to anyone who asks for them," she said, as if Artemis were about to be born again and needed the advice in the labouring room. "Give them to the man the letter names. No one else."

They went up the steps into heat with opinions and a square that wore dignity like a better coat than it could afford. The church had a face that suggested it would slap you if you deserved it. A man with a hat that had seen fewer sins than his boots practiced looking important on a bench.

Father Almeida was where Tomás's letter said he would be: under the side arcade, in a chair that had learned to be his shape, ink under his nails like the remnants of arguments. He was older than he had a right to be and younger in the eyes than a man who stays in one place. He read the letter with his mouth tight, then looked at the seven from behind a pair of spectacles that made honesty look awkward.

"You'll need a *bongo* with a bigger mouth than your own," he said. "And a pilot who doesn't drink the wrong days. I'll write you names they will honour if the wind is in the mood."

"And beyond?" Isidro said. "South. Where the river forgets how to speak Spanish."

Almeida set his thumb on the map's muscle where men have written ORINOCO and then kissed their wives goodbye. "Atabapo," he said. "Temi. Guainía. Or you can pretend the Casiquiare is only a story told by men who like to walk uphill on water." His smile twinged. "Either way the river makes new men out of old ones, or it keeps the parts it likes."

He lifted his eyes to Artemis—not to the others; to her—and saw something that made his jaw knot. "You've been notched," he said quietly. "Be careful where you try the key."

Artemis closed her bleeding hand around the coin
Baptiste had refused. "I am."

He gave them a lodging with walls that didn't know
secrets and a patio where the mosquitoes organized
labour. He gave them a name and a knock for a pilot
with a face like an axe-handle and a soul like a good
rope. He gave them a blessing that tasted of stale wine
and a warning that felt like love reluctant to be named.

Night came and with it the mild courtesy of city dark.
In the courtyard, they inventoried loss: one pot dented,
one coil of rope gone, a third of the quina paste
dissolved by river, a knife that had belonged to a
drowned man and then to a not-drowned woman and
now to fish.

"Buy another," Tamsin said, lying back on her mat,
trousers creased, eyes open. "Make it meaner."

Artemis lay her palm on the oilskin that held the Tower
and the Queen. She counted slow. One, two, three, four,
five, six, seven. The numbers were not kind; they were
not cruel; they were the only stones steady under foot.

A breeze from the river lifted the netting and laid it
down again with the intimacy of a hand. The city's
bells told an hour that did not matter. In her pocket the
spoon lay quiet, as if resting after having chosen blood.

In the thin place between waking and sleep, Artemis
saw again the crossroads of water. But this time, instead
of men with hats and machetes, there were stone faces
under leaves and stairs that had not been asked to carry
feet in a century, and a mouth in the earth that had been
shut with hair and prayer and wanted opening. It had

learned her name and could say it without an accent now.

She woke with her hand on nothing and wanted the knife she didn't have and did not want it in the same breath.

"Count," Séverine said from the dark, because she knew.

Artemis did. At seven, she slept.

Chapter X — The Emerald Labyrinth

"The jungle grows over bones as quickly as over roots."

Father Almeida's pilot knocked like a debt collector and stood in the doorway with his hat in his hands and the river on his clothes. He had the blunt dignity of a stump that had outlived the ax. "Teófilo Aponte," he said. "Teo if the river is quiet." His face had been carved with a dull knife and then sanded by wind. The whites of his eyes showed yellow in the corners. "Your priest writes that you pay and do not argue."

"We pay," Isidro said. "We argue only when dying."

"Everyone argues when dying." Teo tipped his hat to Séverine in an old-fashioned courtesy that did not exclude knives. "We leave at first bell. The *bongo* is wide. She takes weight and secrets."

Weight and secrets. They carried both.

The *bongo* crouched at the foot of the bluff like a brown beast waiting for a prod: broader than the *curiara*, with a low thatch awning half its length, ribs black as old teeth. Two of Teo's men—bare-chested, trousers slick with old water, paddles callused to their palms—stood easy at the stern. A third, a boy with a scar that sharpened one cheekbone, watched Otis watch him and pretended not to be curious.

They loaded with the economy of people who had learned to live out of their hands. Hammocks in a tight roll, netting, quina paste swaddled like a saint's relic, Clara's satchel of needles and ligatures, rope coiled and tied, a pot with a new dent and a story already attached to it. Tamsin slid her pistol into the small of her back under her shirt until its mouth warmed her spine. Artemis cinched her belt until it bit and threaded Éloise's spoon to a rawhide thong around her neck. The small coin Baptiste had pressed on her lay against her collarbone like a stubborn prayer.

"Last ground," Teo said, as if naming a sacrament. "We change language on water."

The *bongo* pushed free. Paddles bit. The bluff slid away like a mask coming off a face. Angostura watched them with a look that said *I knew you when you had cleaner boots*. The river widened and then narrowed under the same sky; men's mouths went quiet to make a space for what water had to say.

They moved days that were also miles and miles that were also years. The Orinoco showed them its moods: a brown broadness with pale sandbars like tongues; cutbanks where the river had been chewing at a hill until the roots hung with the patience of old teeth; backwaters where water stood as if listening. Egrets stepped their long thin righteous steps where shoals hummed fish. Somewhere under the awning a frog learned to live in the pot and had to be evicted every time Clara wanted to boil water.

The heat did not come at them; it sat on them. It taught shirts to cling and trousers to salt-stiffen at the knee. Mosquitoes thrummed, a soft saw across the skin. The netting made its promises and kept some. Clara learned to smear smoke under the eaves of the awning so they could breathe and not be bitten in the same instant; smoke taught everything to taste like itself. Otis learned to sleep in a posture that protected his wrists and ankles. Jonah learned to spit with accuracy without standing up. Tamsin learned to curse in a Spanish that made dogs consider biting and then think better of it.

On the third day Teo raised his paddle and pointed where the river darkened as if a shadow had been poured into it. "Atabapo," he said. "Black water."

Artemis leaned over until Tamsin pinched her belt and pulled her back. The seam was a miracle of manners: the brown on one side, tea-thick, vegetal; the black on the other like smoke dissolved in water, clear as glass and dark as a promise. They slid across it slow, so slow she could lay a palm on the *bongo's* rib and feel the change ease under her bones. The air smelled different, a breath lifted from rotting leaves that had decided to become perfume instead.

"Saints," Tamsin breathed. "It's like stepping from one room into another without a door."

"Don't drink the black," Teo said. "It's clean enough to make you forget your mother. Men drink it and decide to sit down and be leaves."

"What do we drink," Jonah asked, already reaching for the gourd.

"Brown," Teo said. "The brown is a liar you know."

They slept that night on a sand spit that would not keep the shape it had in the morning. Teo's men strung the hammocks between driftwood and cloud and hung netting over all like the idea of prudence. Stars came out one by one, astonished at their own brightness. In the black beyond the fire, something dragged itself along the sand with a sound like a sack of meat. Isidro went to meet it and came back with a turtle and the knowledge of a bite he would not confess had hurt.

"Don't eat," Séverine said gently when Otis made eyes at the meat. "They remember." She crossed herself, not because it worked but because memory deserves to be honored. The turtle watched her with the expression of a philosopher inconvenienced by a practical matter, then went back to the river with the dignity of a bishop refusing soup.

Artemis woke before dawn with her hand stinging as if the night had evicted something from under her skin. She pinned the net back and looked down at her palm. The cut Clara had bound—shallow where the knife hilt had laughed at her—had opened in the night and wept a little line of clear. In the sticky half-light she saw a thing that might have been a white egg of spit laid in the edge of it. Botfly. She ground her teeth.

Clara woke to the sound of her not asking for help and glanced once and didn't sigh. "Hold," she said, took out a sliver of a thing that looked exactly like a sliver of a thing meant to bite pain, and did. The worm came out reluctantly. The pain had the intimate quality of a remembered betrayal. Clara squeezed, quick and obscene, wiped the tiny white thing on a leaf, salted the wound, tied it. "Now we've met that little priest, we won't give him a parish," she said. "Keep the bandage dry and your mouth shut."

"How do I do both on a river," Artemis asked, and got a narrowing of Clara's eyes for answer, which meant *try*.

By noon, the green had settled into its own law. The river gathered itself into channels so perfect they made a geometry of hunger. The canopy leaned until the edges touched like neighbors whispering about sin. Vines ran lines between trees as if mapping a place that had no interest in letting men make maps. The *bongo* slid through like a spoon in a bowl of syrup; everything stuck to everything else.

"Emerald," Tamsin said, sweat painting a new collar around her throat. "If emeralds stank and bit."

Teo eased the boat around what looked like a floating island and was in fact the collected stubbornness of a thousand plants trying to make a floor out of water. A heron watched them pass with professional contempt. "We go slow," he said. "A fast boat here is a boat that wants to forget it is wood."

"God," Jonah murmured, running his fingers along the gunwale. "You talk like a philosophy teacher who owns a knife."

Teo's mouth twitched. "Knives teach philosophy."

They took the right-hand of two equal mouths. Then the left of three. Then the middle of five, because Teo's thumb pressed hard into the wood and the wood answered with a small shiver he recognized as warning. Artemis felt the spoon warm against her sternum. She dipped it once into a cup that held half black-water, half brown, a small blasphemy. Salted it. Held the spoon above.

One—two—three—four—five—six—seven.

On four it ticked. On seven it pointed into a slit where no boat had any business going.

"Teo," Isidro said evenly.

Teo considered her, the spoon, the slit, and the faces of men who had learned to listen to women for reasons that had nothing to do with courtesy. "We could fight the river and be right," he said. "Or we could be wrong with it and live." He swung the bow. "Duck your heads. The leaves bite."

They ducked. Leaves bit. The slit widened reluctantly and then learned how to widen. The light went deeper than green, a glass bottle held up to the sun too long. Things moved in the water without surface. Once the boat rose under them as if a great back had rolled; the ribs complained; Isidro made that small persuasive sound men make to horses, as if the river could be talked into citizenship.

On a low branch overhanging the channel, something hung like a bunch of brown grapes at four feet off the water. Tamsin reached to touch it—beautiful, orderly, ornament—and Isidro smacked the back of her hand so hard she swore in an accent that would have made a priest weep.

"Bullet ants," he said. "Pain that makes men remember all the bad names they have ever been called."

One fell onto the awning with the faintest *tch*. Clara flicked it with a splinter of cane and it landed in the water and sailed away righteous as a magistrate headed for lunch. Tamsin shook her hand with the offended dignity of a woman who has been surprised by reality. "They look like a joke," she said through her teeth.

"The funniest jokes draw blood," Jonah offered, flexing his fingers in sympathy.

The boat slid under a curtain of roots that brushed the tops of their heads like a mother who loved too hard. Something soft touched Artemis's ear. Hair. She jerked, slapped, and came up with three strands caught in her fingers, braided, black, black, white. They were tied to a twig with gut. They had no business being in this channel. They smelled of salt water, of oil, of prayers said in a courtyard an ocean away.

She held them between two fingers. They trembled not because her hand shook. The boat took them forward, forward, until they knocked against the spoon under her shirt like a suggestion.

Séverine watched from under the brim of her hat. "We are being shown doors," she said, and reached out to take the braid and lay it across the gunwale as one lays a problem on a table. "This one is open."

Tamsin's hand went to her pistol. "I don't like to be invited."

"Good," Séverine said. "It means you've been taught manners."

By mid-afternoon the river gave up pretending to be a road and became a room. Thick rafts of vegetation tightened across the face of the water until Teo had to stand and pole the *bongo* like a man forcing a door. The pole came up black to the shoulder. Each inch squeaked with the drowned breath of leaves.

"Deadfall," one of Teo's men muttered. "This place learned how to remember trees."

They came to a strangled neck where two trunks had fallen in a cross, one fresh, one rotting into its own brown sugar. There was no going over—the gap beneath the crosspiece was not high enough to admit boat and breath together. No going back without giving the river the satisfaction of condescension. No going around: the green to either side had decided to be land.

"We cut," Isidro said, with the joy men reserve for problems that have solutions.

Teo measured the trunks, measured the drift, the water's grab. "We portage," he said. "Half-load. The rest we bring like mules."

"Mules bite less," Jonah said, and put his shoulder under the gunwale with the dogged look of an honest thief.

They made the boat light: pots out, satchel, net, quina, rope, hammocks. The *bongo* rose a pleasing inch. Men took it by the ribs. The water took its chance and tried to pull. Isidro swore at it with tenderness. Teo set the pole against the downstream trunk, braced, pushed. For a breath the boat went nowhere and then everywhere: belly sliding across a slime-polished log, ribs squealing, then off and into the dark pool beyond with a hollow chuck that sounded like the boat saying *mind your tone*.

They carried the rest in two relays across a plank-and-root causeway slick as a lie. Jonas slipped once and went to one knee, saved the pot with the reverence of a monk. Otis wobbled and would have gone if Clara hadn't caught the strap of his pack and drawn him back as if tugging at the string on a kite. Under them, water moved in a slow muscular argument with gravity. Something wide and flat nosed up to see. Artemis felt the spoon knock against her sternum like a mouse trapped inside a cupboard. She grabbed for it—and felt her hand do what hands do when curses count down.

It slipped.

The thong snagged her knuckle; the spoon swung, struck wood, skittered, and dropped. It hit the backwater and lay for an obscene heartbeat on the surface like a coin considering which face to show. Then it sank as if called by name.

"No," Artemis said. The word broke in the middle. She went to her knees and jammed her arm between roots without the consent of her survival instinct. The water was tea-cold under the scum, then warmer below, then unguessable. Her fingers met soft leaf and then something that felt like the back of a sleeping animal. She bit a sound that belonged to fear and prayer and pushed deeper.

Tamsin's hand clamped Artemis's belt. "You like those fingers," she hissed. "Keep them."

Artemis found the rim of the spoon with the last joint of her longest finger. The thong had wrapped a root like mercy. She hooked the thong, pulled. Something slid across her knuckles—not teeth, not quite—curious, testing. She made a noise that could have belonged to any creature on earth. The thong gave. She came back with the spoon and half the river on her arm. Teo's man watched the water close and spat neatly into it with the satisfaction of an insult paid.

Clara wrapped Artemis's forearm in a rag soaked in something that smelled like a herb God had made while drunk. "If you lose that spoon," she said, too calm, "Éloise will walk to this forest and beat you with it."

"I know," Artemis said, laughing too hard. The laugh shook her shoulders and then steadied them. She kissed the spoon's cold bowl with the gratitude one gives a relic that is also a tool, knotted the thong twice, then a third time because numbers sometimes obey.

They shoved the *bongo* off the far side and let it settle with a long sigh. The room of water beyond the deadfall opened its green mouth and let them in like a house that had changed its mind.

The day leaned toward evening. The light made a cathedral out of leaves: pillars rising, vaulted shade, small saints of bright birds in the transepts. Something screamed in a key that had no right to exist and then stopped to hear itself. Their shoulders forgot how to be not tired and then remembered.

They came out—abrupt—as if slipped through a fold. The channel widened into a lagoon with water mercifully simple again. Patches of sky showed themselves, blue with a tiredness that matched their own. Teo aimed for a low bank where roots made a ladder and eased the boat in until the sand took it.

"Here," he said. "If we don't die of bites, we sleep."

They strung hammocks between trees that had learned to stand a century without moving their feet. Netting, a tight heaven. Fire coaxed from damp with the patience of old women telling stories they never liked but felt compelled to tell anyway. The pot, dented, faithful, swung from a branch and learned beans again.

Tamsin wandered three steps to piss and came back walking with a precision that suggested pain. She stood, breathing, very upright, very quiet.

"What," Clara said, already reaching.

Tamsin opened her palm. On the pad of her middle finger a puncture had appeared that looked like an innocent sting. The finger trembled in a way that belonged to earthquakes. "One of your jokes," she told Isidro between teeth. "Bullet."

Isidro grunted sympathy that sounded like two brothers insulting each other. "It goes. Then it goes more. Then less. Then you wish for death and remember there are people you don't want to leave your money to."

Clara made a paste with leaf and spit and malice and banded the finger with it. "Breathe," she said. "Scream if you must. I won't tell."

Tamsin didn't scream. She made a sound like metal warming, looked Artemis dead in the eye, and said, "If I die of a bug, tell men with hats I died laughing. Then shoot something. It will help."

"You're not dying," Artemis said, and found the steadiness in her voice that had been hiding all day.

"You're memorizing pain so you can tell stories truer than other women."

Tamsin's mouth jerked. "Always a harvest, even of stings."

Séverine walked the edge of their small circle and shook salt from a horn into a line that could have been prayer or profanity. "We eat," she said. "We sleep. We don't dream."

"Nobody orders dreams," Jonah said, staring into the fire as if card faces might rise. "They come with the house."

They ate beans that had tasted the molecules of every meal ever cooked in that pot. They drank brown water that had learned decency through fire. Otis fell asleep with his hand on the hammock's edge as if afraid it would decide to unlearn its knot and spill him into the mouth below. Teo's men slept in turns, eyes half-open, pectoral muscles making their own slow breathing. The boy with the scar learned Otis's name without asking and didn't say it because names on the river are like meat: you don't waste them.

Artemis lay back. The netting whispered around her like a thousand little audacities. She held the spoon in both hands a moment, not to work it, but to feel it, as one holds a cross without prayer. The braid of hair lay in the oilskin with the Queen and the Tower, wrong and home at once. She did not take it out. She knew better than to ask it to speak twice on the same day.

Sleep came, left, came again. Frogs caroled a liturgy no pope could have understood. Monkeys heckled their own jokes. The river went on moving as if nobody had ever thought to tell it about death.

In the hour when feelings fatten and ideas shrink, Artemis jerked awake certain she was not where she had gone to sleep. The fire had collapsed into a red eye. The air tasted of a damp that did not belong to night. For a long breath she held still, counted—to seven, to seven again—and listened.

Water on both sides.

She slid from the hammock like a thief. The sand underfoot felt unfamiliar in a way sand has no right to feel. She walked three steps, four, and crouched at the margin of the camp's small light.

Ash.

A circle in the dirt. The black of it not-quite-cold. Around the big char of their present fire lay the faint, rain-sagged ghost of another. She pressed two fingers to it. Damp. But when she sniffed them her nose told her a truth her head didn't want: fat-smoke, the scent of beans—*their* beans—forgotten on a boil.

"Teo," she said softly. "Teo."

He came up from sleep like a man surfacing from a long habit. He crouched beside her and put a finger to the ash, then into his mouth, tasting. He didn't speak. He stood and walked ten paces into the dark, then fifteen the other way. He came back with a face that had put on a new crease.

"We camped here," he said. "Either this afternoon or a year ago. The river took us around to return the way it wanted."

Jonah sat up, hair an honest mess. "We've been walking in a city for hours and only just noticed its streets repeat."

Séverine's rosary clicked in the dark like beetle legs. "Labyrinths do not exist to *lose* you," she said. "They exist to make you walk the same questions until you can say the right answer."

"What's the answer," Tamsin asked, her voice thin but stubborn, pain a prayer-bead she refused to give up.

"*Open,*" Artemis said, before she could stop herself, and tasted bile. The hair braid in the oilskin seemed to turn its head under her hand. "Or *no.* Those are the only answers we have learned to say."

Teo stood in the broken light and looked like an old tree that had resisted burning. "We go at first gray," he said. "No better map than habit. If your spoon wants to speak, let it. If your saints want to argue, let them."

Before dawn, a shape moved beyond the camp's edge—low, wide, the careful stalk of a creature that had never learned clumsiness. It paused where their salt line had been. It breathed. It turned away without sound. Séverine watched it go with the etiquette one offers to dangerous guests.

Morning peeled itself off the trees and men became men again instead of ideas of themselves. Teo shoved the *bongo* off the sand with a grunt. The lagoon received them. The channel they would have sworn had not existed the night before opened with the calm assurance of a clerk unlocking a file. The spoon, when Artemis held it over salted water, trembled and turned—not to the center, not to the wide-open brown honesty of river—but toward a green grimace between two stands of trees where roots didn't quite meet.

"The place that doesn't want to be a door," Tamsin said. Her finger throbbed in time with her temper. "So of course we walk through it."

"Yes," Artemis said. She didn't smile. She felt tired down into the arithmetic of her bones and, under that, an iron wire she had not known she'd been drawn around. "We do."

The bow kissed the green mouth. The mouth gave.

Behind them the lagoon lay with their footprints opening and closing on its sand like mouths learning a word. Ahead, water moved with the slow authority of a creature that had no need of speed because it owned the idea of distance.

They slid into it.

Somewhere in the black water beneath, a shape as long as the boat turned and kept pace, unhurried. Frogs fell suddenly silent. Far above, a sloth blinked and, in a gesture slower than a prayer, adjusted one hand.

"Keep your hands in," Clara said, because repetition is a kindness. "And your stories short."

Jonah touched his empty pocket and did not reach for what wasn't in it. "Short story," he said softly, perhaps to himself, perhaps to the river. "We go south. We get what wants us. We come home wrong and alive."

"Short enough," Isidro said.

Artemis held the spoon in one palm and the rawhide thong in the other. She counted the paddles' rhythm without meaning to; she counted the soft knocks under the hull; she counted the places the light broke and came back. The jungle reached to grow over them— over bones, over boats, over names. It would always be faster at that work than they were at the work of keeping their edges.

"Seven," Séverine murmured, not asking for a number but speaking one into the day.

"Seven," Artemis answered, counting them off under her breath. "Still."

For now.

Chapter XI — Fangs in the Water

"The river feeds all things — even the dead."

Morning broke green.

Not the milk-blue of sea dawn, not the brass plate of the llanos, but a green that came from below as much as from above — water reflecting leaves, leaves reflecting water, the two conspiring to make a roof that kept the sky out of the room they'd chosen to live in. Mist clung to the trunks like skin trying to learn a second body. Monkeys worked out their grievances at a distance; frogs practiced scales nobody had commissioned.

Teófilo Aponte — Teo when the river behaved — stood in the *bongo*'s stern and squinted down the narrow, tea-dark reach ahead. "Shoal," he said. "And a bar of teeth under it."

"Teeth?" Tamsin asked, flexing the bullet-ant finger and making a face that could curdle cream. She had bound it with Clara's leaf paste and defied it all night by failing to whimper. Her trousers were rolled to mid-calf, boots lashed to her pack until the day remembered to become land.

"Fish with lawyer manners," Isidro said. "They love a contract written in blood."

Jonah's smile was a coin he couldn't find. "Piranha."

Teo tipped his chin. "And stingrays sunken in the mud. Step heavy, they answer back with iron." He lifted the pole and let it clack against the *bongo's* rib, listening as a doctor listens to lungs. "We lighten and drag," he decided. "Men in the water in pairs. Nobody bleeds if they can help it."

"Nobody plans to," Clara said, which in her voice was a prayer.

They took the *bongo*'s weight down to a story it could carry on human shoulders: packs ashore, then back again; pots slung; rope paid out like a spell. Otis held the coil in both hands and swallowed twice before admitting his fear had teeth of its own. The boy with the scar on his cheek — one of Teo's — watched him with a kind curiosity that wasn't yet friendship. He had a name, but he wore it quietly; in this country, names were meat.

The bar showed itself by not showing itself: a smoothness in the brown that had nothing to do with peace, a hush that meant listening. Teo stepped in first — trousers tied above the knee, pole in both hands like a prayer staff. Isidro followed, the machete looped high across his back. Jonah slung the bowline across his chest and grinned as if it were a lover who might forgive his laziness. Artemis hung back, looped the stern-line thrice around her palm, and breathed to seven until the tremor settled into something that could be used.

"Hands in," Clara said, again, because repetition is a fence.

"Feet sure," Sister Séverine added, voice even. She had wrapped her rosary twice around her wrist, a cuff that could bruise. "And if you feel a mouth, don't snatch away. That's when they take more."

"Persuade the river you're uninteresting," Jonah said, stepping into tea and pretending not to flinch when the chill climbed his calf.

They walked the *bongo* forward under its own long shadow. The sand underfoot shifted the way a thing does when it's considering betrayal. Teo lifted, pushed, set; Isidro set and swore; Jonah swore first, then lifted. A foot's worth of progress. Another. The water made small sugar sounds around their knees.

Artemis watched the men's shins go ghostly in brown, hair pressed by current. She forced her hands not to tighten on the line; she forced the line not to answer by biting. Her palm throbbed under the bandage where the spoon thong had burned a welt; the spoon itself lay cool against her sternum like a truth she hadn't earned.

Something touched her boot.

Not the bump of a branch. Not the curious kiss of a turtle. It was a neat, impersonal tap, like a clerk's finger counting coins.

She didn't move.

Isidro hissed. A thin red thread unwound from his left calf where a thorn-wound had forgotten its lesson. The thread lengthened, bright as a ribbon in the dun. Then the water changed voice. The hush became a whisper; the whisper became a conversation; the conversation broke into a shout of small mouths.

"Back," Teo said calmly, which is how men say *run* when the river is listening.

Too late.

They came silver and gray, unremarkable as pebbles until they were not — a blur of knives with bad intentions. Isidro kicked without thrash, heel grinding down through a face; another face took its place. Jonah yanked the bowline hard; the *bongo* lurched; its belly scraped the bar and complained. The fish found the scrape. For a second the water around the keel went pink. For a second the boat felt lighter in a way that muscles interpret as relief and memory interprets as cost.

Otis tightened on the coil. "Pull!" he yelled, voice cracking.

Artemis set her feet, braced her back, and hauled. The stern slid an inch. Two inches. The line burned. Behind her, Tamsin had the pistol out and then put it away again with the contempt of a woman who knows the wrong tool when it volunteers. "Rope!" she shouted to Clara. "We pull them back by the neck if we must."

Teo's boy — the scarred one — was knee-deep and frowning as if at a math he disliked. A flash of silver at his shin. A ravel of blood. He jerked — not from fear, from reflex — and that was enough invitation. The water at his knee went mad. It looked like boiling without heat.

Clara was already in, trousers dark, sleeves to the shoulder, moving with the economy of a woman whose hands had done hard, precise things before men learned to be grateful. She got her arm under the boy's armpits and lifted, bearing down with her weight to break the bite. Isidro slammed a palm against the boy's calf and the little teeth let go in a sound only he could feel. Jonah and Teo heaved together and put the boy on the *bongo's* low deck with a hoist that had been intended for sacks of maize.

The boy screamed then. Not long. Clara's hand on his thigh cut the sound at the root.

Artemis saw — because someone always has to look — how neatly the river made its argument: a hundred ovals of meat gone from the calf in a tidy crescent, white fat showing under red, strings of fascia snapped like harp gut. No bite was deep. Depth wasn't the point. Multiplicity was.

"Salt," Clara said. "And cloth. Now."

Séverine upended a horn. Salt fell like snow into a world that had never earned it. The boy bucked. Clara's forearm pinned his knee. "Hold him," she said, and Tamsin's palm went flat on the boy's chest, her jaw clenched jack-tight.

Isidro handed his belt. Clara wound it twice above the wound and pulled until the leather creaked. Blood slowed its bright insistence. She filled her mouth with aguardiente, spat it onto the meat, and did not let herself apologize or anyone else say the thing that would make this cruelty into a sin. "Jonah," she said. "Blade."

He had one in his boot and didn't know it until now; his hand found it because hands remember knives even when minds try to be better. He heated it in the cooking flame until it stopped being a piece of metal and started being a verb. Clara took it, kissed her own teeth, and pressed.

The smell was church-wrong: meat, hair, and the memory of wool set too close to a stove. The boy made no sound. He had learned the lesson Tamsin had learned in the night: sometimes pain gets a seat at the table, and you show it you know how to hold a fork.

Artemis's hands were steady now. The counting had done its work. She wrapped a strip torn from her own shirt around the pads of her fingers and tamped where Clara pointed. Salt. Pressure. Breath. The river smacked the hull with small undignified slaps, as if irritated at being thwarted.

"Out," Teo said, face gray under brown. Isidro and Jonah shoved the *bongo* into deeper run, where the small knives had less to argue with. The bottom fell away under their boots; they crawled back aboard with mud knees and the shiver men pretend is cold.

Behind them, the bar looked the same as it had looked before. The red unwound and diluted; silver bodies went back to being unremarkable fish. The water forgot.

They didn't.

Clara bound the boy's leg with linen and bile and a competence that didn't need an audience. She slid two fingers along his femoral pulse and nodded once when it answered. "You keep this," she told him. "You sleep and do not vomit. You piss. You don't get sweet in the wound. If you get sweet, I get mean."

He had the good sense to smile with half his mouth. "Sí, doctora." His name, offered softly, was "Luis."

"Luis," Clara repeated, the way a woman repeats a weight she intends to carry. She tied the last knot with a decisive flick. "You'll limp for your sins. That's all of us."

Otis turned aside and was careful, for once, where he chose to vomit. Séverine put a hand between his shoulder blades and did not make a prayer out loud. Jonah sat hard enough that the plank under his backside expressed an opinion. Isidro ripped his own trouser knee to look at the ribbon in his shin; two bites, neat as a tailor's mark. He salted them like food, then swore with the tenderness a man saves for family.

"Caimans," Teo said, as if calling the next card in a game the river liked to play. He pointed with his chin — not ahead, not behind, but right — to a log that had grown eyes. Yellow, level, old. The log didn't glide. It practiced.

"Of course," Tamsin said. "Of course the river has more mouths, and of course they attend in pairs."

The *bongo* drifted just enough to be impolite. The eyes turned by the smallest degree. A slick of water crossed the knurled back where algae had learned to be comfortable. The jaw was a hinge built to finish sentences.

There's a way a boat quiets that has nothing to do with oars. The men's breathing went small. Jonah's hand moved, slow as winter light, toward the spare pole. Isidro lifted the machete and set its flat against his own thigh — a promise to himself that when he hit, he'd hit like work.

The caiman didn't lunge as boys' stories say they do. It pivoted on invisible hips, floated a hand's breadth closer, and showed a lip. In the black of its mouth, a pale — the inside of a throat that would not gag on them.

"Don't," Séverine breathed, and Artemis, who had been about to move in some direction she hadn't yet chosen, did not.

The second caiman came from under the boat.

Not teeth; not yet. A lift, a heave, ribs creaking, the *bongo*'s belly taking a shove it had not consented to. Clara's palm flattened on Luis's chest to keep him from rolling: pressure on pulse, pressure on breath, pressure on fear. The boat rocked a second time, harder; a wooden slat snapped like a dry wishbone. If the caiman had gotten that grip on meat, the conversation would have ended.

"Shoot," Isidro said softly, and Tamsin did.

The ball hit water two inches shy of an eye and ricocheted into the head behind it; the head jinked, astonishingly fast, and the shot gouged a trench through scutes instead, spending itself in the ancient meat that had learned to ignore knives. The caiman rolled, not in pain — in surprise. Jonah brought the pole down with both hands, a clean, ugly stroke that would have made a priest bless him in any parish. Wood hit skull. The sound was like knocking on a neighbor's door to announce a death in the family.

The caiman's mouth opened, slow as a theater curtain. Isidro put the machete into it at an angle that had no poetry — a black triangle under the jaw as if he were setting a wedge to split cordwood. He leaned his weight. The machete shivered. The mouth closed and tried to keep the blade as part of itself. Isidro swore so gently it could have been a lullaby and stamped his heel on the handle. Something gave. Not bone. Habit.

The caiman slid away, unhappy in a way reptiles do not dignify with sound. The other, the log with eyes, didn't hurry. It sank. The water puffed around its withdrawing shape. The river released air it didn't know it had held.

"Out," Teo said again. His voice had gone hoarse. "Into the middle. If they want us, they'll be honest about it there."

"You keep saying *honest* about this bastard," Tamsin said, re-priming with hands that didn't shake. "I don't think it understands the word."

"Honest means only one thing here," Teo said. "What wants to eat you does it where you can see it."

They pushed off. The bar fell behind. So did the log. So did the place where water had briefly looked like boiling blood. The *bongo* made a sound under them like an old woman finding a chair she'd been permitted to miss.

Artemis sat back on her heels and looked at her fingers. Pink crescents of Luis's blood under the nails, gritty with salt. She wiped them on her trousers and the stain made new geography.

"Drink," Clara ordered, and Artemis did. The brown water tasted of smoke, then of its own honesty. She was light-headed in a familiar way — not hunger, not shock, but the cliff-edge before her body did something she had not given permission for. She made herself breathe slow. She did not ask Séverine what happens after **three — hands drop what they love**. The answer had already been set in the ledger: four. She did not want to write it yet.

They worked the day long with a new tidy silence. The *bongo* bumped drift that had learned to taste. Luis slept; when he woke he was thirsty and then angry and then ashamed of both — all of which Clara accepted as good signs. Otis sat with his back against the awning post and watched the line of the bank with that rapt attention the frightened grant to the word *shore*. Jonah took stock of coins he did not have, then of jokes he could not afford, and finally of the way a pole lives in a man's hands. Isidro sharpened the machete with affection that was not tenderness. Tamsin reloaded and tucked her pistol back into her shirt; her finger throbbed with auras that would have humbled saints. She grinned at it and refused to be small.

Toward evening the river slowed past its own reflection, as if admiring itself in an old mirror. Teo pointed with his chin to a tooth of rock that made a permanent wrinkle in the current. "We beach," he said. "Sand tongue there. Watch the barbs in the mud."

They came in careful; men stepped with iron in their ankles; nobody bled because the day had already paid that bill. The sand took them; the trees approved with a small release of leaves. They made camp under branches stiff with birds that had chosen to compromise with sleep. The fire was reluctant and then righteous.

The pot learned beans again and forgave them for everything.

Séverine broke open a lime and squeezed it over Luis's lips. "This is not a sacrament," she said, "but I will say it like one. Drink, child." He obeyed and did not spit. It stung like honesty.

Tamsin looked across the fire at Artemis. The light took the sickness out of her finger and put it in her face, which she took as proof that light's not a doctor. "Say it," she said. "Whatever your mouth's been hiding since the ship."

Artemis looked at her hands. They lay like obedient animals in her lap. "Four," she said softly, because not saying it out loud made it too much like a prayer. "Seizures."

Clara's head came up. "Not if I pound you with salt and water every hour from here to hell."

"I won't be insulted," Artemis said, and made a smile. It found the shape of her face without asking.

Séverine said nothing for a long breath. Then: "When it comes, it will come when the door thinks you are sleeping."

"Which door," Jonah asked, dry.

"All," Séverine said, which was no comfort and therefore perhaps useful.

They ate beans and the day out of their mouths. The sound of washing pots was almost sweet. Teo's quiet boys split the watches; Isidro lay down like a man who could sleep under cannon; Jonah did his best imitation of a man who didn't dream. Tamsin hung her hammock lower in deliberate defiance of bullet ants and the angry relatives of fish.

Artemis sat a little apart, the spoon cold in her palm. She didn't salt the cup; she didn't ask. She just held the bowl like a coin she refused to spend. The river breathed; the fire breathed faster; the jungle breathed slow and vast. In the black wedge between two roots, two yellow eyes blinked like tired coins and went away, not angry, not hungry — merely inevitable.

She took the braid from the oilskin and laid it across her thigh. Black. Black. White. Sewn through with gut. It had no place to be here. It was here anyway. It lifted in the night's shallow breeze the way hair lifts from a living neck.

"You are not mine," she told it, the way a woman tells a memory to sit. "I am not yours."

The hair lay down flat. It did not answer, because hair never answers; it remembers.

Near midnight, Teo's oldest man woke them with one word, soft: "South."

They sat up like knocked pins. He wasn't pointing, but his face had turned. The air had shifted. It smelled the way copper smells when someone else's blood is near — a penny taste behind the teeth. The water at the edge of camp made a sound that could only be called deliberate. Not a slap. Not a surge. A slow heavy huff, like a great thing deciding how to arrange itself for comfort.

"Caiman," Tamsin said, instinct.

"Not after dark," Teo breathed. "They like shade."

"Jaguar?" Otis whispered, scandalized by the idea a cat could make water sound that way.

"No cat is that lazy," Isidro said.

The huff again. A line went out across the surface from the bank we hadn't named, rolled and did not break, like a drowned log turning to consider a new doctrine.

Artemis felt the spoon move like a heart and then stop. Her own heart stuttered in answer, a fish in the chest. She put her hand flat against the earth and felt it say nothing — which was worse than any warning.

"Sleep," Séverine said, as if commanding a child. "The thing has its business. We have ours. If we give it our eyes, it will take our nights."

They slept because obedience can sometimes hold terror by the belt.

Dawn came gray and then green. Luis's bandage was still clean. Tamsin's finger still throbbed, but at a lower note. Otis had learned, in sleep, to pull his hands into the hollow between chin and chest where no fish could make a contract. They broke camp the way men who mean to live break camp: swiftly, with small insults to the place that had held them, so it wouldn't think to be offended and refuse to let them go.

They pushed off.

The river narrowed again, muttering to itself. Around a
sly bend where roots made a lace, the water darkened
and then stilled. Paddles lifted. They drifted into a room
nobody had been invited to.

The surface looked like nothing living. The surface
looked like a thought that didn't want to become a
sentence. Then the thought changed its mind. A shape
rose under them — a hump wider than the *bongo's*
beam, mottled olive and coal, plated in little shields of
green stone. It didn't breach. It didn't show its head. It
rolled very slightly, a grandmother turning in sleep. The
boat tipped and tipped back. The thing slid ahead,
unhurried, setting its own punctuation.

Teo's mouth opened and closed, not for prayer — for
awe.

Isidro said what men who have walked here say when
the river reveals its old word. "Sucuriju."

Tamsin's whisper carried no bravado now.
"Anaconda."

"Not today," Séverine said. She might have been
talking to a weather, not a beast. "Not here."

The thing sank with the patience of a saint refusing an
argument. Its absence took longer to arrive than its
presence had.

They moved again, alive because the river had other
errands.

Before midday they found a strand of hair tied to a twig overhanging yet another slit of a channel, this one sulking behind a curtain of veils the color of old limes. Black, black, white. Gut stitched through the end like a fisherman's joke.

"Door," Tamsin said. "The kind that eats."

Artemis took the braid without touching it with skin. She folded it into the oilskin like a map she would read only under a roof. She salted the cup, held the spoon, counted — one, two, three, four, five, six, seven. On seven, the spoon turned. Not to the easy bend. Not to the clean reach. Into the slit.

Teo didn't look at her. He'd learned, as all of them had, what it meant to ignore a tool that chose. "Duck your heads," he said.

They slid toward another mouth, another room, another row of teeth.

Behind them the river digested what it had been given and waited for the next course. In its belly, piranha moved like rain you forgot to notice, stingrays lay like regrets in the mud, caiman slept with their appetites set at a constant low flame, an old green body as thick as a man's memory kept its counsel in a coil the size of a chapel. The river would feed all things, including their dead, when the day came.

Not yet.

Artemis rolled her sleeves once, then once again. The spoon lay cool against bone. Her hands obeyed. She counted. "Seven," she breathed, because the number sometimes listened, because she needed it to.

"Seven," Séverine answered at her shoulder, and they went where the water had been pointing since the first time it learned her name.

Chapter XII — Anaconda's Coil

"When the river moves, it is not always water."

They slid into the slit of a channel the spoon chose, a green seam barely wide enough to admit the *bongo* and the stubbornness of ten people. Leaves met overhead like lips. Light came in as droplets rather than beams. The water smelt of iron filings and bruised limes; the air kept secrets in its damp.

"Quiet water," Teo said, and his mouth made it an obscenity. "It's holding its breath."

Bullet-ant fire still pulsed through Tamsin's bandaged finger, but she had her pistol tucked at the small of her back and her long legs braced in trousers as if she were at a gunwale in a more civilized hell. Clara moved like a metronome—check Luis's tourniquet, check Otis's wrists for tremor, check the quina paste as if fury could keep it potent. Sister Séverine sprinkled a pinch of salt from her horn over the *bongo's* bowed nose and said nothing at all.

Artemis held Éloise's spoon to her chest by its rawhide thong, like a saint's relic with less comfort in it. Her palm throbbed where Clara had salted the worm out. She counted under her breath—one, two, three, four, five, six, seven—until numbers became a kind of plank across the water.

A braid of hair swung above the gunwale, gut-threaded to a twig. Black, black, white. It ticked the spoon as they passed, as if they were beads on one rosary.

"Doors," Séverine murmured.

"Teeth," Isidro corrected mildly, easing his machete free.

The channel kinked left and then right, the *bongo* scraping its flanks on roots polished by other uninvited guests. On the far bend, the trunks widened to reveal three stones set like kneeling backs, their faces pecked with shallow, lichen-filled pits—a serpent carved in dotwork, a bowl, a spiral. Between the pits, someone long dead had pressed shards of bottle-green into the rock and the forest had grown a skin over them. It wasn't jade. It wasn't glass. It was the right color to make a throat think *poison, prayer,* or both.

Otis leaned, then remembered and pulled his hands back into the fortress of his chest. "Pretty," he whispered, awed against his will.

"Pretty means altar," Jonah said. "Altar means appetite."

Something changed behind them. Not a splash. Not the hustle of fish. A heaviness. The river's body shifted its weight like a sleeper turning.

"Keep hands in," Clara said, slow as scripture. "And do not name saints you haven't paid."

The surface ahead bulged. Not much. An inch. Two. The kind of swell a tide makes when a ferry noses close in a city far away from here. Then it settled. Teo's pole stopped answering as wood and began answering as bone.

"Sss," Isidro breathed through his teeth. "Sucuriju grande."

"Anaconda," Tamsin translated, as if the English could make it smaller.

The *bongo* slid forward another yard. Another. Leaves brushed crowns, blessed no one. A smell rose: musk, wet rope, cold copper. The water to starboard thickened without changing color.

Then the river stood up.

Not fully. Not in any way that would have satisfied a child's story. But enough. A loop the girth of a wine cask pushed out from under the hull and rose like a green, slicked wall. Scales shingled like small plates. Algae painted the old scars. The loop kept rising. The boat lifted, inched to the left as if set on a shelf.

"Down," Teo said, very quiet.

Two things happened at once. A second loop rose under the stern, shouldered them sideways, and something like a neck drew along the starboard flank, broad as a man's thigh, the skin dark, the pattern low and old as rain. The weight was a thought made meat.

Luis, half-dozing in his pain, pitched. Clara's hand caught his belt and his breath and held them both.

The head showed then—the suggestion of it at least: not fangs, not a hiss, just the shovel-wide wedge easing up out of tea-dark like a grandmothers' apron in the wash. One yellow-lidless eye rolled without hurry and named everything it saw *food* or *not food* with the calm of a very old clerk. The mouth opened a little to taste the air. Pink. Pale.

Tamsin drew and fired in the same breath. The ball kissed the eye's rim, punched a groove through scutes, and spent itself somewhere in the old meat. The head jerked, not in pain—surprise, offended.

"Head or spine!" Isidro shouted, already moving. He and Jonah lunged together, one with steel, one with a pole. Isidro jammed the machete edge along the jaw hinge; Jonah levered the pole against the thick of the throat to keep it off the gunwale.

The snake answered with gravity. The coil under the hull heaved, and the *bongo* came up like bread in an oven. The starboard men—Isidro, Jonah, Teo's older boatman—lost bracing and slid toward the mouth that wasn't open but would be. The older man went first, a clean, unblessed slither into water up to his chest. The river received him like family.

"Hands!" Teo barked.

Jonah threw the pole, grabbed air, got rope. Isidro kept the blade in and leaned his weight. He lost his footing and recovered on a curse with a vowel in it centuries long. The older boatman flailed once, twice, found the hull with ten desperate fingers.

The head came up that last half-cubit and took his forearm into its mouth with such obscenityless ease that nobody had the breath to call it obscene. No strike. No theatrical. Just *in*. The teeth weren't fangs: backward-pointing glass needles meant to keep. He looked at his hand going away and made a small child's noise he would have despised if he'd been allowed to live long enough to remember it.

Clara was moving before her mind permitted it. She had a loop of rope in both fists and threw it like a noose for a bad god. It went over the head slick, caught behind the jaw hinge, snagged on scute. She hauled with something that would have been love if love didn't bleed other names. "Pull!" she snarled, and Teo and Tamsin and Otis pulled, because the word hit their bodies where orders go.

The noose tightened. The mouth opened, an involuntary gape. The boatman's arm came free—but not whole. Not even mostly. The flesh from elbow to wrist was gone to string; the bones showed like wet reeds. He fell against the hull, white to the lips, and slid back as the river claimed what the snake didn't need anymore.

"Get him!" Tamsin shouted, voice breaking like glass.

Jonah got him. One fist in the ragged meat above the elbow, one in the collar of his shirt, hauling a weight that had learned to be more water than man. Isidro drove the machete. The steel scraped bone at the palate and skidded. The head shut down around the blade; his wrist went numb to the elbow. He stamped the machete hilt with his boot. Something gave in a hollow, ancient way.

The coil under the hull cinched. The ribs sang like harp strings. The *bongo* flexed to breaking. Luis screamed once and bit through it. Otis reached for him, then remembered—with a shuddering discipline far too old for him—and wrapped his arms around the awning post instead.

"Pole!" Teo's younger man flung one. Jonah wedged it crosswise between the snake's arching loops and the far rail, a brace made ridiculous only until it worked. The coil tightened again, found no give, fought its own geometry.

"Eyes," Isidro gasped. "If God made a mercy, it's eyes."

He let the machete go and snatched Jonah's belt knife. He went for the yellow. The blade bit. Not enough. Tamsin fired again. The eye roomed red then black. The head writhed, not wildly—resentful, mortally inconvenienced. The coil loosened in the half-inch way that separates life and story.

Clara had the boatman's stump in both hands, fingers locked. Séverine wrapped her rosary around the rope and leaned with both arms, small and furious. Teo planted his pole like a mast and held. Jonah grunted like an animal. Otis clamped his teeth on his own fear and began to haul hand-over-hand on the slack in the noose, making it a winch. The snake rolled. Its back showed as big around as Artemis's waist and then again as big around as her chest. Green plates gleamed like bottle shards sunk in cured leather.

Something inside Artemis's skull hissed like a kettle about to speak. She smelled old musk and bog water and the sweet rot of hair left in a bowl too long.

Open, said a voice that was not the serpent's and not the river's and not any god that loved women.

Her hand released without permission.

The spoon thumped her sternum and dropped to the plank with a clatter too small for the size of anything else. She bent to catch it. The world went soundless for a beat and then came back with a crack. The crack lived inside her. She knew, in the clean instant people know before drowning, that this was *four*.

The first convulsion hit like a door slammed from within. Her chin met her collarbone. Her thighs locked. She went over sideways into Tamsin, who took the weight with her whole body and swore in a litany Clara would have corked if there'd been a cork.

"Hold her head!" Clara shouted without looking away from the stump under her hands. Artemis's skull met Tamsin's palm and Tamsin's knee with the kind of tenderness that leaves bruises later. Foam salted Artemis's lip. Her eyes rolled up until only the whites showed, the pupils trapped under the lids like beetles. She heard the river ask her in a hundred voices whether she wanted rest and she said *no* in a hundred counted numbers.

Séverine let go the rope long enough to strike Artemis—two quick, light slaps that were more for the thing watching than the woman shaking. "Not yours," she told the air. "Not today."

The coil loosened another inch. The noose bit. Teo's older man breathed with the shallowness the dying use when they are trying not to alarm the living. "Mama," he said, and added something in a dialect the river kept for itself.

Isidro lost the knife and found it again in the snake's mouth. He twisted. Jonah drove the pole. The blade went into the brain-pan with a sound like a cork pulled from wet wood. The head convulsed. The coils squeezed once more, hardest, the old killing move, then went limp without admitting defeat. The *bongo* heaved, jolted, dropped.

For a long second everyone breathed like shipwrecked swimmers at the surface—loud, animal, astonished that it hurts. Then movement erupted in its smaller forms: Clara's hands releasing a pressure only to apply a new one, Séverine unwinding the rosary from the rope like a garrote loosed, Teo banging the hull with the pole to convince death not to take the boat in payment.

Artemis's convulsion burned itself out in a series of small jerks. Sweat polished her face. Tamsin wiped the corner of her mouth with two fingers and showed her the spit to make her swallow—it was a trick women teach babies and men. "Breathe," she said. "Because I told you to."

Artemis obeyed, because Tamsin was the sort of woman you obey when you would not obey God. The spoon lay by her ribs. She grabbed it, furious at herself and at whatever counted minutes in her bones. She knotted the thong twice, then again, hands shaking with the shame of having proved a prophecy true.

The snake drifted, heavy as a boat, painted with its own blood. The noose, half cut, rode behind the jaw like jewelry. It slid from under the hull with a nudge from Teo's pole and went away under the leaves to rot in a chapel of ants.

The boatman didn't. He lay on the plank where Clara had hauled him, pulse a weak conversation, mouth blue to the corners. Clara's eyes went flat as slate. "He's going," she said, and did not beg him not to. She gave him water on a limesoaked rag, which he could not swallow. Séverine said a prayer soft and legitimate. Tamsin sat back on her heels and looked at the jungle as if it had offered her an insult she would answer later with interest.

The man inhaled once more through his nose as if remembering a market, a woman's hair, a coin on the tongue. He exhaled and didn't inhale again.

Teo closed his eyes with two fingers and said a single word that might have been a name, might have been *brother,* might have been *river.*

They eased the *bongo* into a pocket of bank where the earth had learned to be soft. Luis, white-lipped, held the spare end of the rope while Clara did what needed doing. They gave the old man to the water the way men give themselves to work: without poetry they hadn't earned. He went under with no struggle. The river swallowed him with the same mistaken kindness it uses for trees.

Otis's shoulders shook once and he made a sound like a boy being told his mother had gone to market and would not come back. Jonah sat with his hands on his knees, back very straight, face turned away, as if privacy could be manufactured by posture.

Séverine's salt made a circle on the plank where he had lain. "Go on then," she told any thing that had lingered. "We are full."

They pushed off. No one spoke until speech became the only thing that kept night out. When words came, they were small and useful.

"Charge," Tamsin said, breaking open the horn of powder, hand steady again by sheer refusal. "One ball left after that shot. We'll need to buy more in a town where men smile too wide."

"Needle," Clara said, and changed the dressing on Luis's calf, which had oozed new anger during the coil. "You will live to teach another boy not to piss in a river."

Luis smiled because she needed him to. "Sí, doctora."

Isidro cleaned the machete with leaves that made his hands smell new and poisonous. "Big," he said softly, not boasting, not frightened. "Big as a story."

Teo nodded once, a broken amen.

Artemis wiped her lip and came away with only spit, not blood. She pressed the spoon to her sternum and the coin to her mouth and counted until counting was a wall again.

"Four," she said when she could trust her voice.

Clara's eyes slashed toward her. "And we'll not have a five. I'll pound you with salt and quina until the devils come out of your ears."

"Fever," Séverine said, not to curse them but to name the next enemy as if that could keep it from sneaking up in false clothes. "It comes when a curse gets hot."

"We move," Teo said. "We find wind tonight. Mosquitoes will eat us otherwise."

They did. The channel melted into a broader brown that admitted breeze and a few honest stars. They beached at a spit of sand no bigger than a saint's coffin; wind worried the mosquitoes off a little; smoke kept the rest at negotiation distance. Clara boiled water and mashed quina, bitter as truth. She doled it out in turns with a lie that it did not taste so bad. They swallowed because refusing would have been letting the river decide their names.

Tamsin, her trousers streaked with green and blood, sat cross-legged and cleaned her pistol like a woman carding wool. She flashed a chip-toothed grin at Artemis without the grin ever touching her eyes. "When we get home," she said, "I'll tell the men at the tailor's that in the jungle the snakes are as polite as gentlemen and the gentlemen as hungry as snakes."

"If we get home," Jonah said.

"When," Tamsin snapped, and she made the word a nail.

Otis ate beans with both hands, then hid his hands under the hammock net again like a child who has learned a nursery rhyme about losing fingers. Luis slept, rattling. Teo watched the river with a displeasure that had nothing to do with grief and everything to do with knowing the river does not own grief and will misuse it.

Artemis laid the braid on her thigh—black, black, white—and the spoon beside it. The hair lifted in the night's thin wind, then lay down, like a shy animal learning new handlers. She didn't ask it. She'd spent a question on it already today.

She said instead to Séverine, low, "Why does it want *open*."

"Because closed things keep power," Séverine said. "And opened things spill it, or share it, or drown in it. We don't yet know which is our verb."

In the breath before sleep they all smelled the first sour-sweet change of sweat that means fever is checking doors. It moved like a rumor through the camp. Clara swore—fervent, practical. "Drink," she said. "Now. Lime. Quina. Again."

Artemis lay back on rough cotton, the spoon cold at her sternum, the coin warming at her throat. She counted. One. Two. Three. Four. Five. Six. Seven.

When sleep took her anyway, it gave her a shape moving under brown water, plated in green stones, not angry, not kind—only inevitable. It brushed a temple of roots where a woman's hair had been braided into the door-lashings centuries ago. It paused, as if listening for her. Then it went on with its business.

In the dark, a little heat woke at the base of her skull and slid forward, sly. Fever is only another river. It feeds all things.

Chapter XIII — Fever Season

"The body burns, and the mind dreams of graves."

Morning came with a sour-sweet tang that didn't belong to rot or river. It was the smell a body makes when something clever has found room inside.

Clara smelled it first. She turned from the cookpot with a face like a padlock. "Quina," she said. "All of you. Now. We don't wait to be asked."

They lined for it like parishioners who distrust their priest. Powder dark as old bark into each tin; a splash of the brown water that had learned smoke; Clara's thumbnail grinding lumps down as if spite could make medicine polite. Men made theater of swallowing. Tamsin tipped hers back in the trousers and shirt that had become her uniform and made a face that would have curdled cream. "If I cough up this bitterness in New Orleans," she said, "do you think it will kill a rat in the street?"

"Drink," Clara said. "Then complain."

Artemis drank. The quina caught in the back of her throat like iron filings and then melted to a bitterness that stained her tongue. She wiped her mouth on her sleeve and had to steady her hand on Éloise's spoon by habit, not ceremony. Her bones had developed a light rattle under the skin, a delicate china sound. She set her jaw against it and counted: one, two, three, four, five, six, seven. The counting walked ahead of the fear the way a lantern walks ahead of a road.

Teo shoved the *bongo* off the sand tongue and let the current take them sideways into the narrow seam

Artemis's spoon had chosen yesterday. Leaves dripped. Frogs practiced scales that didn't belong to anyone's church. Otis hunched with his hands pulled into his shirt like a boy who remembered lessons too late. Luis's bandage held; his breath did, too, stubbornly.

By mid-morning, the rattle inside Artemis's bones had teeth. Her jaw began to chatter between numbers like thin porcelain. She wrapped both hands around the thong of the spoon and pressed the bowl to her sternum as if it could teach her chest the rhythm of living. The sweat came cold. Then the cold went and left heat, sly at the base of the skull, kissing forward. She wiped her upper lip and got only salt. She lifted her eyes to Séverine; the nun's gaze said the number out loud so Artemis didn't have to.

Five.

Tamsin felt it in the air, too. She stretched long legs along the plank with the elegant misery of a woman half a fever ahead of somebody else's. "If the jungle could boil us and drink us, it would," she said. "This is only manners in advance."

"You'll do as you're told," Clara said, without affection and with love. "When you want to leap overboard to cool, you will *not*. When your teeth clack, you will bite your tongue and I will scold you for bleeding. When you want to stop rowing, you will not tell yourself it's because your arms hurt. You will say it is because I am cruel, and I will take that with thanks."

"Cruelty suits you," Jonah murmured, because talking in ordinary tones kept the panic in hobbles. He had learned, in the anaconda-coil, that his jokes were rationed like powder.

They took a right-hand bend that became a bellied silence. Mosquitoes came out of the idea of shade and laid a million little mouth-prints on every seam of shirt and netting. Clara lit a green-smoke cone under the awning that made eyes sting and throats bless her anyway. The smoke brushed the biting cloud into two sullen fringes that waited for wind or blood, whichever arrived first.

The first rigor took Artemis clean. No warning beyond the whisper of china in her bones. Her teeth snapped, jaw jumped as if she were a puppet with a drunken master. She folded inward without asking permission from dignity and hit the plank hard enough to bruise tomorrow. Tamsin was already there, one hand behind the skull, one clamping Artemis's shoulders to the deck. "Breathe," she said. "Count if you can. If you can't, I'll count until I hate numbers."

"One," Artemis said, because she could still lift a finger against something. "Two." On three her hands went to fists and wanted to be claws. She could smell Éloise's courtyard and river musk and the bread smell of a New Orleans morning that had pretended to be kind to her once. Four. Five. Seven. She lied about six because six was a word that felt like a grave.

Séverine's shadow fell over them; the rosary swung. "This is ours," she said to the air. "Find your own woman to lay claim on." Salt ticked the planks like rain.

Clara forced the quina and a little lime-water between Artemis's teeth when the jaw loosened; half went down, half went onto Tamsin's wrist and made her hiss through her teeth, more at the taste than the acid. "Again in an hour," Clara said. "And again after that. We dose the devil until he sours."

The heat came then—the coin under the tongue, the kitchen at the back of the skull. Artemis felt her skin learn to be too small. When she closed her eyes, the jungle wrote a letter behind them in green. When she opened them, the letter didn't stop.

Teo kept the boat moving because stopping invites company. "You sleep," he told Artemis without looking. "The river remembers the way. It doesn't need your eyes to boss it."

"Bossy anyway," Tamsin said softly, stroking the hair back from Artemis's forehead with two fingers as if the gesture could insult fever into leaving.

The heat sharpened. Then softened. Then sharpened again. She threw the blanket because the blanket was the color of a threat and then asked for it because the wind had learned to needle. The shiver set in as if someone had braided it into her ribs. Quina sat like a little bitter saint in her gut and did what saints do: something invisible and insufficient and necessary.

When the worst of the rigor eased, she slid into a dream-shallow that wasn't sleep. New Orleans: beads of wax guttering in a hot courtyard, chalk veves muttering their chalk-mouthed prayers. The ship: bar across the hatch, voices braided like hair—black, black, white—saying *open* the way a lover says *please*. The jungle bent its head and listened to both, judge and jury in green. She saw the serpent idol again, the carved head with its shard eyes, the hair twisted into rope around it—not decorative, not solemn, *binding*. The voice that had taken her mouth in Éloise's house spoke inside the heat and didn't trouble with breath.

The river keeps what the sea cannot. My body is broken. Bring me, or be broken.

She made a small amused sound with lips too dry for humor. "I'm already broken," she said aloud, and Tamsin swore a promise at the fever for making her talk in two worlds.

Around noon, the breeze died of its own boredom. The river got quiet in that listening way that made men work too hard so they wouldn't hear what listened. Teo used the pole, a rhythm like heart. Isidro sweated without commentary. Jonah learned there is a time of day when even clever hands admit to being meat. Otis tried not to cry and did not succeed all the way. Luis slept with the remain of himself.

"Storm," Teo said, reading the color of green and the way birds had learned to move. "Short, hard."

It came from behind a bend with a clap like a door slammed by a god. Rain hammered leaves and water until everything was only water; wind slid under the awning with a knife and took their breath the way men do when they mean to be cruel and not have to admit it later. Tamsin jammed her hat down and laughed a laugh that didn't belong in any church; it made Clara snarl with relief—laughter meant lungs worked.

"Under," Teo barked. "Heads down. Let it talk."

The *bongo* rode it like a horse that had never been broken. The awning tried to leave and was persuaded otherwise with rough language and rope. The storm threw a fist of dead leaves and spiders into the boat as if to make new pets; Otis clutched the awning post and let his eyes be bitten instead of his wrists. Lightning showed them a bank running past too close for good manners, then blackness made a meal of everything again.

Artemis put her cheek to the plank and let the boat be bigger than she was. Fever ran its clever hands along her spine and whispered the word *open* so gently it sounded like *rest*. Séverine's palm touched Artemis's temple, quick as a bee, like a woman stealing a blessing off a sleeping child. "No," she said—mother and blunt god. "Work now. Rest later."

The storm stunned itself in ten minutes and left without apology. Everything dripped. Steam got up and took away any air that had been decent. The mosquitoes held a small cathedral service. Teo pushed the boat into a slack where they could bail and swear with less admiration.

Artemis sat, her back against a rib, and let the shiver write its complaint smaller. The spoon lay cool where it lay. She took the twist of salt from Tamsin and salted the cup and held the spoon over it because ritual is rope: it gives you something to hold, even if you decide not to pull. One—two—three—four—five—six—seven. The spoon turned, unapologetic, toward a seam so narrow Isidro sucked his teeth.

"More doors," he said. "Everything wants us to choose."

"Then we choose," Jonah said, too quickly. He had been handling the medicine bag with the careful dishonesty of a man who knows he will be caught. Clara's eyes found his hands and his hands pretended they had only ever held poles and cards.

She set the bag against her chest and lifted her chin. "Mine," she said. "If I find quina missing without my permission, I will dose you with my fist."

"I was counting," he said, too smoothly. "Rations. Habit."

"Count your sins," Tamsin suggested. "It will keep you busy while we walk."

He gave her a smile that had no home to sit in. "If I must. I'll need more ink."

They went into the seam because the spoon said so and because the day had learned to obey not reason but the small tyrannies that had gotten them here alive. The channel was thick as breath in a sickroom. Roots made the floor; leaves made the ceiling; air made a small emergency of itself. At one point the *bongo* stopped moving because it could not imagine movement. Teo set his shoulder to the pole and persuaded it that imagination was not required: work was.

They sweated until sweat found places it had not known before. Quina sat in their bellies like a grudge. Luis stirred with a little fever of his own and Clara fed him water in a patience that had teeth. Tamsin sang half a London street rhyme and half a New Orleans hymn and made them sit together, ugly as cousins who share only a nose. Séverine walked her eyes over the green for any

shape that meant appetite and sent them away with a
wordless shape of her mouth. Isidro's machete flicked
off opportunistic vines with the joy men reserve for
solvable problems.

Artemis's fever peaked like a cruel tide and broke a
little toward evening. Sweat soaked her shirt; her
trousers clung; a cool came up the spine that wasn't
mercy and wasn't malice and wasn't done with her. She
breathed, slow and greedy. The world returned to
edges. The spoon cooled properly against bone and felt
like metal again instead of a mouth.

"Alive?" Tamsin asked, casual.

"Large as life," Artemis said. "And twice as tired."

"Good." Tamsin wet a rag and laid it on Artemis's
throat with the delicacy of putting a child to bed. "I like
you loud."

"Clara prefers me quiet."

"I prefer you obedient," Clara said, not looking up from
Luis's bandage, which bled only the way anger does
when it has been insulted.

Toward dusk the channel let them out into a reach of
black-water that had remembered how to be a mirror. A
heron stepped through its own face with the purity of a
knife. The breeze came back thin and honest. Teo
steered toward a bank where sand pretended to be a
little beach, and trees pretended to be a roof, and
nothing pretended to be safe.

They made a little fort: hammocks like white smiles between trees, netting that kept more promises than it broke, the quina pot on its rope-swing, the beans forgiving them again for making them dinner. Séverine salted the four corners of their square and the mouth where the *bongo*'s nose touched dirt. She hummed something that had no tune and more power for it.

Artemis lay and sweated and watched the sky find stars through small wounds in the leaves. The fever was not gone. It sat on the edge of the hammock like a relation waiting for an apology and brought its luggage. She said *no* to it in numbers and it smiled like someone who had already bought the house.

When the worst of the heat slid away from her skull, the cold came again and shook her until her teeth plotted escape. Tamsin climbed into the hammock with her and held her like a vice with warmth in it, cursing under her breath with the even rhythm of a lullaby. "If you die," she said, quiet, "I will haunt you across oceans."

"I know," Artemis said, and the little laugh that escaped her cracked like thin ice.

They drank more quina because Clara said it was time, and because their mouths had learned the shape of the cup. Jonah tried to make a joke about love potions and got as far as *heart* before he found his mouth had no coin for the rest of it. He stared at the green and listened for footsteps that wouldn't be feet. Isidro sharpened the machete in case steel had forgotten its profession. Teo counted breaths against the slap of small waves, a man adding his heart to the river's ledger because he wasn't ready to be subtracted.

In the straw-colored hour when the coin flips and chooses darkness, the mosquitoes came like a decision. The smoke drove them back; the wind lent a miserable hand. Still, they fed. They always feed. Clara walked from hammock to hammock and made them swallow more bitterness, as if swallowing could be a profession. "Fever breaks with sweat," she told Artemis, because that's what you tell any woman who needs a door to believe in. "And comes back if you invite it. I'll tie your hands if you try to shake your net free."

"I am not undone by netting," Artemis said. "Only by numbers."

"Then count for me. Make a pen of it."

She did. One. Two. Three. The counting lassoed the night until it could be led.

Near midnight, the sound came again: not splash, not step. A heavy slide in water. A roll—unhurried, immense. Everyone who had sat up during the coil sat up again now. The fire threw a single, rude lick. Eyes shone once and went away. The sound moved on along the bank and left the taste of green stone in their mouths.

"Not hunting," Isidro said. "Not us. Just remembering us."

"Eat a saint," Tamsin whispered to the dark. "Not me."

Dawn came pale and honest, as if night had been a rumor. Artemis woke drenched and light as a woman who has been wrung, the fever run down to a sulk. Her cheeks had color. Her lips had a crack she wanted to lick and didn't. She put the back of her hand to her own temple and tried to be the sort of person who trusts her own skin.

"Better," Clara pronounced, skeptical of any gift not from her own hands. "Not safe. But better."

"Thank you," Artemis said, and meant it to the bitter powder and the woman who forced it and the river that had not taken interest in her last night.

Then Otis coughed. Once, small. Then again, bigger. The boy sat up slowly and the slow was worse than any jerk. His eyes looked glassy in a way that belonged to churches and markets—somewhere clean and cruel. He rubbed his forearms hard enough to make the skin pink and looked at Artemis like a puppy that has learned his name is not a spell that keeps him from death.

"I'm cold," he said. His teeth didn't chatter yet. He said it instead of shivering, as if his body didn't want to admit it had begun.

Clara's face changed in the single way that matters. She turned to the pot. "Then we start with you now," she said. "Lime. Quina. Twice the bitterness because you are young and the fever is greedy when it finds young meat."

Otis drank and didn't make a face because he wanted to be held in the good gaze of the women. Sweat stippled his lip. He breathed as if counting could be done with lungs alone. He pulled his hands back into his shirt again. They came out shaking.

Artemis slid out of her hammock on unsteady legs and touched the spoon with two fingers for proof that work still had a direction. The metal was cool. The thong was stubborn. The coin Baptiste had given her lay against her throat, warm with her own blood. She looked at the boy and felt the number scratch at the door again.

Six, said fear. *Death.*

"Not yet," she told it. "You will not take him when I am still in the room."

The river breathed and said nothing. The jungle said nothing. The day began with the quiet that comes right before a long prayer, the kind where everyone waits to see if the person who leads it has the right voice.

"Load," Teo said, because the river did not care if boys were cold. "We move."

"Count," Séverine told Artemis as she took her place at the bow with the spoon hidden under shirt and coin. The nun's gaze had the weight of a hand between the shoulder blades.

Artemis counted, because obedience can be a sacrament. One for each of them: herself, Tamsin, Jonah, Isidro, Clara, Otis, Séverine. Seven. Still.

For now.

Chapter XIV — The River That Walks Uphill

"Some waters do not flow; they choose."

By midmorning the day had decided on heat with teeth. The black-water lay flat as lacquer between walls of green; every paddle stroke made a slow bruise that closed behind them. Mosquitoes hung in veils that had learned patience. Teo stood in the stern, pole planted like a priest's staff, eyes narrowed into squints that measured color and wind the way other men measure coin.

He pointed with his chin to a seam of darker green ahead, a long wrinkle where the river's skin forgot what direction meant. "There," he said. "The Casiquiare. River that climbs."

Tamsin tilted her hat against the glare and squinted. "Rivers don't climb."

"This one forgets manners," Isidro said, affection in the insult. "It goes from the Orinoco's hip to the Negro's shoulder when it pleases. It remembers two homes and borrows from them both."

Artemis felt the spoon cold at her sternum, the coin warm at her throat. Fever had left her the weight of a wet shirt and the after-taste of bark. Otis flinched under his netting at nothing at all and then at everything. Clara set her palm to his brow and didn't curse because when she holds a boy's head her mouth remembers to be soft.

Sister Séverine dusted a line of salt along the gunwale with her fingertip "Rivers that walk," she said. "Doors that open without hinges."

The spoon wanted out. Artemis salted a cup and held the bowl above, counting with her lips against the inside of her teeth. One, two, three, four, five, six, seven. At seven the spoon turned, slowly, as if reluctant to admit the obvious, toward the seam where water had learned to disobey gravity.

"Up," Teo said. "We lean together. The river will test who means it."

They pushed the *bongo*'s nose into the seam and felt the boat hesitate like an old horse at a bad bridge. Water pressed back with the obstinacy of something that has believed itself a law for too long. The first yard took a prayer. The second took a curse. The third took Tamsin's shoulders and made the tendon there stand like a rope. Jonah dug the pole in and grunted a small truth that had no words. Isidro leaned his weight the way a man leans into a woman who might not forgive him.

The *bongo* slid by inches, then handspans. The water's push softened into a negotiation and then into a sulk. The forest's voice changed. Frog-speech turned from hymn to gossip. A breeze remembered them.

"Up," Teo said again, softer. "You see? She remembers we mean it."

They passed a brown spit where an abandoned mission squatted in the green like a tooth left in the wrong mouth. A low church with a roof half-swallowed by vine; a bell that had forgotten to be a bell, rust eaten through its lip; a cross so eaten by ants it looked like a map of sins. On the steps sat three objects that had outlived their owners: a clay bowl blackened by old fat;

a serpent picked out in dotwork on a stone, the pits filled with bottle-green chips; a braid of hair—black, black, white—tied to the stone with gut and stiff with dried river salt.

Otis made a small sound that might have been prayer.

"Don't touch," Clara said.

"I wasn't going to," he lied.

They eased in. Teo pushed the bow to sand and held it like a man seating a coffin. "Quick," he said. "If there are men who own this place they will watch from shade and decide if we are worth the arrow." He nodded to Séverine, who was already climbing the low steps with skirts that were trousers and a veil tied like a sailor's band.

Inside the church it was cooler and smelled of limes, bats, and a faint stubborn ghost of incense. Saints with flaking faces looked down with the patient disapproval of old women in markets. On the altar someone had carved, long ago or yesterday, a spiral with a serpent's head and pressed green into the grooves until the light found it. Séverine crossed herself out of habit; then touched the spiral with two fingers and sniffed them. "Salt," she said. "And oil. And—" her mouth tightened, "—hair."

Artemis kept her hands to herself because curses keep lists. Outside, Isidro and Jonah walked a short circle with the slow care of men who don't want to step on what remembers. Tamsin stood at the door with her pistol under her shirt and her eyes trying to look like they hadn't already seen enough.

They weren't alone.

A flicker at the edge of green; a shadow shaped like a
man and like a tree at the same time; a rustle that
belonged to leaves and to bare feet. A woman stepped
out first—naked to the waist, paint on her chest that
made a maze; hair cut in a fringe like a knife had been
used with humor. She held a bundle: bark strips, a little
clay bottle stoppered with leaf, a string of teeth that
were not human.

Behind her, two men with faces the color of the river's
good bank. Bows hung easy in hands that had never
learned to tremble. Their eyes were old not in years but
in skill.

Teo lifted his empty palm. "We pass," he said in a
Spanish that knew how to apologize. "We pay for
water."

The woman set down the bundle on the step and did not
look at Artemis or at Séverine. She looked at the braid
on the stone and spat delicately in the dust, a curse too
elegant to translate. With her toe she nudged the braid
so it rolled once over, revealing a knot burned black.
She tapped the knot. She made a circle in the air with
finger and thumb. She drew a line through it. She
pointed—south-west, into a green thicker than anything
should be.

"Not open," Séverine said, reading the sign like a
psalm. "Not here."

The woman's mouth, painted dark with fruit, twitched.
She tipped the clay bottle into her palm, touched its
contents to her tongue, then offered it to Clara with the

care of a surgeon passing a blade. "Bitter," she said in a word that might have been Spanish once or might have been generosity. "For heat." She tapped Otis's chest with two fingers and did not wait to see who objected.

Clara smelled it, nodded once—*quinine cousin*—and tucked it into her satchel like a coin. She put a twist of salt in the woman's palm, and a needle wrapped in cloth, and got back a basket woven so tight water would have to ask permission to pass.

Jonah, who kept his humor for safe moments, kept it now. He bowed. The smallest of the men behind the woman raised one eyebrow with a contempt elegant enough to be art. Then they were gone, back into green that closes like a mouth.

"Told," Isidro said. "Not a blessing. Not a threat. A map."

"A warning," Séverine said. "And proof the serpent you hunt is not only yours."

They left the mission with the hair braid still tied to stone and the bowl still black. Tamsin spit to the side to unstick her mouth. "If I ever see a barber again, I'll kiss him for not saving our leavings."

"Never leave hair where a curse keeps a pantry," Séverine said.

They pushed upstream along the Casiquiare as if pulling a stubborn ox by the horn. The banks came lower, then narrowed, then twisted away as if to hide secrets in polite folds. Every hour Clara made them drink from her bitter bottle and hers; every hour Otis shivered in a more honest way, sweat at the hairline, breath fast. "Look at me," Clara told him when his eyes wandered toward the tree-tops as if they might offer rescue. "Here. On the count—one, two, three—breathe with me. Again."

He obeyed, because he still wanted to be called *good boy* by a woman who would not cheapen the words by using them.

By late afternoon, thunder stacked blue-black over low trees. Teo angled for a sly beach under roots shaped like the hands of saints too thin to help. "We hold for hard rain," he said. "Then we climb again."

They hadn't set the first hammock when men in clean coats stepped from behind the root-walls—three of them, hats wrong for river, boots right enough to have learned. The middle one carried a cane with a silver serpent head, coiled, mouth open in perpetual thirst.

"Señores," he said in the same bored voice that had offered to buy their souls at the side-channel. "Señoras. Don Iñigo's compliments. He requests your papers and your direction. He will keep them safe for you while you go do the difficult work. He is generous that way."

Isidro smiled without humor. "We have a pilot. We have medicine. We have water. The only thing we lack is a liar."

"Then you have yourselves," the man replied with a neatness that made Tamsin itch to put a ball in his coat.

Jonah drifted sideways, casually, toward the bongo's stern where the powder horn sat in a quiet unspoken nest. The emissary's eyes cut to him and away; Jonah's hands kept doing nothing in a very skilled way.

"Your cane's head needs a haircut," Tamsin said. "It keeps sticking its tongue out at ladies."

"Serpents do as they please," the man said. "Right now they please to live in silver and drink the sweat of fools." He held out his palm. "Letters."

Séverine stepped forward with the expression of a woman who had decided to teach a child to stop biting. "No," she said, simply. "Not to you."

"Then to the man behind me with a better hat."

"No."

He sighed, insulted by being made to repeat himself. He lifted the cane, the silver mouth toward Séverine like a threat disguised as a kiss. "Señora," he said. "The jungle is not a place for—"

A twig whispered, then sang. An arrow shook itself in the wood of the cane with a thrumming that made the teeth ache. The emissary stared at it, outraged to find a new rule.

Another arrow pinned his hat by its brim to the root-wall. He laughed once—offended, not afraid—and went to draw his pistol as if the jungle were a salon where gestures mattered and bullets asked to be announced.

Jonah knocked the pistol aside with a flick and brought the powder horn up in the same movement, his other hand already throwing a little gourd—the one Teo kept under the awning—for this very conversation. It hit the root foot of the nearest man and broke open into liquid with the smell of a bad god's breath. Oil. The next arrow found that man's thigh; he screamed; Jonah's flint made a star. Fire climbed the root like it had been waiting to be asked.

"Boat!" Teo snapped.

It was fast—the way good disasters are. Fire glittered up the snake-work of root; the emissary swore in a tone that suggested lawsuits; another arrow took the butt of his pistol and knocked it clean into the water, where the river accepted it with all the courtesy a river reserves for iron.

Tamsin shot the third man in the coat through the soft meat where collar meets shoulder. He went down like paperwork. Isidro kicked the emissary's cane out of his hand and into the flames, which licked the silver with a lover's interest. The emissary chose to live. He ran, more insulted than injured, brought up short only once by the arrow that kept his hat obedient. He left the hat.

They shoved the bongo off while root-fire cracked like little ribs and the sky threw down its own rain to call the matter even. Thunder lay in their mouths. The emissary's curse followed them like a ribbon: "You run to my employer's pockets by another road."

"Let him sew them shut," Tamsin said. "We'll cut them open."

Rain erased the prints they hadn't had time to make. The bank withdrew under a curtain of water. Teo pushed the nose into the center run where current had the decency to be honest. The bongo surged as if sudden purpose had remembered it.

They didn't speak for ten minutes because that's how long the body needs to reassemble after almost dying in a new fashion. When words returned, they were small and expensive.

"Nice throw," Isidro told Jonah without looking, which was his version of trusting a man again for twenty minutes.

"I'm a gentleman," Jonah said, shaking rain out of his hair. "I like to light candles in churches."

"Powder?" Tamsin asked.

"Dry," he said. "For now."

They made a pitch under a bank whose roots were old enough to sign their children's names on the dark. The fire shrank itself to smoke and a small insistence. Otis shivered in a way that made Clara swaddle him in two nets and a blanket and curse the human body for being a wall too eager to open.

"Bitter," she said, and tilted the new clay bottle. He drank and gagged.

"Good," she told him, without gentleness. "If I'm not a monster, it isn't medicine."

"You are a monster," he said, adoring her. It made her mouth try to smile and then un-try because smiling will kill a woman quicker than river fever.

Night came and laid its damp hand on the camp. The rain gave up being theater and became a lullaby with bad lyrics. Teo's boys took the first watch and arranged themselves like furniture that survive earthquakes. Séverine salted a cross on the plank and a circle around the boy. Isidro's blade learned a sharper word. Tamsin oiled her pistol for the hundredth time with a patience that would have looked like love if she had known where to put her eyes.

Artemis, fever-shriveled and stubborn, slid from her hammock and went to the water's lip. She salted the cup, held the spoon, counted. One—two—three—four—five—six—seven. The spoon trembled and turned, as ever, toward a seam nobody sane would have taken. Southwest. Toward the Negro and beyond it, toward the water that turns the world black at midday; toward Manaus; toward the wide brown throat of the Amazon; toward the smaller, meaner mouths—Purus, Ituxí—that had learned to chew without being seen.

"Southwest," she said.

"Of course," Séverine answered behind her, voice tired and fond. "The devil is a cartographer."

They slept like men at work. Somewhere near the edge of camp a line of army ants found the seam in their salt and poured across it like spilled ink. Tamsin woke to the sound of raining leather—tiny feet in number large enough to have music. She struck the line with a burning twist of green leaves and the ants divided and searched for doctrine. Two crawled under the bandage on her finger and bit with the joy of apprentices. She sat very still, let them have their say, then flicked them away with a care that looked like cruelty and was not.

At first light, they lifted their small house and set it back on the boat. Otis's fever sat in him the way an uninvited guest sits at a table: polite, hungry, not going anywhere. Clara kept forcing bitterness down his throat and counting his breaths against the river's. He looked past her once toward Tamsin as if to say *don't let me be the one you bury*. Tamsin put her palm to his cheek as if to wipe dirt and left a kindness there without saying so.

The channel narrowed into a green throat and then widened out into a reach that tasted different—smoky without fire, the air cooler as if a deeper room had been opened. "Negro," Teo said, voice almost reverent. They'd turned the hinge, crossed the river that walks uphill, come into the black water proper—a mirror that made the canopy a ceiling and their faces surprises.

It was quiet in a new way. The mosquitoes were fewer; the birds made other grammar. The banks rose higher. The water tasted less like vegetable soup and more like language.

"Manaus," Isidro said, pointing with his whole jaw downriver as if the city could hear its name and get ready to lie to them. "Days. Then the Amazon. Then the Purus, if you insist on dying in a smaller mouth."

"We insist," Séverine said blandly.

Before noon, a low longhouse on pilings revealed itself around a bend, smoke the color of patience rising. A trading post of sorts: bark cloth hung from a line; gourds; fish strung by the tail; faces that did not arrange themselves to fit European ideas. A man with shoulders like a canoe-chewed log came to the stair-head and regarded them. He had an ax-handle face and eyes that had spent too long not being surprised.

"Powder?" Tamsin asked softly. "Ball?"

"Powder," Jonah said. "If he sells to people who wear trousers without guests inside them."

They laid up at the steps. Teo said things in a language that had borrowed less from priests and more from mosquitoes. The man listened with the generosity of a judge. He took their money at a rate that felt like mercy and probably wasn't. He sold them powder, ball, two new machetes, a length of netting that would fail on a Tuesday, fish smoked to a hardness that would survive bad manners. He eyed Otis and spat to the side, then whistled up a woman child who brought a bundle of leaves and a face like the river when it chooses not to drown you that day. Clara took the leaves like a relic and hid her gratitude in scolding.

In the shade under the longhouse eaves lay a crude map burned into a board: thick line, thinner line, a snake of dots with a wall of triangles where the lines disappeared—hills—and a notch. Someone had shoved green stones into the notch—chips of bottle that had learned to be holy.

Artemis laid her palm on the board and felt the wood say *South*. The spoon in her shirt agreed. The braid in the oilskin lay quiet for once, as if hair could know fatigue.

"Buy a boat with a good mouth in Manaus," the ax-handle man said in broken Spanish. "The river after is a liar. Small mouths tell bigger lies."

"We like liars," Jonah said lightly. "We lie right back."

"Good," the man said, and for a breath his mouth remembered how to be a smile. "Bring stories. We sell those too."

They pushed off again, into black water slick as a polished coffin. Sun struck the mirror and came back confused. The breeze had reprieve in it. Clara fed Otis leaf tea and bark bitterness until he slept without shiver. Tamsin sat with her back to Artemis's and let their heat argue down each other's shadows. Isidro learned the new water with his eyes. Teo smiled once at nothing.

The day went long and then gold and then bruise. Egrets folded themselves down into origami on stilts. Bats unhooked their feet and went about their errands with tidy mouths. The smell of fish rot and flowers rose like a prayer that didn't care if it was heard.

On the reach's far side, half lost in the last light, a shape moved—a boat broad in the beam, canvas patched into a shade-shed, men at the paddles who had been paid to be hands. A flag nobody had taught them to respect hung at the stern. The flash of a cane-head silver and a hat missing its brim told the rest.

"Company," Tamsin said, very calm. "Men who've learned how to follow rivers without learning how to read them."

"Let them," Isidro said. "Money runs faster than legs; greed often runs right past the place where the road turns."

"They will catch us in Manaus with paper and grace,"
Séverine said. "We will answer with trousers and sin."

Clara stirred the pot. "Eat," she said, and the word
made the camp. "Tomorrow you can make enemies.
Tonight you can have beans."

They did. They ate the day off their tongues. They told
no stories they didn't have to. Artemis counted. One for
each living. She did not count the dead out loud. The
number found its shape and sat.

"Seven," she breathed, and for now it was still true.

Southwest, the spoon said against her sternum, polite as
a knife.

Chapter XV — City of Black Water

"Every port is a mask; every mask, a wound."

Manaus—though men here would still call it Barcelos' daughter or simply *a cidade no encontro*—rose from the elbow of black and brown waters like a rumor learning to be a city. Low roofs under palm, a fort's square shoulders, two churches arguing with humidity, a scatter of longhouses on stilts and clapboard shops selling fish, cloth, and sins. Banners bleached to ghost-colors hung from poles; dogs threaded the legs of men who had learned to ignore their own hunger.

The *bongo* slid from ink to coffee where Negro brushed the Amazon and never truly mixed. Black on brown, brown on black—a seam in the world. Teófilo Aponte stood at the stern like a stump that refused to rot. "We tie where men don't sell our boat while we are still in it," he said dryly, and nosed toward a mud lip below a warehouse with a crooked crucifix.

Powder first; rope second; lies third.

Clara tightened the shawl across her sternum and checked Otis's brow. The boy looked hollowed and glassy, his fever-pulse hopping under skin. "Bitter," she told him, tipping leaf brew and quina to his stubborn mouth. "If you spit, I catch it, and make you drink it again."

He didn't spit. He swallowed to make her proud and tasted bark and river and defeat.

Sister Séverine tied her veil like a sailor's kerchief and dusted the boat's nose with salt. "We walk two by two," she said. "Tongues soft. Eyes loud."

Tamsin thumbed her pistol, tucked it again into the curve at her spine, and shook her trousers down over boot tops with deliberate insolence. "If a man in a hat takes offense," she said, "I will sell him a second offense for half-price."

Jonah's grin had more shine than sincerity. "Or we could just buy powder and pretend this is a friendly earth."

Isidro spat into the seam where two rivers argued and made a sign nobody had paid him to learn. "Friendly earth eats slower. That's all."

They climbed the steps into heat that went through cloth and teeth. Manaus—black water on one side, brown on the other—offered its faces: Portuguese in wrinkled linen, caboclos with shoulders like planks, women selling limes with knives that could shave penance, a saint in a niche looking as if no one had told him he was not in Europe anymore. An awning bore a painted snake looped around a chalice. The sight made Artemis's skin crawl like ants learning a word.

"Powder," Tamsin said. "Where men don't water it with river and call it mercy."

Teo led them to a longhouse whose eaves were lined with nets and whose smell was salt, smoke, and the iron tang that clings to men who earn death honestly. Inside, a man with a face like an ax handle—the very cousin of the one on the Negro—raised his eyes and set them on their knives and coin with even justice. He sold them powder dry as gossip, ball in neat paper kisses, flints carved by hands that had not yet learned to lie to themselves. He weighed their silver as if it might try to run. He looked at Otis, clicked once with his tongue, and turned to whistle a girl-child who brought out a packet of bark bound in a leaf and an expression older than her bones. Clara took it and made herself owe no one by scolding the price until both parties grew fond of the quarrel.

Outside, the humidity pressed a wet palm to their mouths. The harbor's voices braided: hawkers, bells, a slapped child, drums. A man in a coat too clean for this latitude leaned against a post with his hat brim low as law. Even from behind, Artemis felt the wrongness— silver glint at the cane's head, serpent's mouth frozen in metal thirst.

"Keep moving," Isidro said, his voice a knife sheathed.

They kept moving. But at the plaza, where the church's whitewashed face pretended innocence and boys played at soldiers with sticks, a woman stepped into their path, her hair braided close to the scalp, eyes like good coffee. She wore a dress hacked short for heat and a pair of trousers under it like defiance. On a string at her throat hung three chips of green glass.

"You're the fools going south," she said in Portuguese that Séverine caught and translated with her eyebrows.

"We're the fools already south," Jonah said lightly. "We're shopping for more south."

The woman laughed once. "My husband took a boat up the Purus. He did not bring my nephew home. He brought me this." She touched the glass chips. "He says there is a city where frogs sing like bells and hair holds doors shut. He wants me to forgive him for loving it more than life."

"We don't forgive men for loving cities," Tamsin said. "We forgive them for coming home."

The woman's mouth went softer around a pain. "Buy a *montaria* with a linesman who knows Igarapés. Don't trust boats with shade roofs; the shade is for the men who will sell you while you sleep. And don't sleep by the fish market. Men with silver canes count dreams there." She looked at Artemis's throat, where Baptiste's coin made a warm, round lie. "If you have a good charm, hide it from women like me. We recognize the weight."

Séverine put a needle wrapped in paper into the woman's palm. The woman put a gourd of oil into Séverine's. Debts changed shape.

They bought a *montaria*—broad-beamed, shallow draft, a good mouth and bad manners—from a man whose eyebrows met like cousins forced to share a bed. They paid twice for the same rope, once to buy it and once to be allowed to leave with it. Teo said, without ceremony, "I turn back at the Negro. The Purus makes men new in ways I don't need to be."

"Then give us a name to curse when the river eats us," Tamsin said.

"Vicente," Teo said. "He stinks of fish and God. He will get you to the Ituxí or sell you with prayer. Either way you arrive."

They found Vicente under a fig, gutting a monstrous pirarucu with the steady intimacy of a long marriage. He had a rosary looped twice around his wrist and a smile that made you want to check your pockets. He listened to Teo's word, measured the seven with eyes that had learned to forgive and forget money's facts, and nodded. "Purus. Ituxí. There are worse sins. I will take you until my wife's dream tells me to stop."

"Your wife has good dreams?" Jonah asked.

"She dreams of me drowning," Vicente said. "And I have not, yet." He wiped his hands on his trousers, patted the rosary like a sleeping dog, and spat neatly. "We leave at first prayer."

They took a room on stilts above a backwater that smelled of fish and flat beer. Hammocks. Nets. The familiar argument of beans on the pot. Séverine salted the windowsill as if windowsills could remember allegiance. Clara set Otis's small bed by the one breeze and tied his wrists lightly to the netting so fever's moods wouldn't tip him into the gap. "If you need to piss," she told him, "I give you a bottle and you give me back something the color of tea. Clear is greed. Brown is negotiation. Red is—don't be red."

He tried to smile. "You are a good mother."

"I am a bad god," she corrected, and kissed his temple like a brand.

Artemis washed in a tin basin and watched the water go gray. She tied her trousers tighter and felt the spoon cool against sternum, the coin warm at the throat, the braid in the oilskin a weight like unspent sin. The city breathed. Somewhere, a drum learned a new word.

They were careful. They went in pairs. They bought nothing with their names.

Care is not a wall; it is a wicker fence.

Near midnight, a hand slipped through that fence. Otis jerked awake to a palm pressed across his mouth that smelled of clove and fish. He fought with all his marrow and almost bit a finger; the net held, the knot gave—Clara's knot would not have, but someone else had looked, later, and retied in haste—and the boy was a bundle lifted out of bed and into night. The hammock swung emptily once and twice.

Séverine woke to the wrong silence. "No," she said, and the word was a bell.

Tamsin was already up, trousers and pistol, at the gap. She saw a shadow slide into an igarapé—one of the narrow black canals that haunt behind cities—and the quick pop of a pole pushed hard. "Thieves," she said, calm as an undertaker.

Jonah slammed through the door in his stockings and no dignity, then grabbed his boots with his hands instead of his feet. Isidro took the machete and nothing else. Artemis clutched the spoon, salted the el cheapo cup at the washstand, and counted to seven like a woman ramming a door with numbers. The spoon turned—to the right, toward the igarapé's black slit, where water hid under mangrove roots like someone keeping secrets before a wedding.

Vicente heard, swore a prayer, and flung his *montaria* off its tether with a shove that broken men would have envied. "In," he snapped. They were.

The igarapé was a vein cut into the city's shadow-meat. Leaves brushed faces; roots gripped air, then let go.

Mosquitoes stitched angry sutures in the one place nets couldn't reach—the mind. Ahead, a ghost of a boat slid without sound, as if the men pushing it had learned to pretend to be eels.

"Otis," Tamsin breathed, and the sound almost made the water shiver.

The spoon nudged Artemis's sternum like a child insisting. She held it like a compass that had once been a mouth and let it think for her. Right-hand fork. Second left. The canal tightened and sneered. Once a rat swam over her boot with insolent hands. Once an alligator's eye tracked them like a coin placed on a priest's tongue.

The kidnappers' boat stalled where a trunk fell low across the cut. There was a hissed curse in Portuguese too clean for these men's pockets, then two silhouettes heaved on the pole. The boy struggled—she saw it then, the small bundle thrash—and a voice that had been trained for begging even when it was singing rasped, "Artemis!"

"Here," she hissed. "Hold."

Tamsin stood in the bow with a pistol that had learned patience and blew out the stern-most man's hatline. The ball took a pinch of crown and made him remember his mother. He dropped the pole with a sound like a small confession. Isidro leaped from their bow like a sin solved with violence and met the second man at the shoulders—the machete's flat kissed his ear; the ear went away without asking the rest of the head. Jonah slid under the low branch, took the bowline of the kidnappers' boat in his teeth like a dog, and passed it to

Vicente, who had the knots of a man married to rivers. The kidnappers' boat was suddenly, marvelously tethered.

"Give me the boy," Clara said, voice enough to direct a ward of drunk sailors. The man who held Otis pressed a knife to the boy's throat and learned what faith is.

There are men who cut quickly; there are men who hesitate. He hesitated—not out of mercy, out of calculation. You could see the coins moving behind his eyes. Jonah put his own knife into that calculation, right through the ledger—between ribs, low, wicked. The man looked surprised to find numbers had pain.

Then the water itself betrayed them.

Not the river's old mouths—no anaconda, no caiman. Igarapés have their own saints: barbed branches, sunken planks, and nails left by men who nail boats and forget their nails. The kidnappers' boat shifted; a nail kissed Otis's forearm and opened a red smile. Not deep. Enough.

The water noticed.

"Hands!" Clara shouted. "Up! Keep them out!" But the boy had already kicked free. Fever and fear make fools. He flailed a hand toward Artemis and found the surface instead. Shining silver bodies materialized—no storm of knives, just a half-dozen neat little mouths, curious accountants checking a red ledger.

Artemis went overboard because love is a stupidity you make into a liturgy. The water took her with the soft throat-sound of a patient lover. She grabbed the boy under his armpits and felt the heat of his fever against her chest even here. "Hold—" she said, and the river answered with its own arithmetic.

Teeth. Pins. The boy gasped; the gasp invited. The mouths came careful and then eager.

Tamsin fired into water to lie to herself that this could help. Isidro beat at the river with the machete's flat as if tormenting a drum. Vicente hauled line and swore a prayer that asked God to pick a side.

Artemis did what math she had: rolled the boy onto his back, lifted his small forearms out of water, pressed her own shins down against the boat's side to give her old bruised abdomen to the mouths instead. She felt the clean bright agony of a dozen little absolutions. "Up," she said, not to him—to the world. "Up, up."

Hands—Tamsin's iron; Isidro's leather; Jonah's gambler's grip—took the boy and drew him into the boat, shivering, bleeding from fine semi-circles like a rosary of cruel little kisses. Clara fell on him with salt and cloth and rage that made her beautiful and terrible. "Put your hands here," she told him, and he did, because he had not learned yet that you can disobey women who save you.

Artemis put her palms on the gunwale and hoisted with the stupid strength of a woman who does not intend to drown yet. Something took a coin of meat from the meat above her knee. She saw the pain, not the blood; she saw the number, not the water. Hands hauled her in. She slid across planks and into Tamsin's lap, laughing a sound with no humor. "There," she said pleasantly. "I still feel my legs. That seems extravagant."

The kidnappers' second man, the one with the ear gone, chose badly. He lunged at Clara. Isidro took his wrist apart with one short wicked turn and fed him his own knife by mistake or intention; it didn't matter. The man spent his blood in the quiet way of people who have not imagined death needs noise.

The first man—the crown clipped—kicked himself free like a crab, floundered into mangrove shadow, and vanished into the number of men with new scars and bad employers.

"Enough," Vicente said, and the word came out older than he was. He cut the kidnappers' boat free and let it rock like a body at vigil. "We go."

They went, retreating from the igarapé's mouth like men backing out of a chapel where something impolite had happened. The city's voice widened again: drums, dogs, trade. Rain found them and forgave them just enough to hide the details on their clothes.

Back in the stilt-room, Clara lit every small lamp, turned every body by the face, and spoke to them with ranked orders. "Salt," she told Séverine. "Boil. Jonah, tip that oil. Isidro, lift. Tamsin—don't shoot the air; save it something to fear tomorrow. Vicente, like a saint, hold the boy's wrists."

Otis shook. Not the obscene rigor of grand mal; a smaller quake that begins in marrow and makes skin look like water. Clara packed salt into each neat crescent and made the boy count with her into a rhythm that reversed the invitation to bleed. The knife nick at his throat was shallow; the arm-wound from the nail deeper than it looked. She cleaned it and bound it and told it, aloud, "You are not a mouth. You are a scar."

Artemis, having used her shins for charity, unrolled her trousers to look. A string of bites across her thighs like bad pearls. Not deep. Multiplicity again. She laughed once and then grimaced when the laugh jostled bite and bruise from the fall. Tamsin dabbed the wounds with brine and vicious tenderness. "You silly woman," she said. "You could have died like a romantic."

"I would have disappointed you," Artemis said.

"Constantly," Tamsin agreed. Her hand shook when she put the lid back on the salt. She hid it by scowling.

Jonah stood in the doorway and watched the backwater for the return of men with hats. None came in the first hour. In the second, a boy with a split lip—cousin to all the boys who sleep under the eaves of cities and learn to trade information like fish—whistled once and tossed a small packet in. Séverine caught it with two fingers and put it on the table without opening. She washed her hands.

Artemis opened it.

Hair.

Black. Black. White.

Gut-thread through the end.

A card from a Spanish deck, the Cup fat as a womb. Across it, a familiar hand: **ABRE.** Open.

Tamsin burned it in a spoon with lamp flame until the hair writhed like something hatching and the smoke smelled of the ship's hold and a woman's comb. She tipped the ash into a cup and salted it and emptied it into river. "Drink that," she told the water. "Choke."

Jonah didn't look at the packet while it burned. He was reading a different paper—a receipt for powder, a note in Portuguese fairer than his hand could manage. He folded it once, twice. He tucked it and looked away so no one had to watch him lie to himself about not lying.

Clara sat between Otis and Artemis like a saint with a sword. "We leave at dawn on the tide the city pretends not to have," she said. "Purus. Ituxí. No more stops where men who smell of silver keep shops."

Teo came to the door and didn't step inside, tired and good. "This is where I leave," he said. "I've buried two men this season and I get no love for three."

"Go," Isidro said, holding out his hand. Teo took it. He looked once at Artemis as if to say *you are a magnet for doors*, then at Séverine as if to say *watch her*. He left with the gracelessness of a man who refuses to rehearse farewells.

Dawn was the color of old tea when they pushed their new *montaria* into the Amazon's wide brown throat. Vicente led and God followed three steps behind, grumbling. The black water let them go with rude courtesy. Manaus turned its face to other fooleries. The men with the silver cane did not appear. The hat stayed pinned to a root by an arrow until some boy made a story of it and a toy.

They had powder. They had ball. They had a pilot who prayed like a liar and lied like a priest. They had a boy who shook and a woman who shook less. They had a spoon, a coin, and a braid that kept not dying. They had seven.

For now.

The Amazon was less a river than an instruction. Its banks learned the word *far*. Its sky learned *big*. The days went ferry-wide and patient; the nights collected teeth. They turned south where Vicente's thumb knew, into a mouth that pretended to be small and was not— Purus, brown and sly, curling like a serpent taught to be courtly. The mosquitoes learned to write their names on forearms again. The forest leaned in as if asking for a secret.

They slept the first night on a bar of sand the color of old bread. Séverine salted arcs against what larger mouths wished. Isidro sharpened silence to an edge. Tamsin, trousers dirt to the knee, oiled her pistol with reverence and a sneer. Jonah played with a coin he no longer had, all muscle memory and no metal. Clara made bitterness and poured it into children of all ages. Artemis lay back and counted the slow wheel of bats flitting like punctuation in a sentence that threatened to run on forever.

Near midnight, Otis woke and sat up, obedient and wan. "Water," he said. "Please."

Clara tipped. He swallowed. He smiled at her—the small crooked smile he had given her the night he stole a sweet and was forgiven.

"Better," she said, bluff and fierce, because sometimes lies are medicine, too.

He lay down. He folded his hands like a boy taught to make peace with God out of habit. He breathed three even breaths, a fourth that snagged, and a fifth that went out as if the person who'd been in the room had stepped away for just a moment and taken all the lights with him.

The quiet was good and cruel. No drama. No scream. The most honest subtraction nature knows.

Clara's hands moved without orders. She pressed—not to bring back, but to be sure of what had already happened. She kept pressing because ritual saves the living. She made no sound. Séverine made the smallest noise a woman can make, a needle of air through teeth, and counted along with no number to catch.

Tamsin's mouth opened and shut twice. She put her fist between her teeth and bit her knuckles hard enough to make blood, then let go.

Jonah looked at the sky and found it the wrong size for the thing in his chest. He said a word that in some languages is also a prayer.

Isidro sat very straight and did nothing for a long time because that was the only thing he could do right.

Artemis was already moving, trousers wet to the knee, hair tight. She lifted the boy the way men lift sacks, not tender because tenderness breaks, and took him to the water's lip. "No," Tamsin said, the word ragged.

"Yes," Séverine said softly. "The river keeps what the sea cannot. It is its work."

Clara stood like a blade. "I will wash him," she said. "And I will put salt in his mouth so that if some small hungry thing envies him, it will remember to be polite." She did. God and anyone else who watched learned new manners that night.

They gave Otis to the river with beans still in the pot and knots still in the rope. Vicente prayed the way a man offers apologies to a piece of wood that will one day be his coffin. The current took the boy not like a thief, but like a midwife. The surface made no ripple at all.

"Seven," Artemis said, somewhere between breath and curse.

"Six," Séverine corrected, because someone must be brave enough to speak numbers as they are. The word cut her mouth.

They sat. They did not sleep much. Toward morning, piranha ticked at the edge of their camp with small impolite sounds. Tamsin rose and threw salt at them the way a woman throws rice at a couple she envies. The fish turned, offended, and went to a different wedding.

When the sun found them, it found six people who looked like seven's shadow. They loaded the boat because work is a sacrament when prayer has turned its face to the wall.

Vicente did not offer comfort. He spat into the water and said, "The Purus takes down, not up. We go to the Ituxí. Your devil is there."

"Our devil," Tamsin said, voice flat as iron.

"Yours," he said again, as if the river had told him something about ownership.

Clara tied the last knot with hands that learned not to shake. She looked smaller and more terrible than any saint. "Go," she told the boat. "Before this place names us, and won't let us leave."

They went.

The river widened and narrowed by its own mood. Monkeys told jokes nobody else enjoyed. A black caiman the size of a pew slid beside them, patient as a creditor. Once, in a sheet of water so still it reflected their shame back at them, a coil as wide as a woman's waist turned, the green plates catching sun like broken glass in a church floor. It did not hunt. It remembered.

They marked a tree at noon with a knife—one notch for the boy and one for the ship's men because numbers will carve whether you tell them not to or not. Séverine kissed the bark where the sap bled and made a small cross with salt. Jonah turned away so no one would see his face like that.

When sleep came, it was a debt collector, not a friend. Artemis woke in the violet hour with the spoon cold and the coin hot. The braid of hair stirred without wind. Somewhere, a drum hidden in roots thudded once and

stopped. The smell of green stone—impossible, real—
rose from the south-west like a breath under a door.

"Count," Séverine whispered from her net.

Artemis countered the shape of grief with arithmetic.
One—herself. Two—Tamsin. Three—Jonah. Four—
Isidro. Five—Clara. Six—Séverine. Seven—emptiness.

"Six," she said aloud, steady, as if steadiness were a
trick you could learn to do on command.

She did not add *for now*.

Chapter XVI — Gate of the Ituxí

"The forest keeps no archives; it writes in scars."

The Purus went on as if it could afford to, brown and
sly, curling around its own bends like a serpent that had
learned to behave in company. Days made themselves
wide. Nights collected teeth. The six of them moved
through both as if days and nights were rooms they did
not own and had no right to furnish.

Vicente's thumb found the water's seam where the Ituxí comes in shy—a mouth under branches, a brown ribbon offering humility and ambush at once. He tapped his rosary twice against his wrist, then raised his chin. "There," he said. "The little liar. Up that throat your devil sleeps or wakes."

Clara stood over the pot with the politeness of a tyrant and rationed bitterness and salt. Otis's place in the boat had become a geography of air; she did not look at the empty quarter-seam and she did not count around it when she counted men's breaths. Séverine's face had learned a new stillness that didn't belong to saints or sinners; it was the hush of a room after a name had been taken down from a wall.

Artemis felt Éloise's spoon cool at her sternum and Baptiste's coin warm at her throat. The braid in the oilskin lay quiet, which was worse than all its small politenesses. She salted the tin cup without asking permission and held the spoon over it—a habit, a rope, a trick to keep the mind from thinking a shape it could not unthink. One—two—three—four—five—six— seven. On seven the bowl turned, sure and little, toward the Ituxí's shade-mouth.

"Up," she said.

"Up," Vicente echoed. He poled the *montaria* into the slit and the river changed its accent. The world narrowed to a corridor of wet leaf and old light; roots made the floor; vines stitched the ceiling. The mosquitoes erected a cathedral and took tithes.

"Hands in," Clara said, again, because repetition is civilized. "And if any god asks a favor, tell him to come to me first."

They worked noon into smoke, smoke into dusk. The Ituxí's grammar was different; it spoke half in mire and half in breath. Rafts of matapí—floating weed islands stitched by stems into deceit—had to be bullied aside with poles; under them, the water moved with a patient intelligence that made men think of teeth.

They camped the first night on a tongue of sand that had learned to keep its shape only because the river wanted to be gracious. Séverine salted corners and mouth. Jonah made a joke he didn't complete. Tamsin sat cross-legged, trousers dark to the knee, and oiled her pistol in strokes that would have been called tender if tenderness did not demand hope. Isidro sharpened the machete until it looked like it could cut ideas.

They did not speak of the boy. They did not need to. In the hour when bats begin to write in the air, a line of army ants discovered the seam in their salt and poured through like a black river small enough to wear boots of chitin. The sound—*sssssssss*—was leather raining on leaves. Tamsin hissed and struck a green bundle; smoke rolled; the line broke and then broke them back in two. The ants chose another creed for the night. Clara, watching the black torrent with clinical respect, said, "If they had found us in our sleep, there would be nothing left of our courtesy by morning."

Sleep came like debt collection. Artemis woke twice to her own hands trying to open and drop—spoon, knife, coin, rope—as if the curse wanted practice. She tied the thong again, a new knot, an uglier one. She counted to seven—not as a charm, as an order to her bones.

In morning light thick as broth, the Ituxí showed them the first of its gates.

Two huge trees had gone down long ago and then again last season, criss-crossed at low water and now pinned in the shallows by their own weight. The gap between trunk and branch was a priest's mouth—narrow, thin-lipped, sick of being asked for money. The current in that throat spun slow as a lie.

"We cut or we carry," Vicente said. "Carry is safer and slower. Cut is quick, unless it's not."

"Prize for honesty," Tamsin said. "Carry."

They lightened the boat to the story it could be on shoulders. Packs went first; rope; beans; powder; nets; quina; the satchel that had turned Clara into God more than once. Isidro and Jonah shouldered the *montaria's* bow and stern while Vicente took the side like a man bracing a door. Roots made stairs where feet had more respect for them. Sweat made clean men out of them all. The boat's belly squeaked over a polished trunk, then went weightless for a second and belly-flopped into the pool beyond with a hollow *guh* that sounded like an insult answered.

Artemis carried lighter loads and counted stumbles instead of steps. The spoon knocked her sternum. The coin warmed her throat. The hair in the oilskin behaved.

On the second portage she learned the ground's repertoire. The mat of leaves over the black water had depth, but not the same depth everywhere; a foot sank, met silt, slid, found a log, found a hole, found the idea of drowning without the convenience of current. She caught herself against a root with her elbows and thought, irrelevantly, of a New Orleans gutter—how it had looked the first time she realized a city could rot and still call itself beautiful. She crawled out swearing with old vocabulary.

Jonah disappeared up to one thigh with a sound that belonged to bad dreams. Isidro hauled him by the armpits, expression unchanged. "This forest likes to eat slowly," he said. "A cook, not a butcher."

They made the pool beyond and breathed like men who had paid for the air with their backs. The *montaria* floated, pleased with the compliment. Vicente spat into the water and made the sign of the cross with his thumb and the paddle. The paddle seemed to approve.

It was there they met the spiders.

Not in a mass, not raining. First a glimmer at eye level that became a face if you were cruel. Then another, bigger, the size of a hand and confident. Then the web between trees was not lace so much as a curtain. A wandering spider—longer than honesty, brown-black, thick-legged—climbed over the gunwale with the polite tread of a small cat and stopped by Tamsin's boot to consider.

Tamsin's mouth thinned. She did not move. "Friend of yours?" she asked the air.

Clara's voice sharpened to surgical. "Don't swat. It will bite where it counts most. I need vinegar I do not have and a clean bed I cannot give. Let it pass."

The spider did not respect either woman. It stepped onto Tamsin's laces like a dowager mounting a step. Tamsin breathed in fours to keep words out. Isidro took the tip of his machete and moved the spider the way you would move a hot coal you didn't want to go out— careful, slow, offering it a better idea. It accepted, reluctantly, and went off the stern into its own business. Tamsin exhaled. "If it had bitten me," she said conversationally, "I would have cursed it to death with language too creative for God."

"It would have made *you* creative," Clara muttered. "You'd have a story for sailors you'd not wish to tell."

"Spare me the details," Tamsin said. "I like my tragedies without jokes that start in trousers."

They moved.

Toward noon, the river's rooms opened out—lagoons under vaults; corridors with birds stepping like priests. Monkeys insulted them in voices that sounded like drinkers in an alley. A black caiman the size of a pew shadowed them for an hour to make the point that appetite is a kind of weather.

The spoon turned when Artemis salted and asked it. It chose seams, not roads; mouths, not avenues. It pointed them toward a low, thick dark under the left bank where vines braided into something that looked almost deliberate. On the root-knee of the biggest tree, someone had pinned three chips of bottle-green with gum. Beside the stones hung a bolt of hair—black, black, white—tied with gut, stiff with old salt.

Séverine touched the tree with two fingers and came away with resin that smelled like a room where prayers have burned too often. She tasted it and her mouth twisted. "Barricade," she said. "Not a door. A *don't*."

Tamsin looked to Artemis. "We disobey?"

"We have made a habit of it," Artemis said, and hated herself for enjoying the honesty of the answer.

They went into the slit. The light went sallow. The air took an extra job of being heavy. After three bends the channel knotted into itself, then unknotted, then shuddered straight. Where its straightness ended a flat stone rose barely out of water—only a foot, only two. On it lay an old bowl black with fat, a coil of hair like rope, and a smear of something that had once been white and was now the color of tea. Salt. It crunched faintly under Jonah's boot when he stepped down to stretch the no-knot in his back. The crunch made Séverine's head snap. "Don't," she said. Too late.

Something in the throat of the trees said *ah* without sound.

"Back," Vicente decided, the instant calculus of men who have lived long by distrusting new arithmetic. "We leave this room polite, before the host notices we didn't bring wine."

They left, not running, because one turns away from some altars the way one backs away from a sleeping dog with a bad history.

By dusk, thunder bunched behind the canopy. Vicente nosed the *montaria* into a shallow under roots and let the boat settle. They hustled the little camp together with practiced ugliness: hammocks, nets, a pot, a small fire that pretended to be a lamp because rain bullied it down into its better manners.

Tamsin took second watch. Rain had just learned a new vocabulary when she hissed: "Feet."

Not beasts. That was the problem. Men make a different music, even barefoot.

They came out of the green as if painted there and someone had wiped the last of the green away: five shapes in coats that knew rain and hats that knew silver. The one in the middle wore his hat bare-headed now—no brim—and carried a replacement cane: another serpent, mouth frozen thirsty, silver like a promise to a whore.

"Evening," he said, Spanish soaked in Portugal and schooling. "The river says you chose the little mouth. Sensible. Big mouths chew."

"You keep buying canes," Tamsin said, pistol on her thigh, voice pleasant. "How long till you learn to buy sense."

His smile didn't move. "Sense is for men who can afford to die poor. Don Iñigo will not. He requires what you seek. You will give me your letters and your directions. You will leave the jungle poorer than you entered it. It will be a mercy."

Jonah was counted and known the last time. He didn't waste tricks twice. He sat as if defeated, his hands on his knees, his mouth quiet. Isidro matched him, the machete a thought near his thigh. Séverine, like a small woman with a large god, stood between the serpent-cane and Artemis with the exact defiance of a door with seven locks.

"Vicente," the emissary said, a courtesy that felt like insult. "A pleasure. Your wife must dream poorly to send you with these."

"She dreams well enough," Vicente said. "Of you drowning." He spat. The rain washed the gesture honest.

The emissary's hatless head tilted. "Choose. Papers. Or a death you won't enjoy."

"We will always choose death," Séverine said, almost gently. "It's the one thing we own."

He sighed, offended by poetry in the wrong month. He lifted the cane. The serpent's open mouth winked with a pale lightning. The men behind him raised pistols like small affirmations.

Tamsin fired first. The shot took the shoulder of the man to the left, rolled him into root-mud with a polite thud. Isidro came up as if the ground had borrowed him and returned him quickly; the machete kissed a wrist. A pistol went off, not his. Splinters blew out of the awning post by Artemis's ear; the world made a sound like paper tearing.

Vicente moved like a decent man taught late in life to kill when insulted. He shoved the *montaria* with a boot against the bank so it would not be pinned; he came up with his own stubby carbine and made the unpleasant music it preferred. A coat danced three steps and fell, a puppet cut. Another coat fired and found Vicente past the third rib under the right breast in that garden where men keep breath.

He made a noise Artemis had never heard and will never forget—a single, surprised *oh*—and sat down as if he'd been asked to. Blood soaked his shirt as if someone had emptied a little sack of red into it. His hand went to the wound and came away glossy. He looked at it with an academic presence/absence, as if reading a letter from a son who had used the wrong salutation.

"Boat!" Isidro barked.

They obeyed with all the dishonor of survivors. Tamsin fired her last, neat and useless except to buy the second that would be necessary for the others to live. Jonah threw the powder-horn out into the rain because wet powder is a democracy. Séverine grabbed Artemis by the arm and pulled, not because Artemis wouldn't have moved but because Séverine needed to touch her with a possession heavier than faith. Clara gripped Vicente's belt with both hands and dragged him with the unlovely strength of a woman who has stopped consulting God.

The emissary did not hurry; he raised the cane and brought it down as if christening a ship. The silver serpent's open mouth hit the gunwale and bit nothing but wood, but the affect was that of a blessing denied. He leaned in; his face was rain-slick, immaculate. "This ends where money ends," he said. "And money is the one river that never dries."

"Tell it to hell," Tamsin said, and cut the painter. The *montaria* thumped free.

Isidro shoved off with the pole. The boat slewed sideways; a pistol-ball ticked a hole through the thatch; another smacked the pot and reduced its future to an ugly dent and a new story. Vicente lay long in the bottom, breathing in short, learning the different geography of a man punctured somewhere below God's better inventions. Clara's hands were already on him. She packed the wound with linen, then with a strip of net that offended both of them. She pressed and he blessed her with a curse. "Hold," she said. "Hold, you old sinner."

In the rain, the emissary's men did not run—a mark of training—but the root-fire from Tamsin's first shot had found fresh fuel. Flare climbed a little spire; an arrow, invisible, came from the green and found the silver snake, pinning it to a root with a sound like a bell struck wrong. The emissary looked down at it with aristocratic confusion; then he looked up and saw only the *montaria's* stern going into dark.

They slid into the Ituxí's throat, where rain is architecture and river is argument. Trees leaned in and hid their sins for them, a courtesy the jungle extends when it thinks you might amuse it.

Clara knelt over Vicente. The blood under her hands was a lake. "He's going," she said, not cruelly. "He is going because the tooth took the one place I can't sew." She put her mouth to his ear. "You don't get confession. You get instruction. Say your wife's name. Say it like a rope and pull."

He said it. The word meant *water* in a language Artemis didn't know and *bread* in every language that matters. He breathed once, twice, a third shallow, and then—because men are obedient to some orders—he obeyed the only one that counts. A last breath shook the netting. The rosary on his wrist lay quiet as if the beads had decided they had been moved enough for one life.

Clara closed his eyes with salt on her thumb. She did not make the sign of the cross. "You drowned where you were dry," she said. "That counts."

They gave Vicente to the river not because they were out of cloth but because the Ituxí had claimed him in a lawful way. Séverine murmured a prayer so small it could have been mistaken for a woman talking to a child; then she straightened and looked at the gap they had left behind them. Rain wrote its own letters between roots. The emissary's fire snuffed itself in that rain-fluent way.

Tamsin leaned her head back and let water wash powder smoke out of her hair. "Five," she said, deadpan—not in despair, not in triumph. As if numbers were horses that must be named aloud or they bolt.

"Five," Artemis agreed. The word walked down her throat and cut her on the way.

They poled. They poled until their backs said new words. The rain lost interest and moved its theater elsewhere. Night made an argument for stopping and then made it into a sentence. The Ituxí opened a room to the right with a low bank that pretended to have fewer teeth than the left. They took the pretense. Hammocks. Nets. No fire. Beans cold, which is to say honest.

Clara sat with her hands on her knees and discovered they could shake if she wasn't using them. She forced them still. She looked at the place where Vicente's body would have made a different silence and then looked away because looking is how rooms keep you.

Isidro set the machete across his thighs and stared at nothing until it learned a new edge from his gaze. Jonah sat with his back against a rib and counted what he had not done too late. Séverine's rosary clicked once—the beetle-sound of beads finding one another—and then was still.

Tamsin reached for Artemis's hand under the net, unseen, and made a fist around it. "If we live through this," she said, "I'm buying a hat just to take it off to myself."

"You'd look hateful in a hat," Artemis said, because gallows humor is also a sacrament.

"Then I'll buy two."

Artemis slid the spoon out from her shirt. She wanted to ask. She wanted to throw it into the river. She salted the cup anyway and held the spoon above like a woman lifting a relic and daring it to fail. One. Two. Three. Four. Five. Six. Seven. The bowl turned. Not back, not downriver, not toward mercy. West-southwest. Into a dark that smelled faintly, impossibly, of cold stone and old women's hair.

"Gate," Séverine said. Not a question.

"Gate," Artemis answered. The word felt like a key she kept in her mouth and did not swallow because to swallow it would be to open without hands.

They slept badly and without dreams they could keep. Cold woke them like a wet hand. Morning had stolen some color and replaced it with a lot of insects. The Ituxí ran under roots with the modesty of a thief carrying a heavy basket. They pushed off again because grief cannot be dignified on a river. Movement is the only etiquette.

The days bent. The river argued. Men watched from shadow and sent a single arrow to pin a silver snake to a root, then no more, because perhaps they had liked that arrow and were sad to see it go. Apes laughed like drunk men in doorways. A tarantula the size of a soup plate sat in the bow for an hour like a bishop and then disembarked.

On the third day from Vicente's death, the Ituxí came to a place where the roots grew across the water in a pattern like a net—interlaced, almost woven. Behind the weave, Artemis saw—for the first time not in dream but in air—a triangle of stone the color of dead limes. Moss wore it; creepers had married it; a fig had chosen it as a father. The line of the triangle's edge was wrong in the way a roofline is wrong when it is not a hill.

"City," Jonah said, very soft, and for once without a joke to sell.

"Door," Séverine said, and her voice had the authority of a woman whose life is a liturgy.

Tamsin spat into the river because spitting is proof of life. "Teeth," she said. "This place has them."

Clara's hands, clean this once, steadied themselves on the gunwale. Her eyes went dark and careful. "If there are traps," she said, "they are old, and old traps are patient. There will be holes pretending to be floors, and stones pretending to be steps that do not wish to be touched."

Isidro stood, set the machete on his shoulder, and smiled the only smile of his that had nothing good in it. "Solveable problems," he said. "I brought blades that also know math."

Artemis did not take the spoon out. She did not need to. It sat against her sternum like a cold yes.

Numbers line up like soldiers when a war wants to start. She counted, because she could not not: one—Artemis; two—Tamsin; three—Jonah; four—Isidro; five—Clara; six—Séverine. Six. Still.

For now.

They poled the *montaria* into the green weave and watched it part not like water but like a crowd learning it has to let a coffin pass.

Chapter XVII — House of the Serpent

"All thresholds are questions; some are asked in teeth."

The weave of roots parted the way crowds do when a coffin passes—reluctant, respectful, eager to close again. The *montaria* nosed through and the river changed its breath. Air went from wet to older-wet. Light came down in coins instead of sheets. The water under them stopped pretending to be a road and became a floor.

There it was.

Not a hill. Not a trick of moss. A triangle of stone shouldered up from the jungle's rib—three faces sloped like a kneeling beast's flanks, their angles softened by creeper and centuries, the visible courses cut into steps too shallow for comfort. A fig had married one corner; the marriage had gone badly for both. On the lowest course, just above the stain-line where floodwater used to lay its claim, a band of carved pits ran like a rosary: dotwork serpents, a spiral, bowls. Chips of glass-green—bottle, maybe, but set with priestly patience—glittered damply in the pits. Between them, braids of hair—black, black, white—had been pressed into gum and salt until they became part of the wall.

"City," Jonah said, reverent for once. The word didn't feel big enough.

"Gate," Sister Séverine corrected. Her voice made a boundary of its own.

Tamsin spat into the water with ceremonial rudeness. "Teeth," she said, trousers dark to the knee, pistol snug against her spine. "Everything here has them."

Vicente would have made a joke about saints who forget their flocks and run off to marry stones. Vicente wasn't here. The Ituxí held his name with the others.

Clara said nothing. She bound her hair back with twine, rolled her sleeves, and touched two fingers to the salt horn at her belt as if asking permission to be cruel where necessary.

Artemis felt Éloise's spoon cool against her sternum and Baptiste's coin warm at her throat. The braid in the oilskin lay quiet like a problem seated politely at the table waiting to be introduced. She salted a tin cup out of habit more than hope and lifted the spoon over it: one, two, three, four, five, six, seven. The bowl ticked and turned, not left where the fig was winning, not right where a channel veined off into shadow, but straight at a wound of a doorway cut low into the triangle's belly: a serpent's mouth flattened to a keyhole.

"Up we go," Isidro said, and smiled the smile you save for solvable problems. The machete rode his shoulder like a pet sin.

They grounded the boat on a tongue of sand that had learned to hold still. Hammocks and nets stayed rolled; the pot, dented and offended, sulked in the bow. They wouldn't need camp if they were clever. Clever people die faster at doors.

Up the first courses: stone slick with its own breath, each step a suggestion rather than a promise. The carved band lay at knee, then thigh. Séverine walked it like a line on a page. She touched a pit set with green and flinched lightly at what came back on her finger— salt and oil and something faintly like combed hair.

"Bindings," she said. "Not saints. Warnings. Do not take off what you didn't put on."

"Noted," Tamsin said, which is different from *obeyed*.

At the mouth, they crouched. It was a throat cut by a patient knife: low, tight, the lintel stone scribed with the spiral and the bowl, the serpent head pecked in dots so shallow they read as rash. The air that breathed out was not rot, not this minute. It smelt of old fat and the breath of stones that cannot stop remembering.

"Let me feel it," Jonah said, and went flat on his belly like a thief with good intentions. He slid the hand with the longest fingers in first, palm open. "Holes," he murmured. "At knee. At shoulder. At mouth-height for a short man."

"Darts," Isidro said. "Or smoke. Or both."

Tamsin drew, cocked, and shot once—high into the left-hand dark. The bang slapped the stone back into the shape of a room; bats blew out like scraps of coat. A breath later the walls answered: a cough of air from the holes, a whispering hiss. Three little bone darts smacked the lintel and stuck there, quivering like offended wasps. Their tips were lacquered black. One wept a bead like an eye.

Clara's mouth flattened. "Enough poison to make a nun write better prayers," she said. "Don't breathe near those."

"Jolly," Tamsin said. "We could drag a net to trigger them as we go."

"Or crawl under," Jonah said. "The bottoms of bad ideas are often smoother."

"Give me rope," Isidro said.

He took the coil, tied a loop, and flung. The loop kissed a spur of stone inside; he set the rope, leaned, and felt for the give a trap loves. The lintel smiled and did nothing.

"Fine," he said. "Jonah, on your belly. I'll be behind you. If you stop, I'll kick. That's love."

"I never doubted you," Jonah said, and went flat again, hands out, head turned and cheek scraping stone, moving like a gambler cheating at prayer.

He found the first trip with his fingertips—gut cord lacquered, stretched ankle-to-knee height. He showed the line to Isidro with a tap and a hiss and cut it with the pocket-knife he kept for lies. No hiss from the wall. Second line, higher. He cut again, kinder. Third line, stupidly low, a joke for hips. He cut. On the fourth, a hair—not cord—caught the knife's edge, stuck, sang.

"Stop," Clara said.

Too late for words to make the past different. The hair sang again, and a breath of air puffed out of a row of new holes Jonah hadn't felt because they were not holes— they were eyes. The darts whispered. He jerked; Isidro's hand closed on the back of his belt and hauled him sideways with a strength that felt like theft. The darts thunked the floor where Jonah's ribs had meant to be.

"Alive," Jonah said, with a disrespectful laugh he didn't feel. "God is bored and wanted theater."

They went in crouched, shoulders tilted, breath wary. The throat didn't go far: a short run to a short room, the size and shape of a stepchild's bed, its walls hung with the teeth of years. On a shelf cut into the far wall sat a bowl black with old fat, and beside it a coil of hair as thick as a man's wrist, bound with gut and hard with salt. Three green chips had been pressed into the hair like eyes. The coil smelled faintly of ship-hold and rosary beads and the iron tang of combs.

"Bindings," Séverine whispered. Her hand lifted and didn't touch. "Leave them."

The floor spoke.

Not loud. A subtle, tired creak like a man lowering himself into his favorite chair. Isidro's eye cut down and left. His boot went light. "Plate," he said. He took a breath, shifted weight onto his back foot, and then— because some doors insist—he stepped.

The room answered like an old machine asked once more for a favor. A counterweight somewhere sighed awake; a slot somewhere grated. From the right-hand wall a stone scythe—no decoration, just ugly, good stone on a pivot—came hissing across at knee.

Isidro jumped, but too late for flesh and not for bone. The blade took him mid-thigh, front to back, a surgeon's amputation done by a jealous husband. He went down without a word, his face suddenly young and practical. Blood went out of him in a sheet that made the floor remember rain. The scythe swung back on its hinge and stopped, smug.

"Move," Clara snapped—a word bigger than prayer. She was inside the room with him before anyone thought about poison; the darts had finished wanting. Tourniquet—the scarf from her own throat into a knot with a timber hitch and fury—high, then higher. She leaned her whole weight into it until her arms shook and the blood went from shining to sulking.

Isidro's eyes found her. He smiled—soft, crooked, his real one. "My leg and I have reached an understanding," he said through his teeth. "We part."

"You'll live," Clara lied ferociously. "And I'll make you a peg that makes whores sentimental."

"Then I'll be taller," he said.

The floor complained again—another plate, Jonah's knee. He froze. The wall to the left spat and something heavy thunked down where a man's head would be if a man had been a little more foolish than Jonah had the right to be today. A block—not huge, but honest. The air burped dust. The room acquired an appetite.

"Back," Séverine said, and her voice had iron at the edges. "Artemis, don't breathe that."

They got Isidro out on the rope and on their arms, bumping over the trap plates like men dancing a dead drunk friend home. Clara's hands were joyless instruments. She packed the stump with cloth that was not clean and would have to do, tightened the knot until the edges of the wound turned the pallor of drowned candlewax, and cursed the lack of heat and iron that might sizzle a vessel shut. "We need fire," she said. "And we can't make smoke here unless you all wish to confess for real."

"We can do it outside," Séverine said. "Under the fig, where the rain takes our sins away."

They took Isidro down the steps like carrying a fallen king. He didn't howl; he swore piously in a dialect that sounded like a farm remembering it had hands. On the sand tongue under the fig, Clara's kit became a cathedral: a little spirit flask, a spoon, a twist of tinder, salt. Tamsin struck flint with a patience that would have made a mother cry. Fire made its small raw room. Clara kissed the edge of a blade and set it to glow. "Hold him," she said.

They did. Isidro bit a strap and still made the old honest sound men make when iron speaks to meat. The stink was church-wrong and necessary: burnt hair, bacon, the memory of wool too near a stove. Tamsin held his shoulders; Jonah held his mouth and counted to seven in a voice like counting lambs. Séverine whispered something in a language that belonged to women who had walked men through childbirth and home from war. Artemis held his hand and felt the shock hit him like a door shut from inside, then recede.

When it was done, the stump was ugly and not bleeding. Clara packed and bound and tied with knots taught by a merciless teacher. "You owe me," she said. "Leg."

He breathed, smiled again, smaller. "I always owed women everything."

"Remember it," she said.

They rested because bodies insist. They fed him beans and rage in alternating spoonfuls. He kept both down because he had decided to. Tamsin sat with her back to the fig, pistol across her thighs, eyes on the green where things that are not men watch men teach themselves to be small.

"Door's not done with us," Séverine said after a thin hour. "If you leave bindings in place now, something that follows us will only have to pull our knot and walk in behind. We cut, or we sleep with our boots on forever."

Artemis knew what she would say even before her mouth said it. "We cut."

Clara looked at her, then at the boy-shaped air the river had claimed. She nodded once. "Then do it clean."

They went back up. The room sulked like a dog thwarted in stealing cake. The scythe hung in its slot with the calm of an old killer. The bowl of fat sat black and patient. The coil of hair—black, black, white— looked deliberate and obscene.

"Don't pull," Séverine said. "It wants reaching."

"Burn," Tamsin suggested, flint already itching.

"Smoke," Clara said. "Darts breathe. We don't."

Artemis untied the rawhide thong from the spoon and looped it through the gut binding so that her fingers wouldn't touch hair. She thought of the Queen of Cups in her oilskin, of Éloise tying hair with salt and mercy, of the men in the hold. *Open,* the voice had said, in New Orleans, in dreams, under the coil of a god.

She said, without moving her mouth, "If I open you, you will not undo me."

The hair didn't answer. It was hair.

She pulled slow. The gut flexed and held; it had been set to last longer than a woman's anger. The thong bit her palm above the old blister with the intimacy of a lover who knows all your bad names. Séverine put her hand on Artemis's shoulder at the exact pressure that says *I could stop you and I am not.* One—two—three—the door behind her counted with its little breaths.

The binding yielded with a small, greedy sigh. The coil unwound into her hands in three stiff loops and a spray of brittle thread. The smell went up: salt, oil, combed women, a priest's mouth.

Something moved, deep in the stone.

Not a mechanism. Not gears. An exhalation. The stale interior breath of a room that had been promised it would be left alone and had not.

A second mouth farther down the throat unlatched itself with a cockroach-quiet click.

They went toward it.

This door was waist-high and broad and had been sealed in a more serious humor. Hair ropes—thicker, older—crossed the hatchway like the bindings on a breakbone. White shell chips, not glass, had been pressed into its knots; they had taken the color of tea from a century of damp. Someone had stamped little cups into the jambs—fat-bellied, Spanish pattern—and the stone around each cup was salt-burned.

"Not local," Jonah said softly. "This is a house with guests."

"Or with hostages," Séverine said.

"Let's see which," Tamsin murmured, and missed because she very deliberately missed reaching for the flint.

"Wait," Clara snapped, and they did, because Clara's *wait* has the weight of a falling block. She took the little gourd the woman in Manaus had given her—the bitter cousin of quina—and daubed it on the knots with a fingertip. "Vinegar," she said. "Sweet vinegar, and oil. Old things. Maybe it will persuade the hair to behave."

Artemis tied the spoon to her wrist because she had learned the lesson of losing it in water. She slid Éloise's bone under the first gut seam and lifted, rocking it like a cradle. The braid creaked like a floorboard in an old house. She saw New Orleans on the backs of her eyes—the courtyard, the chalk, the bowl, the spoon. She counted. She pulled. The hair, stiff with salt and promise, parted—not broken, but unmade. The effect went through the other bindings like a sentence completed.

Inside—at last—an antechamber, low and broad and wrong. Wrong in the way a room is wrong that has been made to feel like a mouth. The floor sloped very slightly down; the walls sucked sound. In each wall, little alcoves—thirty?—held bowls and bundles. The bowls were black with old fat; the bundles, tied hair— blacks and whites, browns ash-gray with age—each threaded with gut and marked with a chip of green. At the far end, another hatch, narrower, sealed with hair turnings that had taken the shape of serpent skin.

Tamsin stood very straight. "This is a pantry," she said, not moved to metaphor.

Clara's chin lifted. "Or a bonesetter's drawer," she answered. "What if each braid binds something you would prefer not to meet."

Séverine stood with her hand on the salt horn and looked older than she ever had, and kind. "This is a chapel," she said. "Of a god that keeps promises the way old women keep combs. If we steal from it, it will steal back."

"We aren't stealing," Artemis said, though the hair in her hands weighed like theft. "We are paying a debt."

"Gods keep different ledgers," Jonah muttered, eyes on the floor. He pointed with a finger. "Step only where the dust lies undisturbed. That clay there—see?—I want to keep my feet."

They went forward as if the floor were a drunk they didn't want to wake. Isidro stayed at the first hatch sitting with his back to stone, breath steady. His face had acquired that peculiar honesty men's faces get when pain teaches them what they do and do not worship. He had his knife on his lap and his stump bandaged high as God. "Go," he said simply. "Bring back the thing that keeps you talking."

They crossed the pantry. The bundles did not whisper, but their presence made an itch between shoulder blades. Twice, Jonah's careful foot felt the give of a plate and he told the rest with a finger. Twice, nothing answered, because this room's traps were of a different kind, older even than stone—the sort that trigger only when breath is held too long in a place that loves breath. The far hatch waited, hair glazed with centuries of handling, gut twine hardened into something like horn.

"Artemis," Séverine said.

"I know," Artemis said. The spoon knocked her wrist once like a child.

She set the bowl under the lowest loop and lifted on the breath between heartbeats, the way Éloise taught when you take a curse off a baby. The gut twanged and the hair gave, a strand at a time, clinging like a lover who has packed. The smell came up—not death, not only— but the ghost of river salt and oil of palms and combs. She did not breathe. On the seventh pull the knot slumped like a body at vigil.

Something heavy on the far side rolled.

Not toward them. Away—right to left—stones negotiating their own old law. The hatch's bottom edge lifted an inch, two. Air came out—dry, colder, like a well's. And underneath that cold, a smell so faint it made the skin crawl anyway: green stone. Hair. Rain that had never seen sky.

"Low," Clara said. "On your bellies. We go in and we come out the way sane men do ridiculous things."

They went in a crawl: Tamsin first because she would not *not*, Artemis next because the spoon was in her hand and the number in her mouth, Séverine on her skirt hem, Clara dragging the satchel, Jonah after with the gentlest elbows on earth. The hatch scraped their spines like a rude hostess. Inside, the floor leveled out abruptly, then tipped down again. The dark had faces; they did not look at them.

Then the room opened like a confession.

It was not large—the size of a saint's reliquary—and full in its small way with teeth and promises. The far wall held a low altar—a box stone, lid off and leaned. On the lid, a spiral had been carved and thumb-oiled until the grooves were smooth. In the box sat the thing that had been calling her since salt broke, since Éloise's finger traced chalk, since a ship had shut a bar across a hatch.

It was ugly.

Not a jewel, not a golden cup. A calabash gourd, blackened, cracked, sewn with gut, studded with green chips dull as bottle, bound twice round with hair— black, black, white—then tarred with something that had once been oil and had learned to be law. Around its neck—if a gourd can have that—had been knotted twelve little brass bells and three teeth human, two animal. A strip of blue cloth rotted against it, stamped once with a French saint's face. Salt had caked in its seams. A Spanish Queen of Cups—Spanish suit, fat-bellied—had been pressed in wet and dried there, its paper dark and mineral-hard, the queen's eyes blind. Wax had spilled across the card and become a rock.

Artemis felt her mouth shape *no* and *yes* at once.

Tamsin said, with admirable politeness, "That's the worst pretty thing I ever saw."

Clara's hands hovered. "Do not drop it," she said, and then because humor would keep her alive a little longer, "or I will hit you with it."

Séverine bowed—not because she thought the thing was holy, but because she was not arrogant enough to assume *she* was. "Do we take it," she asked, the bravest question of the night.

Artemis's coin warmed her throat until it stung. The spoon on her wrist tapped once, twice—*count*. She did. One—two—three—four—five—six—seven. The spoon trembled on five. On seven it lay still, and that stillness was a permission she trusted more than visions.

"We take it," she said.

Tamsin slipped both hands under the gourd as if picking up a baby a mother had not wanted. The bells did not ring. The hair held. The whole had the weight of a human skull and the habit of sucking warmth from skin. For a heartbeat Artemis saw another pair of hands—Éloise's—laying something down on an altar with love and rage married into one serviceable tool. Then the room came back into the size of itself.

The floor shivered.

"Move," Jonah said, quite softly. "Because I have just remembered that rooms like this often dislike the idea of leaving."

They turned. The hatch had decided a century was enough to be open. It was making its decision in quarter-inches, very civil. The air went thinner the way a door makes the air thin when it goes from ajar to polite.

On their bellies again, the gourd tight to Tamsin's ribs, Artemis pushing from her toes, Séverine backing as if out of a confessional, Clara cursing her skirt for not being trousers; Jonah last, shoving the satchel ahead, elbows screaming. The stone kissed Artemis's spine. It kissed Tamsin's boot-heel. It kissed Jonah's hair.

It stopped.

A breath. A mercy. A warning. They slid into the pantry's disgusting safety and lay there with their hearts banging until bang became breath.

Isidro looked up at them from the antechamber, face gray and calm. "Well?" he said.

Tamsin lifted the gourd one inch, as if to offer a toast to a dead man. "We married badly," she said. "We're keeping the child."

Clara wiped her mouth with the back of her wrist and left a streak of somebody else's blood. "Outside," she said. "Before it decides to be more angry."

They retraced every careful step, every plate avoided, every hiss un-triggered by more luck than they had a right to. The first throat breathed darts no more. The serpent's mouth let them go like foreplay: reluctantly but with the satisfaction of appetite proven. They came out under the fig in air as wide as law. The river sounded astonished and then decided to pretend it had expected them.

They sat. Because even thieves sit after stealing from a god.

The gourd lay on canvas like a heart outraged to find itself out of its chest. The little brass bells had no decency to ring and thereby make jokes. The Queen's blind eyes judged no one. The hair bindings had gone soft in the damp, as if ready to be remade or unwound. The smell—salt, oil, combs, old fat—wrote itself into their noses and stayed.

"What is it," Jonah asked, because men need nouns.

"An alarm," Séverine said. "A hinge. A mouth. A hand. A bride-price." She lifted one of the bells with a fingernail and let it drop. It clinked like prayer in a poor parish.

"Don Iñigo's maggot will come the day after we leave," Tamsin said. "Let him. He can rummage in the pantry and feed himself."

"Or he will catch us on the water and ask us again to choose," Isidro said, not complaining. "We will choose again."

Clara adjusted the binding on his stump with the tenderness a bad god uses on a good man. "We're not staying to see what that room does when its toy is missing," she said. "Beans, then pushing off. We make the Purus, then the Amazon, then Negro, then HIDING."

"Hiding," Jonah repeated, tasting the word like a fruit he had thought he didn't like. "And after hiding?"

"Home," Tamsin said. "If home deserves us."

Artemis touched the gourd once, lightly, with the back of her fingers. Heat did not come out of it; cold did not. A presence—ugly and patient and not yet cruel enough to be the only thing in the room—sat still, like a woman at a window counting the feet that pass.

She tied the spoon's thong again, ugly, twice, then twice again. She put Baptiste's coin under the thong to pin it. She folded the Queen that had followed her since salt into the oilskin with the hair-braid the jungle had given. The Queen's mouth looked softer in this light; the Tower felt less like prophecy and more like instruction.

Séverine shook salt in a circle, then a line, then a cross. "If there are doors between this place and the river," she said, "they will have learned our names. One of them will be standing open."

"Then we don't use it," Tamsin said, "and we make our own."

They ate beans because beans insist on being eaten. Isidro took three spoonfuls and a fourth he'd been taught to refuse; he took it anyway and allowed it to stay. Jonah drank water that had learned to be polite and did not make a joke where one belonged. Clara closed her eyes for the length of one measured breath and looked older when she opened them. The jungle leaned in to hear what the gourd would say. It said nothing yet, because saying is a trick and tricks take time.

When night fell, it fell as a lid falls on a pot. The Ituxí breathed out and let its noises organize themselves. Far off, a drum under roots thudded once and then decided it had heard enough. Closer in, something heavy rolled in water without appetite, remembering.

Artemis lay in her hammock, netting whispering in small rude ways, and counted. One—herself. Two—Tamsin. Three—Jonah. Four—Isidro. Five—Clara. Six—Séverine.

Six.

For now.

Chapter XVIII — The Tax of Doors

"Every treasure charges rent; the bill comes due in teeth."

Dawn tried to find them and needed three attempts. Mist shouldered low, the color of pewter rubbed with a rag. Leaves dripped with the self-importance of small gods. The Ituxí breathed like a sleeping beast that had decided to let the fleas worship.

They broke camp as if the ground might complain— quick, without ceremony. Hammocks into green sausages; netting rolled mean and tight; beans scraped into the dented pot with a spoon that knew worse kitchens. Isidro tested the branch Clara had cut and wrapped—crutch, not peg; the stump bandage high under his shorts, knotted with a hatred so precise it looked like love. He stood, swayed once, smiled the private smile of a man who has agreed not to fall in front of a woman who has saved his life. "I am taller," he announced, and nobody laughed because laughter costs.

Clara lifted the canvas-wrapped gourd and felt its weight say *I will be paid.* The brass bells around the neck made no sound—their silence was a ceremony. Salt had caked in the creases of the binding; hair had taken a set like old rope. The Queen's blind face pressed through the wax with the obstinacy of a woman who had cried too much to be decorative.

"Smother it," Séverine said. "Give it less air." Her hands shook once—prayer, or the aftertaste of yesterday's iron—and then they were steady as the habit that made her walk through doors nobody should.

Tamsin made a sling from a strip of sail and her belt and bound the gourd against Artemis's back like a child no one would admit. "If it speaks," she said, "I shall teach it London."

"I shall teach it numbers," Artemis answered, and felt Éloise's spoon tap her sternum once through her shirt as if to say *see that you do*.

The weave of roots at the channel's mouth had knit itself in the night, vines doing their housekeeping. Jonah took the machete with the gentle hands of a thief and cut a polite mouth. The *montaria* nosed out; the river took it with a sullen courtesy. A heron lifted, one-leg-slow, and decided not to care.

They had gone fifty strokes before the forest laid a new sound on the page.

Paddles. Not the whisper men make when they have been taught to live. The tidy slap of men who have not had to learn. Coats. Hats. Silver. The tone of their men.

"Down," Isidro said, and the word spread through muscle: spines bent, heads low, breath lightened, boat shadowed itself against the left bank where roots learned to be kindness.

They came on in twos, three boats abreast, green shade roofed with arrogance. At the foremost prow the emissary stood without his brim, hatless head slick with humidity, cane replaced already—another serpent's open mouth, silver bright as a lie washed clean. His face didn't look like a face; it looked like paper that had never learned how to make a tear.

He did not look toward the left-hand shadow where six breaths organized themselves.

He looked ahead, and—because money makes men prophets—he fired.

Not pistol. Not yet. He lifted the cane and dropped it like a benediction toward the low splash of sand where their fire had been. A pistol ball snapped the air beside his ear and smacked the fig with a grunt. Then another, close, from shadow that was not theirs. An arrow hummed. It struck the cane's head, right through the silver serpent's mouth, and pinned it briefly to the paint of the prow, ringing with the delicate offense of a small church bell. The emissary jerked the stick free, surprised that insult and physics were still on speaking terms.

The woman with the maze painted on her chest—hair cut at the brow like a knife had made a joke—stood twenty paces off under a liana curtain, her bow low, her face amused. Two men ghosted behind her, their arrows already quarter-drawn. She tapped her own teeth, then his with a grin that was older than all the cities he'd ever know. He hid his flinch with etiquette. She vanished into green she had taught how to close.

"Push," Vicente would have said. Vicente lay where rivers keep names. The *montaria* felt the hands on her ribs anyway and sulked into speed.

The emissary's men saw the wake and the push and the shadow. They shouted words that belonged in rooms with flooring and toasts. Paddles bit; gun muzzles lifted; the boats yawed out of their own shadows and made a geometry the river did not like.

"Right-hand slit," Artemis said, before her mouth noticed it was telling people what to do. She salted the cup, held the spoon to the gourd-lump under her sling, counted—one-two-three-four-five-six-seven—and let the bowl take the blame for what her bones already knew. It turned to a seam where a curtain of roots hung like beaded door-strings in a brothel. "There."

Isidro shoved the bow. The *montaria* slid under, low, brushing hair and spider silk that came away like breath. Behind, a pistol cracked and cut a leaf's edge. The leaf forgave.

Inside the slit, the water slowed into thinking. Roots made grids between banks like a net had decided to be furniture. The boat scraped where frogs keep saints. Tamsin took the pole and moved with the efficiency of a woman lifting a bed to chase the roaches. "Hush, hush," she told the river, which is the sort of lie that keeps people alive.

From the mouth a man in a hat fired at the sound; the ball cracked a rib on the *montaria* and said a small word about carpentry. Another ball bit water and went to hell with a complaint. The emissary shouted to turn them, Spanish gone formal with strain. The river answered with a root.

One of the hat boats hit that root with the surprise of a man stepping on a snake. The bow came up and then down where the current had already paid rent to something with eyes. The log beside the root rolled and revealed a jaw with old arguments in it. The hat boat lifted, tipped, coughed men. A caiman the size of a confession closed on a thigh and went backward as if pulled by God. The man screamed a boy's scream.

Piranha beat the water into a colloquy. Another man—clean coat, clean hands—reached for his friend, made the choice not to lose his own hand, and fell backwards into theology.

"Don't watch," Clara said, not unkindly. "We have enough debt."

They made three turns blind and one with malice toward their pursuers. The slit widened into a solemn lane. The river's voice shifted back into conversation. The gourd grew heavier by virtue of being cannot-put-down.

They did not camp.

They learned to move the way men learn to apologize: often, badly, and with practice. The sun stooped; rain shouldered its way in. When the Ituxí delivered them to a room with sand that looked like bread, they stopped long enough for Clara to force bitterness down every stiff throat.

"Your leg," Artemis said to Isidro when the man had used bravado too many minutes in a row. "Sit."

"I sit," he said obediently—because pain is a god with whip and collar—and let her help him settle. Clara peeled back binding enough to look. The edges were pale and furious; the smell belonged to kitchens, not graves. "Good," she said fiercely, as if threatening flesh could keep it in line. "If you rot, I will find a way to rot you myself for disrespect."

He smiled because she needed it. "I am afraid of you."

"Be," she said. "It will keep you alive."

The ground woke while they chewed beans none of them wanted. Not cats. Not men. A sound like rain on leather, only without weather. A *sssssssss* that began as politeness and found a rhythm like liturgy—ants. A black ribbon poured around the trunk of a tree and across the sand, hundreds of thousands of little religions, moving furniture in the world.

"Marabunta," Isidro said, respect in the word. "Army, and hungry."

The column's front reached the salt line Séverine had laid and flowed along it like men do along a property fence, testing for a broken picket. "Add," the nun said. Artemis shook the horn; salt pattered. The ants peeled away, not offended—merely convinced. They split their own river and found a root to use as a bridge instead. They climbed it in two lanes, up and over in competent haste, and poured down the far side like a blessing mispronounced.

Under their feet, a beetle no larger than a thumbnail discovered the cost of being slow. That many small mouths make quick work polite. The column parted around the gourd as water parts around a stone. Ants touched the canvas with sudden caution, tasted, tested, then refused and went around in a clean, even ring, as if the thing emanated a negation.

"They know," Séverine murmured. "Some doors, even ants won't open."

"Excellent," Tamsin said lightly. "We've stolen a piece of the world everything else hates."

After the column passed, the sand remembered where it had been. They pushed off again. The sky bruised into night more quickly than men like. They found a narrow and—because hiding is sometimes dignity—took it, dark, under a ceiling of roots.

Artemis couldn't tow herself out of the knowledge of the gourd against her spine. It drank the warmth from sweat, made a cold that wasn't weather. When the river opened a black mirror to them for a breath, the stars came down to drink and looked shocked to find their faces old. She salted the cup—small ritual, same rope— counted one to seven with lips and mind, let the spoon twitch and point. It led them left, then right, then right again to a run where wind found them. Pursuit drifted behind, faint—paddle rhythms, the price of making men do what they think they want.

Far in the night a cat screamed three streets away in the green—amorous, aggrieved, enormous. They smelled it before they saw it: cat-musk, rotten leaves, iron. "Jaguar," Isidro said, with the grim neighborly pride of a man who has seen an alderman's garden. "Or a ghost of one."

They found it on the portage.

The Ituxí stacked two trees across itself again, crossed like people who always want to stand in doorways, and the water under belonged to teeth or regret. They were already heaving the *montaria* onto ribs; Isidro bared the quartz edge of pain bravely and Tamsin lifted as if muscle could buy miracles. The cat came silent to the lip behind Jonah—gold in the throat, black rosettes like ink prayers. It was bigger than a rumor and more tired than any terror.

It went for meat where meat had a history: Isidro, on the ground, hamstrings exposed, crutch out of reach. It was good hunting, ugly and justified. Tamsin turned on her heel and shot it in the side of the head, quick, even, an economy of mercy.

The ball skated bone; cats have their own saints. The jaguar lurched and struck with rage instead of geometry. Claws found Isidro's crutch, bark and string, and made a new story of it. Clara stepped in—not brave, merely punctual—shoved the hot muzzle of the spirit flask into the cat's nose and flamed its whiskers. The cat sneezed like a god offended and sprang away, wrong, into water where piranha have no politics. The river wrote an ugly paragraph and turned the page. The cat's tail went under with the gravitas of royalty.

Isidro lay shaking and grinning. "I am alive," he said. "Therefore either lucky or unwise."

"Both," Clara said, and leaned her forehead to his for one count of seven as if sharing a coin.

They dragged, shoved, swore, and slid the boat back into its good element. Artemis's hands bled under skin like a bruise that thinks it can argue with a map. Behind them, men in hats had to make the same portage, and they did it louder, with more orders and less grace. The forest remembered.

When they stopped to breathe, Tamsin squatted by Jonah where he tied the painter like a man proposing to monogamy. "You left green-cut marks," she murmured. "Back there. Three leaves slit on the same side of the stem, then a fourth turned. That's a gambler's 'this way.'"

Jonah's jaw exercised. "Old habit. I forget I'm among honest people."

"Funny," she said, not smiling. "You keep forgetting and yet taking our water."

He looked at her, openhanded with his eyes for once. "The emissary has a ledger on me," he said, very low. "From Paraíbas, before you. I am not as good as you think I want to be. I have been leaving crumbs I can also follow if I must choose to live alone."

"Choose better," she said.

He nodded. He did not promise.

Before day rose out of black like a coin out of a priest's palm, rain came back with its club. They ran by night because the emissary ran by day and because the water under their hull approved of bad ideas done confidently. Once the gourd shuddered against Artemis's ribs like a woman trying not to sneeze. Bells did not ring. The hairs in the bindings lifted as if a breeze had an opinion in a room with none.

"Open," it said. Not in her ear. In the pulse, the soft place at the base of the skull where fever liked to sit.

"No," she told it, firm as one scolding a child who is her own too much.

Dawn showed them a new alphabet of water. The Ituxí split into three seams: a clean bend with visible sky, a throat the width of a bed, and an igarapé so shy it was really only a thought the river had not had yet. Spoon over salt said *shy*.

"Right," Artemis breathed.

"We can't fit," Jonah objected, because a sane voice must always audition.

"We can," Isidro said. "We are presently very thin."

They fit. Leaves rubbed their cheeks, rude. Spiders held their coats aside with the offended dignity of dowagers at a ball. They passed under a root-bridge that had taught itself to be a rosary and surprised a sloth into blasphemy. The channel coughed them into a black-water lagoon the size of a small prophecy where the wind had made a habit of visiting. The current forgot them. They listened. No paddles.

"Hold," Séverine said, and her rosary clicked once. "We're in the mouth of something that hasn't decided whether to spit."

They beached on a tongue of mud that pretended at sand. The sky broke into blue at one edge, gray at the other. Clara fed them something that had seen beans in a dream. Tamsin slept with her eyes slit; Jonah dozed like a thief on a church step. Isidro watched the wind.

Artemis followed the itch between shoulder blades to a mangrove knee where a braid hung—small, delicate— black, black, white, threaded with gut, tied to a twig with a shred of blue cloth. French blue, saint's blue, the color of the rag glued to the gourd. She did not touch it. She saluted with two fingers and backed away as from a neighbor who knows your worst story and still lends you salt.

They moved again at noon, bold as sobriety. The lagoon led into a channel that argued south-east, then lost, then went south-west because the spoon said so and because the sun had learned to be treacherous. A shadow moved across the open water beyond—a broad boat with patched canvas and strong arms at the paddles. The emissary's men had circled like creditors. The distance was wrong for pistols, right for curses. A cane flashed.

"Do we run?" Jonah asked.

"We hide," Tamsin said. "Running is telling the world where you are quickly."

They slid the *montaria* into a mat of floating plants stitched tight as a mattress. The leaves closed like cheap acquaintances. Mosquitoes blessed them. The stink of green was intimate and unclean. Séverine drew a tiny cross in salt on the gourd's bulged spine and another on Artemis's crown and a third in the air where she guessed God kept an eye for emergencies.

Paddles went by with the pomp of men who expect to be obeyed by water. Voices—Portuguese tidy with money—bargained with distance. Someone laughed. Not the emissary. He didn't spend coin on laughter. The boats slid on.

Artemis let out a breath in seven pieces and picked them up again.

They came out at evening onto a brown run that remembered being the Purus more than the Ituxí—wider, older, with opinions that did not go with small boats. Vicente's ghost told them where the deep lay and they honored his advice. The sky found a color between fruit and bruise.

A black caiman floated untroubled, eye yellow as a cheap ring. It paced them for an hour the way the truly curious do: without appetite, without malice, with a scholar's detachment. It learned nothing and left.

Night. Fire only a whisper, smoke trained like a dog. Beans. Quina. Salt. The gourd a lump that refused to dream. Artemis lay on her side and let the numbers make cages: one—herself; two—Tamsin; three—Jonah; four—Isidro; five—Clara; six—Séverine.

She was almost asleep when the arrow found the boat.

It didn't hit flesh. It buried itself in the rib below the gourd and quivered with the indignation of a messenger not invited in. A strip of bark was tied under the head with gut; on the bark someone had burned a spiral with a hot wire and pressed three green chips into the lines. **A debt is not paid.**

"From whom," Jonah asked, though he already knew.

Séverine took the arrow out carefully and laid it across her knees as if it were a strange domesticated animal. "From the door," she said. "Or the women who keep it. Or the men who obey them. It is still polite enough to warn."

"What does it want," Tamsin asked, blunt.

"The same thing everything here wants," Clara said, weary and precise. "Obedience."

The jungle settled its weight back onto the bowl of night. They took watches. They did not talk about the way the gourd seemed to make the dark thicker.

Toward false dawn—the hour when mosquitoes lose faith—the fever that had flirted with Artemis since salt first cracked in her mouth returned to lay a cool hand at the base of her skull. Not hot now. Cold. A whisper of the old command: *Open.* She put her teeth together as if holding a small coin there and counted to seven so viciously it felt like blasphemy. It let her go. Not far. Enough.

Morning came with a raptor's cry and the friendly smell of fish dying in the shallows without cause. They moved. They did not look back.

Before noon they came to a choice that had no courtesy to it. The channel ahead narrowed to a reed knot; left opened to a placid reach with sky and men; right became a black throat under roots with no sky, no men, no mercy. The spoon hung cold as a judge.

"Right," Artemis said.

"Of course," Tamsin answered, and flashed a grin at the reach, at the sky, at the invisible hats, as if taking her leave of a party where she'd stolen all the silver.

They went in.

The throat took them the way a snake takes an egg. Light disappeared in a sly, interior way. The water made no noise; their poles learned to be polite or be punished. Twice a blind fish knocked Tamsin's shin and she threatened to marry it. Once the roof of roots dropped low and they slid on their bellies under it like letters in a narrow envelope.

Then, abruptly, the roof lifted and the water learned to breathe again. On the left bank, a tree with bark like a priest's tongue bore a scar a man had cut long ago: a single notch, then two. Beside the notch someone had pressed green chips into sap and let them set. The chips were the exact shade of bottle in a poor parish.

"Z," Jonah breathed. "Zed. Two notches and the stones—Grann's lost man wrote that sign."

"Lost isn't only one direction," Séverine said.

In the middle of the channel a log turned, casual. A snake as long as a boat did the thing serpents do when they are not hungry and not angry and still decide to remember you. The coil lifted an inch, lay down again, and left. The gourd hummed once like a bell heard through walls.

"That's enough," Clara told it, as if cursing a toddler.

They camped at noon in a place that pretended to be safe because the light came in prettily. Isidro slept with his hand on the knife he could throw with either arm. Tamsin snored delicately like a sin with a veil. Jonah lay with his eyes open, teaching himself his bad habits in case he needed them. Séverine sat with her rosary and didn't count   counting is for when numbers will obey. Artemis put her cheek on the canvas that wrapped the gourd and felt nothing, which was worse than feeling.

The day swelled and then broke. They moved while it
bled. At evening they reached a wide brown; the Purus
again, unmistakable in its wide patience, its sly
profundity. South rolled under them like a carpet
designed by an enemy you still respected. They took it.

Behind, paddles in tidy rhythm found their way back
into the story. The emissary does not sleep. The
emissary does not tire. The emissary pays men to do
those things.

"We need weather," Tamsin said. "Or a saint who owes
me."

"We need a door that leads to men who do not like his
face," Isidro said.

The weather obliged in poor humor. Clouds stacked
like a bishop's furniture. The wind remembered its
manners toward boats and misremembered toward hats.
Rain came, hard, without staging. Lightning showed
them the reach, showed them the boats behind like
black teeth, showed them a floating bar of roots ahead
where the river had been collecting its grudges.
Thunder shook the gourd in Artemis's sling until the
bells thought about ringing and chose not to.

"Through or over," Jonah called, water in his mouth.

"Through," Isidro said, his voice all edge.

They shoved the bow into the tangle and let the boat's
mouth innately know wood from not-wood. Roots
scraped their flanks like a crowd. Spiders took their
coats personally. The world narrowed to bark.

A hat boat tried the same trick seven breaths later and met the river's sense of humor. The bar shifted. The hat boat took it broadside in the ribs and learned about leverage from a god. It rolled, gracefully, into brown. Men swore. One fired at the sky by accident. The sky ignored him. A caiman expressed a professional opinion on aim.

They were out the far side before pity could purchase. The rain dressed them all in the same clothes.

When night fell, it fell the way grief does, in one piece and then in shreds. They made a rude camp on a spit that had only just learned to be above water. Tamsin went around it once, twice, with powder in a horn and old sailor's tricks in her hands, laying down a string of little surprises that would make men trying to stalk them cough and swear. Séverine laid salt where powder could not charm.

Clara washed the gourd with a cloth dipped in nothing and squeezed almost dry. "If you go off," she told it, "do it while I'm asleep. I'm nicer when I'm unconscious."

Artemis laughed once and did not startle herself. She counted the living: one—herself; two—Tamsin; three—Jonah; four—Isidro; five—Clara; six—Séverine. She did not count the arrow whose message lay across her lap or the names the river kept.

The night had the taste of pennies. Somewhere far off, drums arranged themselves into a thought and ceased before the thought got rude. Near, something rolled in the shallows and let old breath out.

In the hour when good dreams say they have to go home to their parents, Artemis woke because the spoon had gotten itself into her hand without asking. She had not salted the cup. She had not lifted. But her mouth was moving.

"One—two—three—four—five—six—seven," she said, and the gourd against her spine made a sound like a woman agreeing without liking it.

"Open," the not-voice said, honeyed, persuasive, as if using her own breath to talk to her.

"No," she said, and put the spoon down as one sets down a knife and walks backward away from it. She lay looking up into the net's whisper where the leaves made a little artisan cathedral of shadow.

She did not sleep. Numbers are doors, too, and some nights everything in the world wants to be one.

Chapter IXX — The Emissary's Ledger

"A debt may be settled in ink or in heat."

Morning made the river look honest again. It wasn't.
The Purus widened into a brown page and let wind
write on it; the pen was blunt; the words were teeth.
The sky had iron under its blue. Birds pretended to be
priests on stilts and blessed nothing they couldn't eat.

They moved with that unhandsome prudence grief
teaches. Isidro worked the pole with his good leg
braced and the wrapped stump tied to the thwart so it
wouldn't argue; he was taller by a bark-wrapped inch
and had acquired the cheerful fatalism of a man newly
at war with gravity. Clara rationed bitterness with the
heartless tenderness of a god that causes survival out of
spite. Séverine salted the gunwales like a seamstress
hemming a dress against bad weather. Tamsin wore her
trousers like a dare and kept the pistol in the curve of
her back as if it were a second spine.

Artemis bore the gourd slung against her shoulder-
blades in Tamsin's makeshift harness, the weight like a
child that existed only as a problem. It leeched warmth,
not like stone—stone takes and sits with it—but like a
mouth that doesn't swallow, only holds. The little brass
bells made no sound. Baptiste's coin lay hot at her
throat; Éloise's spoon tapped her sternum once in a
while like a teacher hoping the class was awake.

They kept to cover where cover existed. Where it
didn't, they lay themselves along the *montaria*'s ribs
and became more boat than people until bank and sky
learned boredom. Once, a white heron lifted and chose
not to look at them; once, a black caiman floated beside

like an uninvited chaperone and then lost interest without ever adopting any.

"Left seam," Isidro said, and the boat obeyed his chin. "Fuck the right. It's a lie."

It was. Under the smoothness lay logs that had been learning the language of men's shins for generations. The *montaria* slithered past them without giving them the courtesy of a hello.

"Powder," Tamsin reminded no one in particular. "We have some. We will need more, and we have none to sell to a priest."

"Priests pay in absolution," Jonah said. His mouth made a smile that wouldn't live on his eyes. "It buys nothing but funerals."

Artemis watched him over her shoulder because watching men who trained their hands to secrets becomes habit. He didn't meet her gaze. He had been leaving marks again: three leaves slit on the same side of the stem; a fern turned just so; a scrape on bark the height of a tall man's hand. If she hadn't learned to read door-signs out of hair and salt, she might have called it nervousness. As it was, she called it *bread crumbs*, and she looked at Tamsin once. Tamsin's mouth made not a line but a wire.

They stopped just long enough to piss and heat beans into civility at midday under a stand of castanheiras— Brazil-nut giants, the sort of trees that make the word *age* look foolish. Long after, men would call this country rubber; now it was nuts and little fish and the smell of smoke where men had tried to convince green to be useful. Here and there the forest remembered a camp: a lean-to skeleton; a ladder into a tree cut with the immodesty of men who don't believe trees are taller than they are; a rack for drying things nobody needed today. It had that loneliness things get when they remember songs no one sings.

The old rack had a roof of palm and a smell of past fires that had agreed to become religion. Clara eyed it and approved. "We can boil water without the sky spitting in the pot."

"Also, it's a stage," Jonah said, smiling his coinless smile. "For theatricals."

"Don't play," Tamsin said. "You lose your own money too much when you play."

They boiled, salted, swallowed; they pushed off. A band of rain passed like a broom dragging dust. In the clearing left behind, a sound took the place of birds.

Paddles, neat. Voices trimmed to look expensive. The **emissary** had not learned to be bored.

They cut into a sly vein of igapó and let the trees keep their sins for them. The hat boats went by with all the dignity of a magistrate late to dinner. There were fewer hats than yesterday. The river had been paid a little. Not enough.

They came out where the forest had been chewed into a clearing and allowed to scar: one of those shell settlements men make of their stubbornness, half mission and half trading post, half-abandoned and half too proud to admit it. A cross leaned against a wall of mud-brick like a drunk who'd been asked to leave; a smokehouse on stilts drooled old fat; a shed remembered powder in the smell and had learned to pretend it was only flour. A low bell hung by a rope, its rim notched by ants.

Isidro sniffed. "Castanha camp. They leave when flood laughs at their bridges."

"Or when money moved downstream," Jonah said. His voice said nothing about the way his eyes went everywhere at once, mapping doors, counting men who might return, remembering debts.

Séverine tilted her head. It wasn't the bell that had called her attention. It was a hair-braid, gut-threaded, tied to the corner post of the smokehouse beneath a nail. Black, black, white. Stiff with salt. The knot had been burned clean once with a coal, and then retied by a hand that didn't believe in fire.

"Do not take what is not yours," Séverine translated the knot, because knots have language. The line of her mouth said *do not take it anyway*.

"We need powder," Tamsin said. "And flour. And oil. We can pay in brass and knives and stories and—" her eyes made the smallest flick toward the canvas lump on Artemis's back—"nothing at all."

Clara set the pot under the slatted roof of the rack, listening to heat the way midwives listen to women. "Quick then," she said. "If there are men who loved this place, they will come back to see if the bones have learned politeness yet."

Jonah took the role that suited him: the man who knows where things are kept in any room because he has been asked to find them and sometimes not asked to bring them back. He went into the powder shed with his shoulders slouched like a harmless uncle. The door protested with a little cough. The smell inside was the smell of funerals said nicely: saltpeter, old cork, flour pretending to be explosive, rats pretending to be merchants.

Tamsin counted hats that were not present; she didn't trust their absence. Isidro shifted with that small obscene grunt of a man teaching pain its place. Séverine stood at the corner with her veil tied pirate-tight and let the rosary beads click once as if to say *I brought witnesses*. Artemis moved like a woman whose back could feel teeth.

"Found," Jonah called, easy as a card flipping. "Dry as gossip and twice as reliable." He came out with two horns and a parcel of paper kisses. He did not meet anyone's eye.

Artemis tasted metal in her mouth and counted without lifting the spoon. One — two — three — four — five — six. Not seven. She told herself numbers were not god. She told herself god was not numbers. She failed to be persuaded.

They worked their own refit: tied a new length of net to replace old lies; swapped the *montaria*'s cracked paddle for one less disillusioned; cut a twist of dried fish that would survive sin and rain and men. Tamsin paid the camp with salt and a knife left on the step in the old code: leave something, take something, lie only to people.

That was when a hat appeared at the far edge of the clearing, held at a man's side by two fingers—a sign for truce if the fingers belonged to a gentleman. The emissary wasn't a gentleman; he had learned to look like one.

"Señores," he said, voice dry in the heat. "Señoras. You continue to misunderstand the situation. The jungle is expensive. Don Iñigo pays his bills."

"Then let him pay the river," Tamsin said, planting her boot on the rack's lower crosspiece. "We don't do credit."

He smiled with the weary kindness men wear when their teeth want to show. "The boy was an accident. Your boatman, a regret. Your pilot, an inevitability. The artifact—" he did not point at Artemis, but his eyes touched her shoulders as if his hand had learned the habit—"belongs to a man who knows how to care for it."

"Like money knows how to care for hunger," Séverine said.

Isidro lifted the machete the way one lifts up a child to play. "You keep buying canes," he observed. "Have you considered buying sense? Tamsin has some."

The emissary sighed as if scolding nephews. He lifted his free hand, palm open in parlor peace. "I don't want to shoot you," he said. "It offends me to lower myself. Give me your directions, your coordinates, your priestess's little tricks. I will leave you a boat and a sack of maize and the liberty to return to your hovels having failed at something no one could have expected you to accomplish."

Jonah made an odd, strangled sound. A man hearing his own name on a ledger read aloud.

Artemis felt the line in the world where the place broke. It had nothing to do with his offer; it was the itch between her shoulder-blades that comes when a door swings behind you and someone you love stands on the threshold and does not follow. She turned too late.

Jonah had put the powder horns down and was walking toward the emissary with his hands up and his smile tucked away like money. "Señor," he said, and the old city under his Caribbean Spanish came out like a slipped accent. "We make a trade. You erase the book you hold on me. I give you the road. A map you can keep even when men die."

Tamsin's pistol was in her hand before his second word finished being treachery. She didn't raise it. She had learned to conserve bullets as well as kindness. "Don't," she said. "You will be stupider than you know and he will still kill you."

The emissary's mouth made sympathy the way a clerk makes letters. "A ledgerman." He nodded, as if at a lesson attended. "Yes. Come, then." He withdrew a paper from the breast of his coat with the delicacy of a man handling a holy relic. It was only a receipt, only a letter, only a promise made in Paraíbas or Belém or a courtyard in an honest city and broken in an ugly one. "Bring me your map."

Jonah looked span-long, thin as a lie that has been starved—boy again where he had learned to be man because men will not save boys without being paid. He took three steps into the open where powder makes theater. He opened his mouth to say the price.

The emissary threw the receipt into the smokehouse door.

He did it idly, as if he were sick of the game and swatting a fly. The paper fluttered like a bird and caught at old grease. It did not burn at once. It thought about it. It decided.

Tamsin didn't need instruction. She was already moving—flint, steel, oil. Vicente's old trick married to a new hate. She struck a star on a rag that had once cost a saint her candle and tossed it where the receipt had landed. Fire remembers old fat. It clung. It licked the black slats. It found the powder left by other men's bad housekeeping and decided to write an ending in a quicker hand.

"Back," Clara snapped. The word contained a whole grammar of surviving.

The smokehouse sighed like a sick ox and then coughed flame through its seams. Men in hats stepped back with the injured dignity of people who prefer their violence directional. One fired into the orange out of principle. The emissary's face, for the first time, looked like a face.

Jonah hadn't moved.

He was looking at the door where the paper had gone as if time could be bent into a shape that allowed both his survival and his dignity. "My name," he said, and laughed once, poor and beautiful. He ran for the smokehouse with his hands bare.

"Jonah!" Tamsin's voice broke on a letter. She lunged, too late.

He got one foot onto the ladder, then two. Heat took the air out of his mouth and gave back ash. A beam shifted with a sound like a rib. He went inside anyway— because some men would rather die picking their names out of fire than live with the wrong ones.

The little powder the rats had not gotten discovered flame just as Jonah discovered the nonsense he had made of his life. The blast wasn't grand—the store had been scavenged and the shed had leaks. But it blew the door outward with a kind punctuation and threw Jonah backward like a card losing interest in a trick.

He hit the ground on his side and rolled twice and a half. He came up to his knees and then to his elbows and then stopped halfway to breath. The left side of his face was no longer a face; it was an example. Skin blistered into handwriting. Hair burned into icon. Eye gone. The right side wept apology. He grinned with broken lips and showed a tooth that did not belong to him anymore.

"Tamsin," he said, very pleasantly. "Tell me I died gambling."

"You died idiot," she said, and got her hands under his shoulders because there are things you do even when the words have done quitting you. Clara slid in with a roll, linen, the calm of skill. She could keep him from bleeding out fast. She could not keep him from what fire had already written on the page.

The emissary kept his men steady with one lifted palm and a face that had learned to keep score of other people's screams. He did not shoot. He waited to see if the fire would finish his accounts for him.

Artemis lifted the spoon to her mouth without salt and counted until the room in her head filled with numbers and left no space for pity that could make her step into a bullet. One—two—three—four—five—six—seven. She didn't ask a door. She asked her legs.

"Boat," she said. "Now."

Isidro shouldered Jonah with a grunt that sounded like love and regret and a debt paid late. Tamsin took the other side, her jaw writing curses with no ink. Séverine lifted the powder parcel and the half-horn and the rosary and made of them a gospel of obscenity. Clara took the gourd from Artemis's back and thrust it at her again because hands remember their enemies. Artemis shoved it into the sling and felt the bells think about ringing and again not.

A shot cracked. Another. The emissary had gotten bored with letting the world do his work. Splinters flipped off the rack's legs; a dry gourd hopped and then lay down in an interesting position; a palm leaf learned how to be a sieve.

"Go," Tamsin snarled through her teeth, gutting the *montaria* with her hands to get it into water. "Or I will make dying take longer for each of you for disobeying me."

They went. The boat took them the way boats take people who mean it. Isidro and Tamsin laid Jonah in the bottom as if making a bed for a man they disliked and loved.

The emissary stood alone in the cleared place where men try to make the world reasonable and did not smile. He lifted his serpent cane and brought it down in a motion that could have been baptism if baptism were hissed through teeth. A ball sang past Artemis's ear like a wasp and erased a mosquito. The world tilted a little in gratitude.

River, roots, a bend where the water had decided to be clever. They slid behind it like thieves. Bullets thudded into bank and made ants reconsider theology. The smokehouse sighed itself collapsed in two parts like an old kneeler deciding to become a bench with a last rude cough.

No one spoke for a long swath of reeds. The boat learned to breathe again.

Jonah breathed too, against probability. Not well. Clara held his face between both ink-stained hands and did the ugly little things that make breath agree to remain. He watched her with the remaining eye and came in and out of the room.

"Tell me," he whispered when speech remembered him long enough to do kindness. The right corner of his mouth tried a grin and managed the idea of one. "Tell me I was…almost…good."

Tamsin sat cross-legged in her wash of gunpowder stink and blood and stared hard at the place where the sky decided to be green. "You were," she said. "Once. That was the problem."

He laughed. It was beautiful; it fell apart halfway through. "Do I get a saint."

"You get salt," Séverine said softly, and touched the grains to his lip with her thumb. "It is better for you."

He nodded without nodding. "Artemis," he said. His eye found her with a surprising accuracy, as if he had always known where she would be, always this place in any room. "I left…bread. Turned it after. Go wrong where I marked right, and right where I marked wrong. I'd hate to be useful."

"You won't be," Artemis said, and felt the coin heat her throat along with shame. "Rest."

He did.

Not sweet and not slow, but not as ugly as fire could have made it. His breath stepped down a stair too quickly and then forgot a step and then another and then let go of the banister. His face, a ruin, learned how to be a boy again for half a second before it stopped trying. When it was done, it was done the way clean work is done.

Clara closed what could be closed and left alone what couldn't. She wiped her hands on the inside of her own skirt and will never forgive herself for that, because hands that have done useful things should not be cleaned on anything but worthy cloth. She kissed two fingers and set them on his forehead where the hair had burned to curl. "Go pay your debts where men are kinder," she said, which was the mercy she could imagine.

Isidro looked out at the reach and counted in his head the things he would not say. Tamsin bent forward until her forehead touched the plank and made the smallest sound she had made in years, one that belonged in a London cupboard or a New Orleans theater, never here. Séverine sat back on her heels and took the arrow with its message and snapped it once in the middle and tucked it into the stern under the coil of rope, as if to say *we saw you and we will keep reading*.

Artemis put her palm flat over the gourd slung at her back and felt nothing. That made her angry in a new way. She wanted it to hum or sting or weep. She wanted it to ring its little bells like a puppet of a church. It did none of that. It sat like a hand on her spine and asked for rent.

"We put him in now," Isidro said.

"No," Clara said, and there was steel under the soft rot in her voice. "He goes under the fig when the sky lets us have dirt. I won't feed this bastard river another boy without making it admit it is a grave."

They buried Jonah at dusk under a bank that pretended to be an altar. There was no fig, but there was a root with a bend in it like a woman's arm resting and that was enough. Séverine said a prayer that had gotten very small and very good since New Orleans and then said nothing, which was better. Tamsin tried to say a thing and could not; she untied the red kerchief she wore some days to keep sweat out of her eyes and tied it to a twig above his head. The river learned a new color that night and took it downstream to tell to other bends.

They ran until the stars lost interest and the moon decided she had been asked to stay too late. They stopped only when stopping was already something that had happened to them. They ate nothing. They drank the river boiled into something like a promise. They slept like debt.

Before dawn, Artemis woke because the gourd had learned another trick. The hair in its binding flexed once under her palm as if remembering the old law of *pull to open*. The little bells did not ring but they knew they could. The not-voice in the soft part of her head between fear and the number said, gentler now that it knew where she lived, *Open.*

"No," she said, with the pleasant firmness of a woman denying a child a knife.

Tamsin shifted in the hammock beside her and found her hand without waking fully. "Say it again," she murmured against sleep.

"No," Artemis said, and the word felt like a stake you put in the ground to tell the world where names stop.

When morning came, it came like a debt collector, polite and early. They moved. The river made less commentary. The emissary's rhythm behind them had changed. Fewer boats. Fewer shouts. Patient now. He had learned something about the price of being impolite to water.

They reached a confluence where the Purus flirted with a smaller run and then refused to go home with it. The spoon lay cold and sure at Artemis's sternum. She salted the cup because ritual is a rope you carry even when you're not sure there will be anything to tie to. One—two—three—four—five—six—seven. The bowl turned toward the stubborn little run.

"Smaller mouth," Tamsin said, standing to stretch, trousers damp, eyes smarter than any bank. "Liar's road."

"Lies we can read," Isidro said, and smiled with half a face.

"Lies I prefer," Clara muttered, binding a fresh strip of cloth over the place where ash had found a resting place between finger and fate the night before.

Séverine looked back once—south, toward the place where the smokehouse had written its last parable. She had an arrow under her arm like a useless hymn. "Five," she said, not cruelly, not softly. It was not for counting the living. It was for remembering there are numbers that behave only when spoken aloud.

"Five," Artemis answered, and lifted the spoon as if it were a candle whose light only her bones could see.

They turned into the smaller mouth.

The river closed around their ribs like a door drawn shut by a patient hand that meant to charge them for passage.

Chapter 20 — Ledger in the Narrows

"Some debts are collected where a river cannot breathe."

The small mouth closed behind them like lips reconsidering a kiss. Overhead, roots laced into a low ceiling; underfoot, the water lost its habit of behaving like a road and turned into a hallway with poor lighting. Even the mosquitoes changed their tone—as if a choir director had lifted two fingers and asked for minor keys.

"Slow," Isidro said. His voice had gone from blade to wicker since the cut. He braced himself mid-boat, crutch wedged, good leg pressed to rib. The bandage high under his shorts was clean for the hour and trying to forget it had been meat once.

Artemis salted the tin cup because ritual is a rope you carry even when you don't know if there will be anything to tie to. One—two—three—four—five—six—seven. Éloise's spoon turned not right, not left, but into a seam so mean even the frogs sounded offended. The gourd on her back drank warmth without swallowing. Baptiste's coin at her throat stayed hot, a small defiance.

"Always the worst door," Tamsin murmured. She stood in the bow, trousers slick to the thigh, pistol tucked in the curve of her spine like a second vertebra. She shoved the pole gently and the *montaria* slid under a curtain of vines that had learned to behave like hair. Spider silk kissed her jaw. She did not flinch; she did not give them that story.

The Ituxí's child-throat made a bend and then another, the boat scraping where tree knees learned to be furniture. Séverine ran two fingers along the gunwale, dusting salt as if hemming a dress against rain. Her veil was tied pirate-tight. Her rosary clicked once, the sound a beetle makes when it remembers it has wings.

Clara eyed Isidro's color and made the face she saved for pupils who argued with knives. "Tell me if the pain learns a new language."

"It says church," he said, almost cheerful. "I tell it I am atheist."

"You are Catholic when I say so," she answered, and he grinned because obedience under duress is the poor man's flirtation.

They weren't first to name this throat.

Hair hung from a low branch ahead—black, black, white—threaded with gut, stiff with salt. Three green chips were pressed into the bark beside the knot, each smeared with oil that would not come off with rain. Below, in the water, a small raft of palm rib drifted with something arranged upon it: a bowl black with old fat and a single human tooth placed like a star.

"Threshold," Séverine said.

"Tax," Tamsin corrected.

"Watch for men," Isidro added, because all thresholds have accountants.

They came. Not with guns and hats. With paint and silence. The woman with the maze on her breast stepped out of leaf like a punctuation mark; two men slid through water to either side of the boat, shoulders barely rippling it, blowpipes lazy in hands that had learned never to shake. A third man appeared on a root span above them, arrows already real in the bow.

The woman did not look at the gourd, didn't make the indecency of curiosity. She looked at Artemis's face, then at Séverine's salt horn, then at Clara's hands. She spoke five words in a language the river likes better than Portuguese. Séverine listened, then answered in Spanish.

"She says: you took bread from a god's mouth. The god will take a tongue in payment. Will you pay your own or do you prefer we choose?"

Clara, without asking anyone's permission, unknotted the scarf from her throat and held it up like a flag of surrender. "Hair," she said to Séverine. "Tell her hair. Not tongue. We have words still to spend."

The woman smiled like a knife laid on a table by a friend. She pointed at Artemis, then at herself, then mimed cutting. She tilted her head as if to offer a bargain old women make with combs.

Artemis reached up and took hold of the plait she'd kept tight since New Orleans—the one that had survived brine and anaconda musk and smokehouse fire. She slid the thong free. Tamsin hissed a little; Artemis met her look and shrugged. *If I am a door, let some things close.*

Clara took out her knife—a blade when the world was civil—and cut clean. The hair was heavy with river and bark and the smell of salt that wasn't ocean. Artemis wound the plait once around her wrist, felt the old innocence of that gesture pull at something under the breastbone, and let it go. The woman caught it like a midwife, twined gut through one end with a skill that made the act a sacrament, pressed three chips of green into a knot, and tied it to the low branch alongside the others. She tapped the knot twice, then Artemis's throat once, gentle as a warning and as precise.

Séverine said, low, "She says: your mouth still owes."

"I'll pay with other parts," Artemis answered. "Tongues have work left."

The men in the water tipped the *montaria* gently with open hands and let it right itself: a benediction or an inspection, it didn't matter. On the root bridge, the archer lowered his bow. The woman took a pinch of powder from a gourd and shook it into the water beside the floating bowl. Fish rose and rolled white-bellied where it touched them, the poison polite, quick, and thorough.

"Respect," Clara murmured. "We won't eat here."

They passed. The braid bobbed in their wake like a very small door left ajar.

"Good," Tamsin said, light. "Now we've paid our toll to the women who actually own the world, perhaps the men will stop trying to collect interest."

"The men will try harder," Isidro said.

He was right.

The throat spat them into a narrow lane with roots like ribs. On the far side, the river gathered itself into a harmless-looking comb of floating logs, bound by current and accident. Innocent. Arranged perfectly for a jam if someone up-current tugged the right string.

"Not natural," Isidro said.

"Nothing here is," Séverine replied.

A swallow flicked the air and died of it. A moment later—soft, distant—the noise a saw makes when it stops being useful and becomes an argument. Then paddles, in a rhythm that thinks it's a law.

"Push," Tamsin said. Not loud. The kind of push people do when they mean to be gone before their own ghosts catch up.

The *montaria* nosed into the comb. Poles slid between logs and found the lie that holds all lies together. Artemis counted to seven because counting kept her body from trying to run without her. The gourd dragged at her bones, a cold child. Baptiste's coin burned her throat like a promise no one had the right to make.

The first tug from upstream was not obvious. A little jerk. Then another. The comb of logs tightened like a jaw.

"Back," Isidro said, too late for grace. "Cut free."

A line had found them. Not rope—vine, thick as a wrist, wet as language. It snared the bow and took hold like a cuff. The comb shifted to humor the tug. The *montaria* slewed. Clara slammed both palms down on the gourd to keep it from rolling and earned a bruise that would be a story. Tamsin reached for the pole and found it already bit into the seam between two logs like a thin truth jammed in a door.

Artemis crawled forward on her knees and threw her weight against the vine. It gave not at all. She slid a knife under it and sawed; sap bled like clean snot and made everything too honest to hold.

The second tug was harder. The comb closed like a book on an ugly chapter. The logs were not alive; they moved like it anyway. The bow rose, then dropped. The stern answered with a sulk. The boat became a coin stuck in a bad slot.

The emissary's men came into view up the lane—hats lowered against insects, coats learned to love the rain. The emissary stood in the bow of the center boat, cane upright like a standard. He raised a hand and his men stopped. He had not come to get wet. He had come to watch.

"Cut, cut, cut," Tamsin sang between her teeth, knife sawing with fury and art.

Isidro made the decision men make when they have been given exactly one new life already. He unknotted the scarf from his thigh, flung the crutch aside, and crawled forward over the ribs. "Hold me," he said to no one and everyone, and before any woman could disagree he swung himself over the bow like a soldier in a story and went into water that is not a road.

"No," Clara began, automatic.

"Yes," he said, already hands-deep in the snarl, shoulders heaving. He didn't kick; he had learned that lesson. He went under to his armpits and let the logs talk to his spine. The stump, wrapped savage-tight, stayed out of the teeth by inches and a prayer he did not say.

He wrapped both arms around the vine where it fitted the *montaria*'s nose and braced one palm on the bow, the other on a log, skin the color of men who work for their food shifting over rope like a story about to end. "On three," he said, smile flashing in the spray because he was a man even now. "One—"

The next tug pulled like a priest taking a bottle from a table. The log to Isidro's left rolled; the one under his right hand rose like a breath. The boat's nose went down as if seeking confession. The vine tightened with the glee of a strangler fig. The emissary lifted his cane and half bowed as if the river were his example.

Isidro roared. Not a word, not a name. Noise that scares cats and wakes birds and makes children grow up. He shoved up on the log, down on the bow, and threw his weight into the place where the vine bit. Tamsin's knife found that exact weak measure and bit too. Sap spat. The vine thinned. The bow came up one inch, then two.

A shot. Then another. The emissary's men had decided that watching was not efficient. A ball struck the log by Isidro's ear and stung it into tipping; water came up shouting. The next ball bit the bank beyond and killed a fern that had never wronged anyone.

"Head down!" Clara barked, and Isidro laughed while under, which is how men drown. He came up and coughed, grin wiped away. "Cut," he said again.

Artemis cut skin off her knuckles that had never known their use until now. Tamsin's blade did the better part. The vine frayed. The comb groaned. A log slipped. The boat bucked like a saint refusing a miracle. Isidro slid deeper and clamped his teeth on a curse he had been saving for marriage.

The emissary fired his own pistol.

It was a gentleman's shot: careful, bored. The ball found Isidro's left shoulder in that narrow triangle where collarbone and breath keep their secrets. It went through very neatly, not to kill a bull but to make a man stop lifting.

Isidro stopped lifting.

He did not drop. He set his jaw like a branch set against a door and pushed again with his whole back as if his bones had decided to help. He made a sound that wasn't human and then remembered how to be one to say, courteously, "Now."

Tamsin cut the last strip. The vine gave up with the little song a prisoner sings on the gallows. The comb loosened the way a fist does when a man is dead. The *montaria* leaped like a fish beaten and freed. It slewed. It slammed Isidro in the ribs with its own joy and would have taken him under if Artemis hadn't grabbed his belt with one hand and the gourd-sling with the other and simply refused.

Clara had him by the armpits before pride could yank anyone's hands back. Together they dragged him over the bow like a deer stolen from a mean god. He fell into the bottom in a wet heap and smiled because he didn't know how not to.

"Pretend it's nothing," he said.

"It is nothing," Clara lied. "You are uninteresting. Bleed quietly."

Behind them, the emissary's boats discovered their own vine's humor. Tamsin had not been the only person with a knife this morning; the women under the leaves had been busy last night as well. A tug on the wrong string at the wrong second delivered a hat boat into a mouth it had been warned about. Men swore. A paddle vanished like a joke; the river used it elsewhere. Someone shouted to cut, cut, cut, and the river corrected his grammar.

"Row," Tamsin said, though there were no oars. They rowed with poles and breath and the wish to be away from arithmetic.

They made a room of backwater under saplings frail enough to hide their sins and sat in it breathing until breath learned to behave again. The gourd cooled one degree and then warmed, as if pleased to be in a place where men had bled and not died of it yet.

Clara's hands did what they had been made to do and then remade by war: plug, bind, swear, threaten, coax. She propped Isidro's shoulder open with two fingers and spat into it with spirits and salt. He bit Tamsin's scarf like a holy object and did not make a sound any more blasphemous than necessary. The stump held, a mean little fist of survival.

"Good," Clara said, which in her mouth is mercy. "You will live until the river asks different."

"Until then," he said, pale and upright and old in the way a man gets old all at once in a day, "I will be obedient."

"See that you are," she said, and kissed his forehead like a brand.

They didn't move far. The narrows demanded more tolls: a veil of vines so thick it felt like sleeping in someone else's hair; a raft of ants moving house with all their kittens; a wasp nest shaped like a priest's fist, which they took wide with more respect than any bishop deserved.

By afternoon, the sky stitched itself shut. Rain came all at once without choreography. The world went white for ten breaths—lightning setting all their bones into x-rays—and then it went black again like a mended lie. The emissary's men lost their rhythm for the length of the storm and had to find it again when the river gave it back. They sounded farther—fewer oaths, more orders. He was learning his patience. That was worse than any bullet.

They camped mean. A sand tongue no bigger than a saint's coffin. Nets low. Hammocks higher than any ant's ambition. Smoke disciplined to a whisper. Séverine salted a circle within a circle—small magic inside old. Tamsin set little strings of powder where men would try to put feet and left them unlit because rain remembered everything. The gourd lay under canvas with its bells not ringing and its hair waking sometimes as if dreaming of being pulled.

Artemis dozed with her jaw clenched and woke because numbers had chosen to work for the other side for a breath. The spoon was in her hand and her mouth had practiced *one-two-three*, as if counting could be made into a kind of surrender. She put the spoon down like a weapon and lay flat on her back under the net and looked up until her eyes had learned how to have a ceiling again.

She heard it before anyone else did: wood on wood, polite, almost apologizing. A paddle dipped where there should not have been water enough for paddles. A cough—a gentleman's, played to ask pardon for arriving late to dinner. The emissary had come around by a channel they had not seen, or by one he had paid for with other men's ribs.

"Tamsin," she whispered.

Tamsin's eyes were open already. She said nothing. She moved the way cats do when they accept gravity but intend to renegotiate. Pistol. Powder. Breath. She cocked and smiled at no one. The smile would have curdled milk.

Clara's hand found Isidro's chest and pressed him back down with the same authority with which she had given him a new life. Séverine's rosary made the smallest sound and then stopped because beads learn discipline when men bring guns to church.

They didn't light a fire. They didn't have to. The emissary brought his own. He lifted a lantern on a pole—glass dull, light resentful—and made a small show of being a man who prefers to see what he buys.

He stood in the bow of his boat with the serpent cane upright between his shoes like a spouse. The men behind him did not enjoy their work. Their faces had learned new truths about water. Their hats drooped as if the day had been long enough to teach manners.

He did not clear his throat. He had the room.

"Señoras," he said, tone pleasant with mildew. "Señor. You have cut my men twice today with your river's teeth. I regret the cost, which I do not pay. I am moved to offer mercy."

"I am moved," Tamsin said, even lighter, "to offer you a wet grave."

He smiled because she amused him and he preferred being amused to being honest. "You carry something that belongs to my employer. You do not know how to care for it. I do. You are poor in all the ways that matter. He is rich in the only way that does. Give me your road and the thing. I will leave you a boat and two barrels of flour and a letter that will see you past any soldier you meet from here to Pará. You will tell your grandchildren you almost did something clever once, and you will have all your teeth."

Séverine stood up in the dark and the lantern found her face and made it a small white moon. "We have no grandchildren," she said. "We have a debt to pay that is not to men."

He tilted the lamp a little in appreciation for theater. Water made a sound near the *montaria*'s stern that might have been a fish kissing air and might have been a hand taking hold.

Artemis said, before the gourd could speak with her mouth, "No."

The emissary sighed, disappointed in the way men are when they have to do violence they've already written into their diaries. "Then I will take payment for inconvenience." He pointed with the cane, lazy. "The man."

Isidro grinned and showed him all his teeth. "I am expensive."

"Not to me," the emissary said, and lifted two fingers.

Two shadows rose out of the water like part-time saints. They did not take Isidro. They took the boat by the stern and tipped it with a practiced, elegant cruelty that had nothing to do with anger. The *montaria* shifted. Water ate its shadow. Hands in—Artemis yanked the gourd under her chest with a hiss; Tamsin fired from a moving world and took a hat off a head in a way that would be funny in any other century. Clara's palm was already on Isidro's belt. Séverine threw salt. The emissary looked bored.

Something old and without politics rose under the boat: not the river's jaw, a breath. The gourd hummed once without making sound. The hair in its binding lifted like a woman whose lover has come home drunk and banging at the door.

"Open," the not-voice offered, with all the sweetness of a sin you haven't tried yet.

Artemis's mouth formed the number that fits no god. "Seven," she whispered, and put her palm on the gourd's cold hide and held like a jailer.

A crack. Not thunder. Not wood. The assistant in the third boat had found his powder dry and his aim good and his soul indifferent. The ball hit Isidro in the side—the unruined side, just under ribs—where a man hides a small store of courage. He jerked once, beautifully, and lay back as if a hand he respected had pressed his chest and told him to rest.

Clara was already over him with both hands and her rage. "No," she informed him, and the emissary, and the river. "No. Not this ledger."

He smiled up at her with nothing dramatic in it, only a tired love. "Obedient," he said, like a joke they had shared.

"Be," she ordered, and pressed down, and in pressing knew as well as any saint that there is a force that does not yield to will. He was obedient for one breath more. Then he paid a tax nobody returns from and made no fuss about it.

"Shoot," Tamsin said, not crying. She had very little powder worth the name and used it the way women use days when men insist they are not owners: well. A coat made a noise and lay down. The emissary ducked for the first time and swore with tidy diction.

"Enough," he said, and dropped the lantern to smash it. Fire winked out with a small cat's cry. Darkness came back with indifference. The bow rocked as the men let go and allowed their employer not to die for a while longer. The boats slid back into the throat whispering about accounts.

No one spoke. Not even Séverine. The only sound was Clara's hands confessing to uselessness on Isidro's chest, and then even that learned silence.

They took their dead man to a root where the river would remember. There were no figs. There was a bend in wood that had learned to hold, and that was enough. Salt. Two words that don't belong to any priest. The stump bandage still neat—the stubborn little fist. Tamsin put her palm on his hair and said a London word that made the water consider teaching itself English to understand it. Séverine pressed an arrow— the one with the spiral message—under the root like a notice. **A debt is not paid.**

They went, because grief on a river is not a house you can sit down in. The *montaria* had the line of a boat that has decided not to drown yet out of sheer disgust. The gourd lay under Artemis's breastbone and learned how to wait. The spoon tapped her sternum once like a teacher insisting that class is not dismissed.

When morning rinsed night off the leaves, the world had one fewer man in it and more mosquitoes. They ate beans. They did not taste them. Clara sat without moving for a long minute with her hands on her knees and the color in her face gone to paper. Then she turned her head as if listening to a street two centuries away and stood up because the living ask to be served whether the dead are finished or not.

"Four," Séverine said softly, because someone has to keep the accounts even when the numbers refuse to cooperate with kindness.

"Four," Tamsin answered, careful, as if the word were a weapon that might go off.

Artemis salted the cup and lifted the spoon and counted to seven until numbers behaved. The bowl turned, unkind and faithful, toward a seam where the river promised new thresholds. The coin at her throat warmed, and she knew with a calm that was all rage that the road to New Orleans would not be a road at all—it would be more mouths, more doors, more ledgers.

"Southwest," she said.

"Of course," Séverine replied, and picked up the salt.

They pushed into a morning that already knew their names.

Chapter 21 — The Tongue-Tithe

"Some oaths are signed in the mouth."

The small run learned their names by listening to their breath. It forgot them again when it pleased. Light came down in coins and ran away. Roots stitched the roof so low Tamsin had to keep her hat off or wear it in the wrong place on her body.

They moved as people move who have four lives and too many debts. Isidro's absence had a shape; the *montaria* rode higher; the world made room where it had not before. The gourd drank warmth off Artemis's back with the practised greed of a babe raised on famine. Éloise's spoon tapped her sternum once like a teacher insisting on the lesson. Baptiste's coin lay hot against the hollow at her throat, a round lie with edges.

"Left seam," Tamsin said. She had a way of standing in the bow that made the river look like it worked for her and resented doing so. Her trousers were soaked to the thigh; the pistol in the curve of her back had become a part of her spine.

Clara counted breaths she didn't own. Her hands moved over nothing—over air and rope and the memory of flesh—checking the places where a world can open without permission. The bandage on her forearm, where a piranha had tried to write its name in her, held. Her jaw worked like someone chewing a prayer too long to swallow.

Sister Séverine dusted salt along the gunwales, thumb and first finger. The rosary made its beetle-click once, then learned silence again. Under her veil her mouth looked like a line drawn by a steady hand.

The river gave them signs whether they asked or not. Hair hung on a low branch—black, black, white—gut-threaded, salt-stiff, three bottle-green chips pressed into the knot. Below, a bowl black with fat floated on a raft of palm rib with a single human tooth on its lip; a small star with bad manners.

"Another threshold," Séverine said. Her voice made the word a wall.

"Another shopfront," Tamsin muttered. "What does the proprietor sell?"

"Permission," Clara answered. She untied the scarf from her throat with the temper of a surgeon forced to barter. "Hair again. Offer ours before someone asks for our wrists."

The woman with the maze painted across her chest appeared as if the green had been peeled back to reveal her. Two men slid in the water at either flank of the boat, bare shoulders, blowpipes that needed no powder. A third balanced on a root span above them, arrow lazy but awake. Their eyes were old in the way skill makes eyes old.

The woman didn't look at the lump on Artemis's back as indecent curiosity would have demanded. She looked at Artemis's face, at Séverine's salt horn, at Clara's hands, at Tamsin's pistol, and found the ledger in that sum. She spoke five words. The river understood them. So did Séverine.

"She says: you took bread from a god's mouth. Mouths keep books. Pay your tongue or we collect."

"Hair," Clara said to Séverine. "Offer hair. We need tongues for later."

Séverine relayed with all the politeness of a woman who can ask a favor without making a wound. The woman listened, measured, nodded once. She tapped her own teeth, then touched Artemis's throat, a light bell-push of a finger: not now. Soon.

Artemis took the thong off her plait. It had kept salt, smoke, and men's hands out of her hair since New Orleans; it made a small sound when she unbound it, like a door that has learned to admit only what can pay. Clara cut clean. The weight in Artemis's palm felt like a childhood she had eaten already.

The woman caught the braid like a midwife, threaded gut through the end with the speed of a verb, pressed three green chips into the knot until resin took them, and tied it to the low branch beside the others. She touched the knot twice, then Artemis's lower lip once, a courtesy and a warning both. One of the men in the water raised a palm, pushed the *montaria* gently by the bow as if to see if it had teeth, and let it go.

They passed. The braid bobbed once in their wake and then lay still, learning a new weather.

"Paid for now," Tamsin said. "We'll get a bill at the door."

They did—the kind not written on paper.

The channel pinched into a narrow where logs lay in a comb, so neat it looked accidental. If you've never had a river set a trap for you, you might mistake it for drift. If you have, you can smell the twine under the leaves.

"Not a god's joke," Isidro would have said. He wasn't there to say it. Isidro was downstream, making the current remember his name.

"Cut if I say cut," Tamsin told the air. "And if I don't say it, cut anyway."

They nosed in. The first tug on a vine line was perfunctory, like a shopkeep clearing his throat. The second wrote *now* in their ribs. The logs snugged with the appetite of a well-run mouth. The bow dropped. The stern got ideas.

Clara went to her knees with both palms on the gourd to keep it from rolling into idiocy. Tamsin got the vine under her knife and made it smaller with insults. Artemis slid forward and put her weight over the bow, the coin at her throat burning like a promise made by a man who can afford to tell the truth. The *montaria* sulked against the comb.

Up-channel the emissary came neat as a receipt—three boats, fewer men than yesterday, their faces set in that tight look that belongs to men who have learned the price of disobedience. He stood in the bow, hat gone to manners, serpent cane upright between shoes. He watched. Watching is a profession.

They cut the line before the river could say *please*. The comb loosened its teeth by inches; the boat came up like a bad idea abandoned. A shot cut a fern to education; another grazed the *montaria's* rib and taught it religion. They didn't look up. They left. The emissary lifted his cane without annoyance and let them go as a man lets a card pass because the deck is marked for later.

The run knotted, unknoted, bent the way a patient argues with a doctor. The sky stitched itself shut and ripped open again. Heat learned rain. Voices behind them got smaller. The day turned into two hours you could stagger across.

They made a camp you could pick up in the time it takes to fumble a pistol cap. Hammocks like pale mouths. Nets like cracked stained glass. No fire. Smoke had been a signature too often and too recently.

Artemis lay with the gourd under her spine and learned how to breathe around it. The bells on its neck thought about ringing and didn't. The hair in its binding lifted once, as if remembering wet fingers. The not-voice in the soft part of her head said *open* in the accent of a kind aunt who has never told a good truth in her life.

She put the spoon between her teeth like a coin and counted until numbers grew claws.

Sometime deep in the hour when mosquitoes lose faith, the smell of smoke tried the camp, sniffing, then committed. Not their smoke. New smoke, sweet—palm, fat, and something else: green stone. The women with the hair-knots had sent a messenger or a warning, and it came in a flavor.

Séverine sat up under her net and raised one hand for silence in case silence needed reminding. She listened to the smell the way other people listen to rain. "It wants the tithe," she said, voice flat. "If we don't pay with hair, the bill moves to mouth."

"I'll tell it to send an invoice," Tamsin muttered.

"No," Séverine said. "It's old enough to collect at the door."

She took out her knife—the clean one she used for fruit and babies—and put her thumb on the flat. She didn't ask permission. She did not look at the others because looking is how you make witnesses out of kin.

"Don't you—" Clara began, too late for anything but insult.

Séverine stuck her tongue out and cut the tip off neatly.

It wasn't brave. It wasn't hysterical. It was exact. The pain jumped her eyes to water and sat in them like a bright animal. Blood pooled mortar-red. She caught it with her other hand and smeared it on the hair-binding of the gourd, on the tiny brass bells, on the blind eyes of the Spanish Queen pressed into the tar. She made a cross without liking crosses. She made a circle without trusting circles.

"It takes less when you pay first," she said, the words thick. "Later, it takes what it wants."

"Rinse," Clara snapped, handing her a cup. "Salt. Hard." She tipped brine into Séverine's mouth and Séverine took it the way saints take nails: with intent.

The gourd stopped its tiny dreaming. The hair lay down like a tame thing. The bells learned modesty. The river exhaled once through the roots of the world and left them to sleep.

Morning had a bruise under one eye. They moved. Séverine didn't speak unless she had to, and when she had to she sounded like a woman who had just learned a new language and was prepared to be rude in it. Tamsin looked at her with that particular tenderness rough women have only for other women who bleed on purpose.

"You could have cut mine," Tamsin said. "Mine swears enough to pay any bill."

"It wanted one that prays," Séverine said, and laughed once, short—*ah*—because laughing cost.

They found the Purus again by smell and by sky. The black-water niceties dropped their skirts; the brown went wide and old. Wind came down it with ideas. A steamer's far rumor lived on the air the way the memory of a bell lives in a church. Not here— downriver. Time catching up.

"East," Tamsin said. "Manaus. Then the long road downriver. Then the sea. Then a boat that doesn't taste like teeth."

"And a man with silver will be at every corner asking to see our pockets," Clara said.

"We show him our empty ones," Tamsin said. "And our pistol. And your hands."

"We show him our dead," Séverine added, not unkindly. "Accounts collect interest." She pressed her fingers to her mouth. The cut had stopped seeping. It would be a scar that taught vowels to limp.

They held close to banks that had been taught to be furniture and not theatre. The emissary's beat moved behind them—patient, diminished, never absent. Once, in a high bend, they saw smoke where men had gathered to make trade and songs. They slid under the outermost root and let other fools be seen.

Before noon, the river set a different price.

They poled into a reach where the current went lazy and the spiders had bored themselves into engineering. The web spanned from palm to cecropia to a stump, a curtain the size of a rich man's bedsheet. In the middle, hanging with the confidence of a bishop, sat a spider the size of a soup bowl, banded legs like polished wood, abdomen with a bright nick in it where something larger had tried and failed.

"Darling," Tamsin said, under her breath. "You are in our way."

"Don't swat," Clara said reflexively. "They bite like men with small souls."

The spider raised two forelegs very slightly in a position that could only be read as *and what if I do*. The thread the boat pressed against drew a note you could feel through bone. The web swayed. Under the web, gold ants ran a congress up and down a liana with the clockwork economy that makes men fear republics. A small bird skeleton hung in lace, reduced to an idea.

"Pay," Séverine said.

"We've paid hair and tongue," Tamsin said. "Shall I tip the spiders as well?"

"Salt," Séverine said. "Pay with the sea."

Artemis shook a small handful of grains into her palm. She didn't fling them. She *offered*—hand up, wrist bent, as if asking a dancer to come down from a chair. The crystals hit the web at the closest anchor point and made small white stars. The silk sang. The spider stepped sideways with the sullen grace of a woman asked to change seats for a man's convenience. It took one strand in long forelegs and cut it itself, then another, then waited to be admired.

The boat slipped through the new seam. The spider made a sound like an old lady disapproving of onions and set to mending the insult.

"Bless you," Tamsin told it, and meant it.

Midday turned itself over and became a heat you could chew. The sky went coin-bright. They came upon a stand of *juçara* with a ladder cut into the nearest—men climb it for hearts of palm and to see if the world is smaller from up there. A dog trotted out onto the bank and barked once at them, polite. The man who would have shushed the dog was dead or drunk or downriver. A canvas hung from a line with a child-sized shirt clipped to it with carved pegs. Clara looked at it too long and deliberately looked away. Tamsin didn't look at all. Séverine crossed herself with her eyes only.

They didn't stop.

The emissary's boats slid onto the reach half an hour later, tidy again, diminished—two now, not three. One of the men wore a sling. The emissary had a new cane. He had not gotten tired of buying serpents.

He didn't hurry. He had learned not to. He waited for the river to simplify the problem.

It obliged at dusk with the honesty of a trap sprung by nobody's hand.

A tangle of floating roots and logs had been collecting all afternoon at a bend where the current forgot itself and then remembered abruptly. Down the back of the pile ran the small, black waterfall the Purus makes when it wants to laugh at you. The *montaria* slipped into the vee with the seduction you get when wood pretends to be water. The bow rose as if for a better view. The stern made a decision.

"Off!" Tamsin snapped. "On the right. Step where the ants aren't. Hold the line."

They moved because obedience, under some women, is religion. Clara got the gourd off Artemis's back before anything could instruct her hands for her, slung it in low and mean against her own spine; numbers don't own all women. Séverine got the coil, made it into a sentence, threw the first clause around a stump. Artemis stepped onto the root and sank clean to her shin in a rot that smelled like a wardrobe's breath. She laughed once without humor and hauled.

The boat, unburdened by people and still burdened by beans, decided to leave. Tamsin said a word that in some languages is cousin to a prayer and took the

painter in both fists as if intending to play tug-of-war
with a minor god. The line sang. The log under
Artemis's foot rolled. She went to her hip. The gourd
on Clara's back knocked wood and traced a bruise that
would heal in the shape of a bell.

The emissary's men saw and began the moral
arithmetic of pursuit versus spectacle. The emissary
added numbers with eyebrows. He did not lift a pistol.
He did not need to. The river was being instructed.

They got the *montaria* out of the vee because four
women can steal anything out of anybody's mouth if
the timing is right. The painter squealed; the bow came
up; the stern banged something like a man's knee. The
whole slid sideways into the kind of water you can
forgive. They flopped into it after, all knees and elbows
and the impolite noises bodies make when they refuse
to die gracefully.

"Go—" Clara began.

"—and don't look back," Séverine finished, spitting
pink into a leaf and not making a calendar of it.

They went, because staying is a luxury and only rich
people deserve it.

Night came honest and fast. They made a camp on a
spit so small it could have been a saint's coffin. No fire.
Powder is a liar in rain and a thief in light. Tamsin laid
two little strings of pleasant inventions across the track
where a man too proud of his boots would put a foot.
Séverine salted a circle in a circle and a cross where the
montaria's nose kissed mud. Clara set the gourd under
the awning in shadow like a baby no one had agreed to

love. Artemis lay on her side and counted until the numbers stopped shaking hands with ghosts.

In the hour when true dreams go home to put on day clothes, a paddle bumped wood politely. A lantern climbed a pole and showed a circle of light like a coin held up to tavern eyes.

"Evening," the emissary said. He hadn't tired of it. His voice had mildew and manners. "You are unfair to me. You make me work too late."

"You're paid by the hour," Tamsin said, and the pistol was in her hand at the end of the sentence.

He smiled. He had learned to straighten it so it looked like a line and not a bite. "Give me the artifact and the road and I will leave you flour and a letter and a story you can tell grandchildren."

"We are short of grandchildren," Séverine said, her words thick on the new geography of her mouth.

He looked at her not with contempt but with the puzzled interest men reserve for women who do not arrange themselves to be useful. Then he lifted two fingers. The men behind him put their paddles into water.

What happened after had the quickness of a ledger-line subtracted. The stern sucked; the bow lifted; hands found wood; feet found mud; the boat decided to invert its morals. Tamsin fired and took the lantern's glass; darkness came down with a cat's snarl. A ball from the third boat found the place in Isidro's body where breath

had once been paid; he was not there to collect it. It hit
the log beyond and ricocheted into the water like a lie.

"Hold," Clara told the world and the gourd and the men
in hats and the women laying traps and the number that
keeps trying to be seven and the river that keeps
forgetting it owes nothing. She put her whole body into
the word and the world obeyed long enough for them to
become a moving object again.

They didn't sleep after. They held their lives like plates
you can't afford to drop. Dawn made everything
smaller without making any of it kinder.

"East," Tamsin said through teeth. "Manaus. Men. A
steamer if God owes me something I can spend."

"God owes me nothing," Séverine said.

"Then men," Tamsin said, and spat, and smiled without
humor. "I can spend men."

They moved. The Purus widened. The running behind
them took on the tired measure of men who have
learned how long a jungle is. The day made promises it
had no intention of keeping.

At noon they came to a place where the river had
decided to be honest in a new way. The bank to the
right had been bitten hard. A tree the size of a church
lay in the water, roots up, red clay on them like flesh.
On the bank men had built a small shrine out of what
the river had vomited: a doorframe nailed to nothing, a
child's shoe, a bottle with a ribbon in it, a plank burned
with the word **Zé**. Three green glass chips were pressed

into the ribbon, and a braid—black, black, white—hung from a nail that didn't belong to any of it.

"Bad luck makes its own altar," Clara said softly.

"Z," Jonah had said, in a different hour. He was gone; the letter stayed.

They pushed off into a reach that was almost river and not yet sea. The air tasted of iron and austerity. Manaus was days away but you could smell cities the way you can smell rain long before it arrives.

Artemis counted and found only four. She counted again and found only four. She said it anyway, small: "Four."

"Four," Tamsin answered. The number lay between them like a knife where girls teach each other to cut bread.

The gourd lay quiet under canvas. The bells didn't ring. The hair lay down. Séverine's mouth bled one clean line of salt brine and healed a little. Clara's hands did not stop being busy even when there was nothing to do. Tamsin's eyes scouted a horizon that had not yet learned to be water colored like money.

Late light turned gold with a bruise under it. In the bend ahead, a whistle—thin, arrogant, new. Not a bird. A boiler learning to speak.

"Listen," Tamsin said, and her grin became wicked for the first time in days. "A boat that doesn't taste like teeth."

"Or a mouth you can't spit out of," Clara said.

The steamer came around the point as if a boy had pushed it. Low, ugly, with a stack like a finger scolding God. Men on its deck wore coats too clean for this latitude. On its stern a flag—the wrong flag—hung like a promise. At the fore, a gentleman's cane flashed silver and small.

"Of course," Séverine said thickly. "He bought a river that makes its own steam."

"We'll steal it," Tamsin said briskly, as if explaining a domestic economy. "Or we'll burn it after using it to go where we need." She checked her pistol as if that settled the physics.

Artemis lifted the spoon and counted because even when a door is metal and runs on fire, a woman can still negotiate with numbers.

One. Two. Three. Four. Five. Six. Seven.

The bowl turned toward the uglier water, as it always did.

They went to meet it.

Chapter 22 — Fire Under the Tongue

"Engines are only hearts that forgot to be afraid."

The steamer came around the bend with its own weather. Stack smoke kneaded the sky; the paddlewheel beat a law into the brown water; brass on the rail shone like a tooth that means it. Men in clean shirts stood at attention because engines make armies out of fools. At the bow a gentleman leaned on a serpent-headed cane, hatless as a sermon, and regarded the world as inventory.

"Of course he bought a boiler," Tamsin said, mouth crooked. "Men like that marry anything that hisses."

"Heat kills as clean as ink," Clara muttered. "Don Iñigo has learned his alphabet."

Sister Séverine's tongue-tip was a new geography— healed enough to make consonants obey, vowels limp. "Steam makes cowards fast," she said. "But fast cowards are still cowards."

Éloise's spoon tapped Artemis's sternum once, twice— *count*. Baptiste's coin warmed the hollow at her throat until it stung like truth. The gourd on her back drank heat with practiced greed. She salted the tin cup—small rope, same knot—and lifted the spoon. One—two— three—four—five—six—seven. The bowl turned not to safety but to a seam where the river's skin slicked darker and the current ran sly under a scatter of roots: shallows with a window, a door in the bottom the steamer would misread.

"Lure him," she said, not liking the taste of command and taking it anyway. "Make him think he has our backs to the bend."

Tamsin grinned without humor. "Strut and flirt? I've had worse gigs."

They ran the *montaria* parallel to the steamer's run, then cut across its nose in a swallow's curve that made the paddlers look up and the engineer check his gauge out of habit. Tamsin stood in the bow, trousers rucked, hat off, hair like a flag. She cupped both hands to her mouth and shouted a word the Thames had taught her that means three things at once: insult, proposal, challenge. Anyone who has worked a river knows the sound and will die answering it.

The emissary raised his serpent cane a hair's breadth in acknowledgement—the bored courtier's bow. He turned his head slightly. Orders went down a chain one man long; pressure built the rest of the way. The paddles bit with new malice. The steamer's nose swung for them.

"Left," Artemis said, and Tamsin put the pole where numbers wanted it to be. The *montaria* slid into the seam as if money had given permission. From the deck, the cut of water read as open. From the spoon, it read as *no* spelled by logs and biblical roots.

"Your cane won't teach you the river," Séverine said to the gentleman no one let hear her. "You need to learn it by losing a tooth."

The steamer came in proud and patient, trust invested in iron and men it could afford to burn. Its paddle churned the seam to gravy. Under the bow the window closed; the river found the old joke it had planned. The paddle bit silt; the nose kissed a buried log with the wet thud of a hand slapping a child. The hull jarred. Crate and man stumbled together; dignity spilled like powder. The engineer's whistle shrieked two notes and a prayer. Reverse, but river is not a ballroom and iron is not light on its feet. The steamer slid up on its own mistake like a man forced to sit where he never meant to.

"Grounded," Isidro would have said, satisfied. Four of them said it with their faces instead.

On the bow the emissary did not stoop to look, because people with money do not bend in public. He set the cane's silver mouth on the cap-rail and leaned. "Cute," Tamsin imagined him saying, a word he'd never learned to allow. Out loud—enough—he lifted two fingers. Rifles came up along the rail like teeth.

"Down," Clara said, and they flattened, obedient because obedience to some women is a sacrament. Ball chewed leaves and threw splinters; the *montaria's* gunwale learned a lesson it didn't deserve. The steamer's engine labored in reverse, wheel slapping mud with the petulance of a trapped saint.

"Two minutes," Artemis said, tasting the river's comedy as if it were salt on her wrist. "Maybe three. Then he'll wriggle free."

"Two minutes is a long time if you know how to be someone else," Tamsin said, all bright London wickedness sharpening to a point. "We climb."

Clara made a knife-noise with her teeth. "You are not thieves of boats you cannot run."

"I can run anything with valves," Tamsin said. "I've danced with uglier fire on the Lea. You feed her. I'll teach her manners for long enough to insult a tyrant."

Séverine tied her veil back as if dragging a net and made a mouth for numbers. "We don't own victory," she said. "We can borrow time."

They slipped along the grounded steamer's flank in the blind angle between the wheel-house and the eye of men who don't expect fish to grow hands. The *montaria* bumped iron with a small kiss that called nobody mother. Tamsin sprang first—hands, boot-heel, rail, up with the grace of a girl who learned to outrun dock police. Artemis after, the coin burning, the spoon knocking her sternum like a small bell. Séverine shut her jaw on pain and followed, shoe-smart, skirts already trousers. Clara, last, slung the gourd down off her back and under the awning on the *montaria* where salt and a little prayer made a poor house for gods, then came up with the ugly economy of a woman who knows how to ignore what skin says.

Deck: tar and brass and men startled into being prey. Two of them—boys, the kind money breeds—went for pistols because that's what theater demands. Tamsin's pistol had six proper endings left in it. She spent one to erase a hand. Spent another to erase a plan. The third she kept in her teeth and used as punctuation.

"Don't be heroes," she told them, and they understood because even bullies know the tone midwives use when telling men to get out of the room.

The emissary didn't flinch. He watched with a scholar's calm, as if measuring strokes on water. "Again," he said to the engineer, voice flat through the glass of class. The wheel dug; the hull groaned. The trapped log changed its mind a finger's width. Another minute, and the river would go back to being diplomatic.

Artemis went forward. He saw her then.

"Señora," he said, serpent cane between his shoes, as if speaking to a woman at the edge of a dance. "If you hand me my employer's property now, I will allow you to live long enough to discover how meaningless that is."

She was tired enough to like him for telling the truth. "You have nothing I want," she said, and her voice sounded like a courtyard in New Orleans and a door that never belonged to any priest.

He showed teeth without smiling. The silver mouth of the cane winked river-light. "You have nothing I won't take."

"Take this," Tamsin said pleasantly, and kicked him in the knee as if he were a boy who had upset a pail.

He staggered like a gentleman remembering he was meat. The cane clattered once on the deck; a bronze bell in the wheel-house rang out of sympathy. Séverine slid past Artemis low and quick and threw a handful of salt, not in his eyes—that would be theater—but along the cane where it lay, crusting the seam at the jaw. The silver serpent's mouth, touched, looked briefly as if it had learned humility.

Clara was already down the companion into the belly where iron sweated and men forgot God. The engine room had two hearts: furnace and wheel. The firebox roared like a wedding no one consented to; billets, stacked like army coffins, waited to be burned into obedience. The man tending the door blinked once at Clara's knife and decided life was longer without lines across it. He stepped back. She fed green wood instead of cured, and wet, and dragged a sack of river sand into the fire like a bad aunt. Glass in the sight blew a blasphemous note. Pressure learned the new grammar of spite.

"Whistle!" the engineer shouted, because some men's first love is noise. He spun the wheel. Steam shrieked to sky. The wheelhouse bell clanged again, confused to find its own mouth making that sound.

On deck the emissary recovered poise. He drew his pistol as if removing a thorn and leveled it at Tamsin's face. She smiled at him with interest, altogether alive. "Three left," she said mildly, though the count was for her own hand.

He fired. The ball flattened itself into the iron of the ventilator by her ear like a beetle denied a door. Séverine's second handful of salt hissed where the serpent cane stood; the silver mouth's hinge stuck an instant. It was enough for a woman raised among clever doors. Artemis booted the cane under the rail with a kick that had learned its manners from London. It went overboard like a bad thought.

The emissary looked at the loss as if someone had changed an arithmetic sign on him. He raised the empty hand, palm neat. "Men," he said.

Men obliged. Two rushed with lengths of belaying pin polished by other fights. One came with a rope like a priest with a loud opinion. Tamsin took the first pin on the arm and called the man a pet name in a language that likes consonants. Artemis slid in on hands and knees, low as a bad idea, and took the legs out from under the rope-holder with a sweep learned at the edge of a boxing ring where girls aren't allowed. The deck jumped; somebody's skull found wood and decided to nap. Séverine smashed the little brass ship's bell off its hook and swung it by the tongue like a cudgel, a choir-girl making new liturgy. The bell sang once, twice; men found God. One lay down and didn't get up.

"Pressure dropping!" a stranger's voice howled from below, which is how engines pray.

"Backwash!" the engineer countered.

Clara kicked the backwash valve with a neat boot and spun the injector wheel half-open with a wrist knife-hidden. River water shoved cold into a throat hot enough to swear. The boiler shuddered like a sweating bull. If you know how to make a boiler weep, you know how to keep it from screaming. Clara knew despair better than any engine alive. She patted its iron cheek once—there, there—then threw a last scoop of sand into its red mouth, a recipe of charity.

On deck the paddles clawed mud and let go. The hull shifted half a hand's breadth backward and stopped as if the river had demanded tithe and been given only gossip. The emissary looked at his engine-room door, then at the woman between him and the stair. He measured three lives and found them insolent. He stepped in. Artemis let him, because she didn't own men's deaths and refused to pretend.

He lunged for the stair, pivoted, and slammed his shoulder into her in a motion that would have broken a smaller saint. Baptiste's coin cut her collarbone where leather dragged; the spoon thumped her sternum like a knuckle. She bit off the number that wanted to spend itself—*six*—and said *no* out of principle. Tamsin swung the pin she had stolen and missed his skull out of bad luck; it hit his ear and made a new, red religion of it. He stumbled, cursed in a Lisbon that belonged to lawsuits, and ran below.

Clara met him at the top of the ladder with a mouthful of steam. He lowered an arm and shoved like money erasing names. She went down two steps and caught herself with the kind of hand that doesn't drop things people give it. He passed, spitting, to the heart of his purchase and found it offended.

"Spill feed," he snapped to the engineer, who looked at him as if men had stopped making sense. "Shut her down."

"You'll ground us!" the man cried, though the day had already made that choice.

"I will buy dirt," the emissary said, savagely elegant, and spun a wheel himself with fingers that had never earned strength. Iron obeyed—the way beasts obey the wrong men for a while. The padlock on the safety valve, pretty as a brooch, clicked. He paid attention to the wrong sound.

Up top, Séverine threw the bell at a head that needed warning. Tamsin dragged Artemis by the belt to the rail and pointed with her chin to the bow seam: the *montaria* afloat, faithful, nose in. "Drop," Tamsin said. "On your count."

Artemis salted the cup with quick, mean fingers. One—two—three—four—five—six—seven. They went on the seven the spoon had already chosen. Gravity and friendship caught them. The *montaria* took in two women with a grunt and a wet slap; Séverine rolled in alive and laughing once the way saints aren't supposed to. Clara came last, deliberate, satchel first, dignity second. A man with a rifle leaned out to be dramatic and Tamsin shot his hat. The hat flopped into river with all the grace it had held on a head, and a caiman accepted it as replacement dignity.

They shoved off. Behind them the steamer exhaled like a woman insulted once too often and settled her weight into the mistake the river had prepared. The wheel turned once, twice, slowly, then stuck with a righteousness that belonged to saints and stumps. A thin scream rose from the engine-room—the sound of iron learning limits. It faded fast. Clara had not come to blow a boiler; she had come to make a point, and she had made it hard enough to buy them river.

The emissary came back to the rail, face cut at the ear, hair neat elsewhere. He had found another cane somewhere —how many serpents can a man keep on retainer?—and leaned on it lightly as if it were a wit. His gaze slid over the four of them, counted, saw the subtraction, and did not smile. He lifted the cane a fraction, courteous as murder. "Tomorrow," his posture said. "I am rich enough to have tomorrows."

"Not if I steal them first," Tamsin called, cheerful, already tucked back into petty larceny with the stern painter gathered at her foot.

They ran the *montaria* into vines, let the river erase their wake, and breathed like thieves who have found a church with no god in it. The sky decided to be generous and threw two minutes of clean rain at their faces. Even mosquitoes staggered under the gift.

"Powder?" Tamsin asked, because business makes grief behave.

"Enough to be insulted," Clara said. She laid a hand flat on the gourd and felt nothing. That was worst. "He will follow at three-quarter steam by evening, when he bribes the river with wood and men."

"We bribe women instead," Séverine said, tasting her new consonants, making peace with them. She nodded toward a braid swung low from a branch—black, black, white, three green chips pressed into a knot, a tooth placed on a palm-rib raft below. "Door."

They paid before being asked. Tamsin cut a coin's width of her own hair and tied it with gut learned from watching; Séverine pressed a chip into resin like a stamp; Clara touched the knot with salt for *stay closed*. Artemis set her thumb to her own lip and left a red print small as any child's. The braid accepted their economy. The raft spun once like a lazy priest.

Toward noon the sky balanced between iron and mercy. They found a slough where water learned to talk to itself. The wind held its breath. A scent like cold stone rose—impossible, inland—green, mineral, remembered. The gourd flexed under canvas once like a sleeping animal having a wicked thought.

"Open," it said, honey and poison together, in the soft plank of Artemis's head between fever and math.

"No," Artemis told it, and because she was tired of politeness she did not say please.

They ate beans because beans demand to be eaten. They drank water that had learned a little shame through boiling. Séverine rinsed her mouth and cursed—in proper French this once—when salt kissed the cut. Tamsin counted cartridges like a gambler with a dying habit. Clara lay on her side an inch from the gourd and stared at it as if her gaze could scratch it.

"Manaus," Tamsin said. "Steamer stage. Men with bad hats. A real boat that goes east." She lifted her chin. "We take it."

"Buy it?" Clara asked, bleak and funny.

"Steal it," Tamsin said. "Or stow under something that smells like fish until the sea agrees to have us."

Séverine smiled with her eyes because smiling with her mouth would have hurt. "We will be the saints of rats."

"Artemis," Clara said, and the tone had more mercy than orders ever do. "Count for us. If numbers are doors, then we need the one that gets us to bread and not to teeth."

Artemis salted, lifted, counted. One—two—three—four—five—six—seven. The spoon turned toward the uglier water again, toward a tongue of black that pushed under the right bank where men with money don't look because there's nothing to buy there.

They went.

Behind them something new spoke on the river—the steamer's whistle, arrogant even when it had been made humble for a while. Not close. Not far enough. The emissary's ledger had turned a page. The coil of hair under canvas lay quiet, patient as a loan shark.

Evening grayed out of the canopy like someone aging in a painting. They slipped into a backwater that would be called a harbor when river learned to have cities. A scatter of canoes with their noses on mud. A rick of billets cut and stacked with love. A boy with grease on his chin and a salt wrist, three fingers missing from the old accident nobody mentions, watching them with the flat curiosity poverty gives.

"Powder?" Tamsin asked him in a Portuguese taught by sales and fists.

He nodded and scowled, which is how poor boys say *yes, with terms.* He pointed with his chin at a shack that had been taught to pretend to be a shop. Inside, barrels, sacks, a woman with a knife at her belt that meant business and a saint's picture hung by a nail that meant spite.

Clara put coin on the barrel and asked for bark and salt and the lie that is called sugar when you need a man to get up who wishes to be down. The woman took coin and added a flask of lamp oil without looking like it was charity. "You smell like the wrong story," she said to Séverine's face, and nodded at the way the nun's mouth had learned to be smaller. "Don't die in my doorway. It blocks trade."

"We will die elsewhere," Séverine promised, gracious.

Outside, wind shifted—the exquisite, heart-stopping shiver from west to east that means a broad water is breathing. The Negro's breath, honest as a slap. Manaus by smell. East beyond that with its iron sugar, its sea and its diseases. Men and ships and letters.

"Tomorrow," Tamsin said.

"Tonight," Artemis said, because numbers had put the word in her mouth. "He sleeps with steam up. He will be here at the hour when men think God owes them a gentle watch." She looked at the billet stack: dry heartwood in lengths a steamer could eat. She looked at the shack: oil, rags, matches. She looked at the boy with grease and salt wrist. She took the coin out of Baptiste's work—a coin that had been promised to other doors in other cities—and set it in the boy's palm.

"We owe you a mess," she said. "And a story."

He closed his hand without ceremony—as if men had given him that before and they had all been bastards. He nodded once. He began to carry billets—three at a time because boys love proving their bones—toward a place where a boat could feed without witnesses.

"Artemis," Clara said, gentle and grim and tenderly: *don't make yourself new sins.*

"I will make us distance," Artemis said. "It spends the same."

Night found them under black wing, powder thin as good lies, oil in a rag that did not belong to any saint. The whistle spoke again, closer. The river carried it like gossip. Tamsin took the rag, set a small polite fire where billets would feed better hot than cold, nodded to the boy to leave, and did not run. A minute. Two. Heat taught the stack to be news. Flame made theater for men who wanted to be distracted into pride.

They slid the *montaria* into a seam the spoon had had the courtesy to keep for them and let the river write the next line in its own handwriting.

The steamer came high and pleased, paddles clapping. Men shouted the things men shout to impress engines; engines listened to no one but heat. Then a small bright rose in the night where wood lay and became a tongue and then a mouth and then a fact. Men at the rail laughed because other men's fires are pretty. Then someone realized that pretty burns. Orders. Buckets. The emissary, impeccable, leaning on his third cane with a look that said *what an inconvenience,* and *how human.* The steamer slowed to feed itself. The river disagreed with slow.

"Go," Tamsin breathed, though they were already moving. Séverine lifted the salt horn like a ciborium and traced a cross on the gourd without asking whether God got a vote. Clara watched the fire show grow into an alibi.

Artemis counted. Not to control, only to make her bones decide which way was forward. One—two—three—four—five—six—seven.

The *montaria* kissed the Negro's breath and laughed like a woman who has left a man with all his pride and none of his answers.

Chapter 23 — Where Black Marries Brown

"At a confluence, the wise steer for the seam; names wash off there."

The Negro's breath came cool, thumbed across their cheeks, and brought with it a smell like wet iron and old tea. Ahead, the world divided itself into two honest colors: on the left, coffee with milk; on the right, ink. They ran side by side and refused to mix, two strangers walking the same road with their shoulders almost touching and a hatred polite enough to be physics.

"Keep to the line," Tamsin said from the bow, voice low, trousers plastered to her thighs, pistol a vertebra in her back. "Here. Where the world can't decide what it is."

Artemis felt Éloise's spoon tap her sternum once— *count*—and obeyed not because she needed permission but because ritual makes the hands agree to live. One— two—three—four—five—six—seven. The bowl turned—neither ink nor coffee—right down the knife-edge seam where the waters argued in whispers and the surface went wrinkled as an old woman's palm.

Behind, the steamer's whistle bragged. Smoke muscled the sky. Brass winked. The emissary's hatless head held its neat disdain; his new serpent cane gleamed like a lie freshly polished.

"Let him try the seam," Séverine murmured. Her tongue-tip had mended enough to make R's behave like obedient sinners. "Engines assume truth. Seams aren't."

The *montaria* skimmed the border, the hull half on black, half on brown; the boat trembled but agreed. The steamer turned to cut them off and entered the marriage at the wrong angle. The right paddle bit warm mud; the left clawed cold glass. The wheelhouse bell rang its complaint; the hull yawed with the gracelessness only iron can achieve.

"Good boy," Tamsin told the river, and the river pretended not to preen.

They slid past the mouth of the black water into a corridor of stilt houses and warehouses nailed to faith. Manaus—still shabby enough to be charming, already arrogant enough to be expensive—unrolled itself: wharf posts furred with barnacles; rope; boys with salt wrists; women selling limes; a priest making a cross that looked like an apology; a painted sign whose snake looped a chalice like a joke understood by too many.

"Eyes," Clara warned, looking small and terrible as a god in a poor parish. She carried the gourd under a patch of canvas as if it were a quarrel that could not be postponed. The bells around its neck behaved; the hair lay like dead things when nobody asks them to dance.

They tied up where Teófilo had taught them to tie the first time: a mud lip under a warehouse with a crooked crucifix. The *montaria* sighed against the post like a tired animal. Artemis slung the gourd into a rag-and-rope sling Tamsin had made and felt it drink heat through her shirt. Baptiste's coin burned her sternum. The spoon tapped once and went silent, as if impressed by the seam.

The harbor's voices braided themselves into a single rope: men, dogs, fish, the shop-bell's thin dignity, the whistle's arrogant throat. They kept to shade. They kept to being nobody.

"Powder. Rope. Lies," Tamsin said, counting their needs like rosary beads.

"Passage east," Séverine added. "And a place to put our backs while men with letters remember our names wrong."

The woman with coffee eyes who'd warned them before stood under a green awning slicing limes with a blade that could shave grief. She saw the four of them and arranged her face into good manners instead of surprise. "I told you not to sleep by the fish market," she said without preamble. "You slept somewhere worse."

"We paid for the lesson," Tamsin said. "We'd like to rent another."

The woman sniffed, considered the sky, the steamer, the set of the men's hats, the way Artemis carried weight. Then she whistled a boy out of a crate shadow: salt wrist, three fingers missing from an old accident, eyes that knew where the pockets were and which ones were empty. "Costa," she said. "Saint of rats. Take the ladies to Capitaine Olavo, who sells space under salt fish for people who choose to become jokes. If any man asks, they are matrons from Beruri on pilgrimage to the saint who lives inside barrels."

Costa grinned without showing teeth—respect. "This way," he said, and threaded them through a seam of city narrower than any river: past a stack of billets cut and stacked like little coffins; past a woman beating laundry from a barrel while her baby chewed sugarcane and contemplated rebellion; past a brass plate with a name—**Companhia do Alto Amazonas**—that pretended to be destiny and was only a company.

The steamer's whistle flattered itself again. In the slice of sky between roofs, the stack blurred black; the paddle beat; men with money leaned on rail and made their faces into judgments.

"Quick," Clara said, and Costa made quick happen.

Capitaine Olavo's kingdom was a shed with ideas above its station: tar barrels, salt crates, half a mast for repairs, a lamp whose soot had stories. Olavo himself had the look of a man who'd been paid in teeth too many times; he wore a neckerchief and a frown and nothing like conscience. He took Tamsin in with one blink and Artemis with the next, saw the gourd-shaped fact under canvas, and did not let his eyes show greed. That earned him the chance to negotiate.

"Downriver," he said. "Belém. Two days from now on the *Flor do Pará* if the boiler keeps its vows. I can put you under salt high and dry, and you can pretend to be barrels. The captain will not count. He barely can. I will."

"Price," Tamsin said.

Olavo named a number that would steal a saint's ring finger. Tamsin named a number that would shame a thief. He laughed; she did not. They met in the middle of the river where both could drown. He added another price—silence tax—and Tamsin added a kindness tax— three men carried under with them who didn't have coin but had lungs that deserved air. He shrugged, as if generosity were a stain he couldn't get out of his shirt, and agreed.

"Tonight," he said. "After the last light. The *Flor* loads rubber and lies. Bring none of the second if you can help it."

Clara had been listening like a midwife. "We need a room," she said. "High. Quiet. With a basin. And a door that doesn't open for men with hats."

"Old Carmo," the lime woman said, appearing with appropriation that looked like magic and was only women. "The sisters take sailors with knife work. They'll take nuns that bleed by choice."

Séverine touched her lower lip with two fingers in acknowledgement and made a smile that hurt to look at. "I only need water and heat and space to lay salt."

"Then you need a kitchen," the lime woman said. "Come."

The Carmo had fallen out of fashion with God and men both and survived on pity and garlic. The nun at the door took one look at Séverine's veil, Clara's hands, Tamsin's trousers, and Artemis's problem, and made the sign of the cross with an exhausted sincerity that made Artemis like her. "Up," she said. "Third gallery. No men. God will wait downstairs."

They climbed past saints who had learned to keep their eyes to themselves. In the little cell the sister gave them, Clara unwrapped the gourd and set it on a folded blanket. It sat like a heart outraged to be outside its chest. The little brass bells had found a religion of silence. The hair had stiffened again, as if remembering its job and offering to do it without complaint. The blind Queen of Cups glared through wax like a woman who has forgiven nothing and sees no reason to start.

"Open?" the not-voice offered, sweet as the first bad idea.

"No," Artemis said, gentler than she felt, and pushed cloth around the thing like a mother who knows the child will cry anyway.

Séverine boiled water. Salt hissed in it like gossip. She rinsed her mouth, winced, pressed lips together thin as linen, and said, when she could: "We owe hair already. We paid. We owe more later. We will not pay with tongues again if we can help it."

"Speak for yourself," Tamsin said, and tied a spare kerchief around Séverine's jaw in an insultingly tender knot. "I'd shave my mouth clean if it made this thing shut up."

"It won't," Clara said. "It wants what it wants. It will want it until someone wiser than money tells it otherwise." She rolled her sleeves. "Now. We change our smell."

"What?"

"Barrels," Clara said, and opened a jar Olavo's boy Costa had fetched from the fish market with magisterial glee. The burst of rot that emerged from it had a color; it staggered the saints on the walls. "If a man with silver brings dogs, dogs will salute this and leave us to our own sins."

Tamsin swore delightedly. "Marry me."

Clara raised one eyebrow. "I don't husband women with pockets for bullets."

"Shame."

They worked until the light cut itself thin. Fish oil on canvas. Salt rubbed into hair. A smear of brine under each eye where the smell will sit and baffle. Séverine drew a circle with her salt horn in an old sailor's sign on the floorboards where the blanket lay, then another outside it, then a third across them both. "If this door wants to be used, it can open for the river between dusk and dawn," she said. "Not for men."

The harbor below went into evening grammar: clink, curse, dog, bell. The steamer's whistle came stubborn and pleased; the paddle slopped an arrogance into the Negro. Artemis went to the gallery rail and saw the emissary's boat slide past the Carmo's low wall, neat as a receipt. He stood with his hand on the serpent cane, mouth a line, ear bandaged from Tamsin's opinion. His eyes ticked once over the convent's roof, quietly amused that poverty kept secrets too. He told his men, with a nod, to search elsewhere for now. He wasn't worried. Money hires tomorrows.

"Tonight," Tamsin said behind her shoulder.

"Tonight," Artemis agreed.

They slept like women who have chores after midnight. When Costa rattled a pebble against the gallery post, the city had gone quiet enough for a heron to sound like a crime. They lifted the gourd. It hummed once in protest like a child woken and forgave them because they were decisive.

At the shed, Olavo had made the *Flor do Pará* into an animal with its mouth open. Men's shadows moved like spelling mistakes along the rail; a foreman counted under his breath and got more wrong the more he cared. Rubber smoked in black loaves on one side; salt fish went into the hold in a long, complaining river; a barrel rolled wrong and took a boy's shin skin with it; he swore, was blessed, and kept working.

"Here," Olavo said, not looking at the shape under Artemis's canvas. He pointed to a row of casks with their bellies already full of stink. He pried the head off one with a lover's care. Salt and oil breathed out; under them, clean boards had been laid like a small lie. "Down. Then I put the lid back and you say nothing until we smell Belém. If you fart, fart modestly."

Tamsin laughed once and then got serious. "Jonah would have enjoyed this," she said quietly.

"He would have ruined it," Clara said.

They went into the barrel world: dark, close, blessedly specific. Fish lied about everything. The gourd lay between Artemis and Clara like the third person in a marriage. Séverine pressed her hand once to Artemis's wrist and then withdrew it because some comforts make things worse.

Boarded. Lids. The world became wood and the slow drum of men's labor. Nails bit. Ropes sang. The smell took their noses hostage and negotiated for their souls. The deck above became law and the bilge below became hymn. They breathed with discipline.

Footsteps. The particular neat step of authority.

"Open that one," a voice like clean coin said.

"Salt fish, senhor," Olavo answered with abusive respect. "Your men will smell like saints if they go poking."

"They smell like sin already," the emissary said. Under the wood, Artemis felt the shape of his mouth in her bones: the way men make smiles that don't include eyes. He tapped a cane lightly on staves. The barrel answered like a drum in a mean church. "Open it."

Pry. Light leapt in a bright wound. A crowbar scraped the rim. A lid came free. Light blanked her eyes; salt ate her breath. Tamsin's shoulder touched hers in the dark and didn't quite press. A face appeared above—Olavo's, upside down, grin professional. "You like my saints?" he said to someone who wasn't looking. He dipped two fingers to the wrist and flicked brine; it spattered and ran. "See? All holiness. All day."

The emissary peered into someone else's barrel—thank all fish—and recoiled with aristocratic offense. "Close that. And wash your hands before you touch any other property I may have to purchase."

Lids went down. Hammers found their old lovers. Artemis let her jaw go slack and counted backwards until the pulse in her ear stopped making itself into the engines of boats sent to do murder.

They made the *Flor* in the second hour of the night, when men prefer to be asleep and are not allowed. The hold took them into itself with the indifference of a belly. Above, the whistle blew for the pleasure of it; ropes slapped; a bell rang as if absolution were being sold cheaper for the evening crowd.

"Gates," Séverine breathed against Artemis's hair. "All we do is pass them."

"Then pass faster," Tamsin breathed back, and someone—Clara, of course—hushed them without wasting tenderness.

The *Flor* moved with a sigh. Planks took up a new story. The hull shifted from **I will** to **I am**. Outside, men on the emissary's boat swore in three languages at once: the river had laid a raft of drift across their nose with a timing even money cannot buy.

Under barrels, the four of them held hands because there are sacraments older than churches. The blackwater slipped away; the brown took them; the Negro and Solimões turned their backs politely, and the Amazon learned their names without admitting it.

It wasn't over.

Midnight and a little, the floor became a drum under someone else's heel. He had the step of a man who thinks he owns all rooms he enters. The pry of iron. The scream of nails. Lids up. Light. A face: not Olavo's. A soldier with a uniform that had learned to look clean

even when wrong. Behind him, the emissary's ear
bandage neat enough to be an insult.

"Contraband," the soldier announced, as if inventory
had been his mother. He shoved his rifle's muzzle into
the space under their lids with an intimacy that felt like
prayer spoken into the wrong ear. "Show me what sins
you carry."

Olavo sighed as if men had paid him to be patient.
"Fish," he said. "Which is to say, the dead made useful,
Your Excellency."

Tamsin's hand found Artemis's. Artemis found the
spoon with her thumb and put it between her teeth, the
way a woman rides out a pain and refuses to curse the
wrong god. One—two—three—four—five—six—
seven. She could not use it for anything but holding.
She used it to pretend her mouth could change the angle
of guns.

Clara did not waste numbers. She used stink and
theater.

She coughed once, small. Then she made the cough into
a sermon—deep, wet, patient. She put her fingers in the
jar of pig's blood she had smuggled in a cloth twist and
dabbed two neat spots high on her cheeks where fever
makes saints. She rolled her eyes just enough to remind
men of the last time they'd seen yellow go through a
camp and take names down. She groaned the word that
gets doors shut in a hundred ports: "Vómito."

The soldier flinched so sharply he almost shot the floor.
He stepped back. The emissary didn't; he watched,
pleased in the way a man is when the world behaves as

predicted. "Cholera," he said, regretful as a clerk. "Or the other one that makes your tongue black. Either way, put the lid down."

Olavo, professional, slammed the lid. Hammers. Nails. Hammer. The soldier's boots retreated because men who enforce laws have mothers who told them not to bring certain things home. The emissary stayed one more heartbeat—long enough to let the cane tap once on the head of Artemis's barrel, a love-tap from a man who will come to the house next week with flowers and a priest—and then left.

The *Flor* gathered herself and ran beside the brown water's sure shoulder. Above, the lamplight on deck did its exhausted moth-dance. Inside, four women lay with their hands still touching and let the numbers move in their mouths without making sounds.

Dawn under salt comes as a smell before it admits light. Fish went from obscene to ordinary. Boards warmed around their shoulders. The boat found a rhythm that said **downriver** and kept it. When Olavo pried them out two hours after sun, the world's colors had decided to be day again and Manaus lay behind like a story you tell about someone else.

"Change," he said, and threw down two shirts out of kindness or habit. "You smell like saints and I need the hold to smell like commerce. The deck's yours for ten minutes. After that you are barrels again."

They emerged like a birth that wanted to be quiet and failed. Wind. Sky. The banks going by with their shoulder bones showing. A pair of pink dolphins rose and rolled, blunt-headed and happy as mistakes forgiven. Tamsin laughed outright; it made the deck decide to like her.

Clara stood with her hands on the rail and let wind burn the last of pig's blood off her cheeks. Séverine put her fingers to her mouth and discovered the cut had gone from wound to order: her consonants would behave, her prayers might limp, she would still make both. Artemis put a hand to the canvas-wrapped gourd and felt it lying there like a fact the future would not argue out of.

"East," Tamsin said.

"East," Artemis agreed.

Olavo came to stand at the rail beside them with the air of a man who dislikes being thanked and intends to avoid it by charging extra later. He looked downriver, squinted, and spat into the seam where current changed its mind. "Your gentleman will hire a faster tomorrow," he said conversationally. "Money buys speed, not luck. If you want more of the second than the first, talk to Dona Estefânia in Belém. She runs cargo that sometimes includes trouble. She likes women who make it interesting."

"We make everything interesting," Tamsin said, and grinned with all the teeth she was prepared to risk.

Artemis watched the river widen until even grief looked small on it. She put the spoon away because her mouth didn't need the bit anymore to remember what not to say. She counted anyway. One—Artemis. Two—Tamsin. Three—Clara. Four—Séverine.

Four.

For now.

Behind them, far upriver, a whistle learned to be patient. Ahead, the Amazon flattened into a road too wide to own.

That evening, the sky put all its cheap jewelry on and then took it off one piece at a time. Tamsin counted cartridges. Clara mended a shirt she would bleed into later. Séverine salted a little cross at the bow and another beside Artemis's elbow where the gourd sat and made no demands until it did. Artemis stood at the rail and watched the black of night meet the brown of river and choose not to mix.

"Open," the not-voice breathed, a suggestion in honey.

"No," she said, firmly, with all the patience of a woman who will not be hurried into a ruin. "Not until I call your name."

The bells slept. The hair lay. The gourd rode out the evening like a secret someone had paid too much to keep.

They went east.

"Ports promise absolution; they deliver witnesses."

Belém rose out of the brown with a mouth full of knives. Piers like teeth. Warehouses with shutters for eyelids. A market that smelled of sweet rot and brine and the money men make by naming decay *trade*. The fort squinted downriver with old European suspicion; a white church bared its chalk to sun and pretended it had never bargained for rubber or souls.

The *Flor do Pará* found her berth with the weary entitlement of things that push water for a living. Lines went across; curses followed; a boy leaped and almost missed and was not allowed to. Olavo cracked his back and his knuckles and his conscience in the same motion and pried their barrel open.

"Up," he grunted. "Breathe like you intend to do it tomorrow as well."

They came into day salted to disguise and aching from being furniture. Wind put a hand on their faces and decided to be friend. Below the rail in brown and glare, pink dolphins turned like jokes and made even Tamsin's tight mouth soften.

"Smoke downriver," Olavo said, chin. "Company boats. Your gentleman buys everything that floats except the reasons not to."

"Then we buy reasons," Tamsin said. "Women's currency."

He had given them a name before: **Dona Estefânia**, who moved cargo and scandal and preferred both salted. Costa—salt wrist, three fingers missing—met them at the gangway with the heroic seriousness boys wear when employed. He threaded them through Belém's seams: past *Ver-o-Peso* market where fish lay like wheel-ruts in ice; past baskets of açaí like bruises; past a chain of boats unloading rubber that looked like black lungs; under a balcony where a woman with a fan watched them with the professional melancholy of those who sell hope and keep their own.

Estefânia kept court in a warehouse that had learned to smell like pepper and law. She was small, immaculate, and amused; her hair was pinned with a silver thorn. Men on her floor labored with the suspicious devotion of debtors who had been treated fairly and could not forgive it. She did not look surprised by four women in trousers with a problem wrapped in canvas; surprise is for the poor.

"Ladies," she said, and meant *gentlemen.* "You smell like saints and lies. I like one and detest the other. Which is which depends on the hour."

"Passage," Tamsin said. "Tonight if not faster. East along the coast, then north, then west to the Gulf. Or a ship to Cayenne and a chain of worse decisions."

Estefânia's mouth did a math. "A *charrua* to Cayenne by way of Salinas and Macapá, the captain a fool, the owner a thief, the cook sentimental. Or a brig out of São Luis bound for Havana that will sell deck space and regret nothing. Which would you rather be, smuggled or illegal?"

"We are already both," Séverine said, tongue mended enough to keep the salt on her words. "We prefer not to be dead."

"Dead is a document I can usually forge," Estefânia said, and smiled like the knife in her hair. Her gaze dropped once to the awkward canvas package that never left Artemis's side. She did not ask. "The brig leaves at moonrise from the outer mole. The captain will not wait for saints. If you are not there, his conscience will be clear by morning. He sharpens it nightly like a knife."

"Price," Tamsin said.

"Two men's passage and two barrels of salt," Estefânia said, "and the promise you will never bring this kind of weather through my doors again."

"Done," Tamsin said before the river could argue.

"The gentleman in the steamer?" Estefânia continued, almost bored. "He will hire the *Guarda Nacional* to search, then conclude that bribes go farther than oaths. He will look for men who smell like powder and women who smell like fear. Make yourselves smell like neither."

"We smell like fish," Clara said. "It's a start."

"Good," Estefânia said. "Costa will guide you to the mole at dusk. Before then, it would be polite to disappear."

She made them disappear with the efficient magic of women who own their neighborhood. A back gallery. A wash basin. A sack of cassava so their stomachs would choose to live. A little lamp whose light made spies waste time and the honest prefer darkness.

"Sleep in shifts," Clara said. Her voice had learned command in a bad school. "I need a pot and oil and a scrap of cloth that is not blasphemy."

"You will waste it," Estefânia warned. "I forgive you in advance." She left them a twist of lamp oil thick as sin.

Clara oiled the gourd's rope-sling, checked knots, rewound the canvas that made a lie of its shape, and put her hand flat against it as if daring it to hum. The hair binding lay quiet. The tiny bells pretended to be brass carved on a saint's reliquary and not made to ring. The not-voice in Artemis's head—the honeyed one that lives where numbers cannot light their candles—offered its polite obscenity. *Open.*

"No," Artemis said, out loud because secrecy makes some things real. She put Éloise's spoon between her teeth and chewed patience while her bones learned not to listen.

They slept in turns. Séverine prayed without noises; salt made its beetle-click; Tamsin counted cartridges like small sins; Clara made knots in string the way surgeons think about veins when their hands are idle. The hour before dusk brought the lighthouse's breath and men who had been paid to erect a law; it brought also the steamer's whistle—new coal, new arrogance.

"Now," Costa hissed, an alley boy turned saint by need. He led them through scent and tin and gossip. Past a line of conscripts loaded with sabers and confusion.

Past a priest who blessed nobody and expected a tip. Past a stall where a woman sold sugar-sour *taperebá* juice and insulted every man who took it. Down to the mole: stone slabs, tide chewing the edges, a brig riding low and restless with cargo men will die to protect and captains sell for half-price if the right face smiles.

The brig's name was a joke—*Santa Dolores*—because there is no saint for sorrow; sorrow works without intercession. Her captain had a coat and a sharp profile and a habit of tasting the air with his teeth. He looked at four women with a canvas baby and Estefânia's boy hovering and named a price that took marriage into account. Tamsin narrowed it into something money could bear without later violence; he liked her for it and did not show it.

"Deck space," he said. "Under the longboat. If rain comes, you will be rain. If men fight, you will be deck. We will put you off at Havana and you will be somebody else's problem. If you die on my ship, I will owe no man more coin than the cost of a sheet."

"Bless you," Tamsin said solemnly and meant the opposite.

"Bring the thing," he said, not asking what it was because secrets cost extra. He turned to shout at an officer in a dialect of Portuguese learned in courts and whorehouses both. Lines creaked. The tide set its jaw. The sky stood with its arms folded, waiting to see which way the argument would go.

They were three steps from the gangway when the emissary arrived with the law.

He did not run. He did not shout. The *Guarda Nacional* fanned around him like a thought they were ashamed to think. He raised the serpent-headed cane he had found to replace the one Artemis had given to river and pointed it lazily at the brig as if choosing a pastry.

"Contraband inspection," the officer announced, as if the request had come from God's neat handwriting. "All holds. All persons. Ord—" He didn't finish. Séverine's elbow found his ribs precisely where old bruises keep their coats; his breath negotiated with itself.

The emissary's eyes found Artemis the way accountants find familiar debt. "Señora," he said, pleased to be where the air smelled like sails instead of insects. "You are in luck. The ocean is larger than the jungle. The drowning is cleaner. Give me my employer's property and take your friends' lives as change."

He had learned the city. A sergeant peeled right to cut off the dock's back stair. Two men moved to the gangway. A third started up the brig's ladder to tell the captain who owned his soul now. The tide bit at stone and laughed. Something under the gourd moved the wrong way in Artemis's hands. *Open* it said, sweet as poison, and tried a little flex as if to help.

"Not yours," Artemis said, and wrapped both arms around the canvas like an ugly infant hungry for law.

"We need mess," Tamsin said, almost conversational. "And witnesses who prefer seeing to doing."

Clara delivered both in one act.

She stepped into the officer's space with a cloth twist in her hand, a surgeon's neatness in her jaw, and all of her contempt gathered like hair. "Sir," she said, perfect Portuguese—for once—and let the twist fall. Pig's blood splashed his boots and the stone, bright, convincing, patient. Then she coughed into her elbow once—wet, charitable—and put two fingers to her temple as if to steady a fever. "*Vómito*," she said, the Belém word for the bad plague; she curled her tongue over it so the accent belonged to sailors. "My sister just died in the Carmo. We came for air."

Men do not fear God. Men fear filth. The sergeant recoiled as if she had put a live coal down his collar. The enlisted men recoiled double. Two-blue uniforms put hands to mouths in an exact mirror of two women on a different river remembering a boy. The emissary did not flinch. He had learned to keep his face when his boots stepped in muck. His cane tapped once on stone, thinking.

Tamsin slid on the beat. Up the gangway, narrow, casual, a girl accustomed to giving orders to men who only realize later that a woman is not supposed to do that. "Captain!" she called, bright. "Inspection for filth, not for sins. We'd like to leave before virtue gets contagious."

The captain of the *Santa Dolores* had a strong dislike of virtue. He had a stronger dislike of official boots on his deck. He lifted one arm and waved; lines snugged; men at the capstan looked hopeful. He wanted to be persuaded to sail; the world had just consented.

The emissary put two fingers up and the law reconsidered its appetite. The sergeant moved right, then left, then found the only direction men with orders can stomach: forward. He came for Clara. She waited. Violence was going to be a fact; she preferred to choose where it would sit.

Séverine moved between them with her jaw bound in the will Tamsin had tied. "No," she said to the sergeant. Just *no*—a mother word that frightens even men who have none. He hesitated out of old habit. In the breath that opened, Costa shoved a barrel off a hand-cart with all the idiotic strength of boys; it rolled—oh, blessed gravity—and caught the sergeant on the shin. He hopped, cursed, and forgot to be an idea.

The emissary stopped being amused.

He lifted his pistol as if taking up a pen and wrote a small, neat line in the air. The shot cracked off the water and made a gull change its politics. A nun in the Carmo's high gallery flinched far away. Séverine took the ball low in the side.

It wasn't theatrical. No scream. A sound as tidy as the bullet that made it. She folded like a woman kneeling to pull a boy out from under a table and sat down on the stones hard enough to jar her teeth. Red ran under her in a very clean hurry.

"No," Clara informed the world, and went to her on knees that had never learned to consult anyone. Her hands were on the wound before blood could do what it loves. Tourniquet—skirt, cinch; plug—cloth, salt, pressure. Séverine's breath came obediently through the pain. She looked at Artemis and grinned with her eyes because her mouth was busy.

"Go," she said, as if dismissing children from a pew. "I will be late. Tell God I am coming; I do not rush for men."

The emissary re-primed with aristocratic economy. The second shot was for the canvas in Artemis's arms. He did not mind breaking the thing he wanted; men with money trust glue.

Tamsin's bullet met his out of courtesy. She had saved that cartridge for a tyrant; she spent it with interest. His pistol jumped; his hat fell; the cane clattered and made a little silver cry. The second ball struck the brig's gangway stanchion, splintered, went somewhere no one is keeping accounts for.

"Move!" Tamsin barked, her voice the color of London brick after rain. Artemis ran because obedience to that voice is its own liturgy. Up the ladder, canvas to ribs, spoon biting her teeth, coin burning her throat like honesty. On the deck, men swore loud theology and let lines fly because the captain had made a sign under his breath that meant *we are leaving without explaining why.*

Clara did not move. She spared her hands for Séverine's blood and her mouth for lying to those hands about how much time they had. "Hold," she told the wound. "Hold, you bastard. I'm not done with you."

"Clara," Séverine said, gently, as if chiding a student. "Don't be impolite. Say goodbye."

Clara shook her head once. "I have two hands and salt. I don't say goodbye with half a kit."

"Then I say it," Séverine breathed. She reached up, wet, and gripped Clara's wrist with a strength that is only given to women who have decided they are done with asking permission. "You cannot keep me. Keep her. Keep numbers. Keep your own tongue. Don't give the world more than it will pay for."

The captain's whistle cut the air. A deckhand bucked the stern line free and shoved with his boot in the same motion. The *Santa Dolores* took the tide like a thief takes an unwatched purse. The ship moved. The dock did not. The distance that kills friendships opened like a mouth.

Tamsin leaned over the rail, pistol in the curve of her spine, two hands on the canvas rope that made the gangway a last chance. "Clara!" she shouted, a word like a nail. "Now!"

Clara looked at Séverine and did the only courtesy left. She kissed the nun's forehead, put a grain of salt on her tongue-tip as if anointing a child, and tore the tourniquet free so blood would not argue with decks long. She stood up and ran with her face little and clean.

The emissary fired at her back in tidy malice. The ball made a familiar sound and did unfamiliar things around mercy. It cut the knot on the longboat tackle with mechanical piety. The boat swung out and down and caught Clara along the shoulders and spun her into the air. She hit the gangway with both palms and one foot and the canvas that held the gourd skidded toward the gap out of inclination, not malice.

Artemis dropped to her knees and got both hands on the package—and on Clara, who could be convinced to live only if grabbed and insulted. Tamsin's grip came over both. Men on deck swore in Portuguese and God and hauled because hauling is men's one reliable sacrament. The ship bent its back. The gangway bit rope and did not break.

They got Clara over the rail with as much grace as a sack of flour. She lay with her cheek to deck and breathed like someone who had just remembered there will be tomorrow. Blood stamped both her shins where wood had voted; her hands were raw coins.

On the mole, Séverine sat in an enlarging sermon on stone and smiled toward the Carmo because she had always liked good houses. She put two fingers to the braid she wore inside her sleeve—black, black, white— and tied it around her own wrist with the last strength given to women who have decided to finish well. The emissary watched her like a man considering whether to swat a fly or let it prove a point. He did not shoot again. One of the *Guarda* knelt beside her because some men remember how to kneel even in the wrong uniform. She said something small and rude in French, laughed once, and then paid the due that closes books.

The *Santa Dolores* turned her shoulder to Belém and showed the city her rude stern. The river took the brig and forgave it for every future sin. Men on the mole shouted that the law was offended. The law shouted back that men were offended. The emissary did neither. He removed his hat with impeccable economy, as if at an acquaintance's funeral, and put it back on again to do business.

Clara crawled to the rail and made a noise the color of rope. "I'll go back," she said, like a woman having a bad idea on purpose. "I'll swim."

"You'll drown," Tamsin said, not cruel. "She told you not to."

Clara put her hand on Artemis's knee and squeezed hard enough to make the coin at Artemis's throat feel like a lie. "Keep her," Clara said, meaning Séverine, meaning a thing that could not be kept. "Then keep this." She slapped the gourd lightly, as a doctor slaps a child's bottom to make it breathe. "Make it hurt somebody worth hurting."

The not-voice in Artemis's skull acquiesced as only hunger acquiesces. *Open,* it offered, sweet as a badly intentioned lullaby.

"No," Artemis said, and the *no* was a brick she placed in a wall she intended to live behind.

They crowded under the longboat amid the smell of tar and ropes and men who hadn't been told girls don't belong here. The captain came, looked like an accountant discovering a ledger full of poetry, and rolled his eyes until heaven counted. "If anyone asks," he told them, "you are ballast."

"Bless you," Tamsin said, again meaning the opposite and making it an affection.

Night turned Belém into a collection of lamps in a story you tell yourself to keep from remembering the knives. The fort blinked; the church sulked; the market folded into itself like a tired animal. The steamer's whistle sounded one last impolite paragraph upriver. The tide said it had other appointments.

Under the longboat, the four became three. Numbers make their own grammar. Artemis counted and found only three and then counted again to be sure grief hadn't miscounted for her. One—herself. Two—Tamsin. Three—Clara. Séverine lay in the ledger where rivers keep the names of people who have paid exactly what they owed.

Clara put her forehead to the plank and prayed with her mouth open and no words. Tamsin sat with her back to the gourd as if daring it to try anything. Artemis wrapped both hands in the sling and felt the bells under the canvas think about ringing and decide not to.

"East to São Luís," the captain said to the night, to the wind, to his crew, to the simple math of tide. "Then north. Then Cuba, if the saints will sell us weather cheap."

"And after Cuba," Tamsin murmured, for Artemis alone, "home."

"Home," Artemis said, and let the word be a door with a hard hinge.

The river widened until it was a rumor of sea. Air changed; salt grew an edge. A small storm walked along the horizon the way a woman of sense walks a bad street—swiftly, with a knife in her palm. The *Santa Dolores* leaned into it like a soldier and spoke in the creaks and groans and small humilities of a thing that prefers obedience to glory.

In her skull, the honeyed not-voice learned patience from grief.

Open, it said, very softly, as if practicing being harmless.

"No," Artemis said again, and for the first time did not have to count to make the word stay.

Near midnight, a flying fish misjudged distance and slapped Clara's shin with a wet apology and died of it. She laughed—a short, obscene little miracle of sound— and shared the fish raw with Tamsin like girls who are making bad decisions because the good ones are gone for the day. Salt on their tongues tasted like wages.

Ahead, the Atlantic was a door you could not mistake. Behind, the emissary counted his money and bought another tomorrow. On the mole a nun's blood had dried in the shape of a salt mark. Costa would step around it and remember where stories change direction. Estefânia would balance her ledgers, write a note, and be owed by the future.

Under the longboat, Artemis laid her cheek to the canvas and whispered, not to the gourd, not to any god that rented rooms on earth, but to the number that had not abandoned her.

"Three," she said. "For now."

The brig found the seam where river stops pretending to be land and made a choice. So did they.

Chapter 25 — The Mouth that Eats Ships

"If you must wake a god, name what you will let it take."

The river widened until it forgot the word for knees.
Salt came into the breath; the water's color thinned; the
sky turned iron where it meant to be generous. The
Santa Dolores leaned into a swell like a soldier dying
politely. Ropes spoke; spars answered. Under the
longboat, Artemis, Tamsin, and Clara held their small
kingdom of tar and fish-stink and will.

By noon, the Atlantic had taught the brig its manners.
The Gulf took over the lesson—warmer, slyer, full of
old lies. Tamsin sat with her back to the canvas-
wrapped gourd, trousers salted stiff, jaw a hinged insult.
Clara bound her bruised shins, checked her hands for
bones that might have been persuaded to wander, tied a
fresh knot in her own hair and scowled at the horizon as
if daring it to invent new physics. Artemis felt Éloise's
spoon a steady throb against her sternum, the coin at
her throat a small round *still here.*

The wind, by late afternoon, began to write long-armed
sentences. The captain sniffed and scaled his voice to
bigger weather. "Dirty," he said, to no one and ropes.
"We'll run before her."

Behind them, toward the east, a coal-smudge fattened
into cloud. A steamer's whistle bragged once, too far to
be manners. The emissary had bought his tomorrow,
and it had come with a new hull and a better appetite.
The *Santa Dolores*'s mate peered through a speaking-
trumpet, swore a sea oath, and spat starboard.
"Sidewheel," he said. "Low in water. Nose like a lie.
Cuban paint. Spanish crew."

"Of course," Tamsin said, and took her pistol apart with love. "Men who can't row buy engines. Men who can't pray buy saints."

Clara watched the horizon where two weathers were negotiating a treaty. "We cannot outrun both," she said. "Not the storm and the man."

"Then we marry them," Tamsin replied, eyes bright. "Introduce them at the worst party of their lives."

Wind agreed with that plan with an untidy shove. The brig's nose went down, came up with dignity; spray bit. The captain shortened sail a point, then two, then reconsidered and put the second reef in with the care of a man signing his own name on a document that can hang him later. The *Santa Dolores* began to run—a little less stubborn, a little more humble.

The steamer came on low and cocky, paddleboards slapping. On her bow the emissary stood spare as a ledger-line, hatless, ear bandaged neat from Tamsin's previous opinion, a fourth serpent cane between his shoes like a supplicant. He didn't shout. He had men for that. Rifles made long thin threats that wind shredded into gossip.

The first shot skated across the brig's waterline and kicked a fish into air. The second took a splinter off the quarter-rail and made the captain call the saint whose name he did not believe in.

"Under," he ordered them as if he feared he'd learned their names. "And tie your hands to something that can pay for you."

They went under the longboat because that was their
church. Wood around; salt in the mouth; the gourd
between Artemis's knees like a question no priest
would answer. The honeyed not-voice was patient now.
It had learned her pronoun. *Open, Artemis. It will be
easy. You are tired. You deserve it.*

"No," she said, pleasant as contempt.

The Gulf inhaled once and revealed how much air the
world can misplace. The sky cracked itself end-to-end,
white on iron. The lash of rain came sideways, thick,
unruly. In that white moment Artemis saw the
steamer's nose slice toward starboard to cut the brig off
and drive her into shoals only men who own charts
dare, and she knew the emissary would use the storm
the way he used pistols: neat, impersonal, efficient.

"Captain!" Tamsin bawled from under wood, as if the
deck and the rain were only two more girls to flirt with.
"Bear south into the teeth. Let him take the lee. Make
him choose in water he doesn't pay."

The captain was not a complete fool. He loved his hull
greedily. He spun the wheel half a spoke, then another.
The *Santa Dolores* yawed, rode a slope, shouldered a
wave. The steamer corrected with arrogance—engines
teach that. His port wheel bit foam; his starboard
clawed brown. The bruise of the storm rolled forward
and set both boats in its mouth.

"Artemis," Clara said, without looking at her. "If you
call that thing, name what you will not give. Order it
like a dog. You must never whisper to it. You must tell
it the grammar of the room."

"I have been telling it *no* since the forest," Artemis answered. "It has manners now. It can keep them."

The Gulf laughed hard and hit the brig sideways. Spars yelled. A sea tore free, ran along the deck like a horse let out in a church, and threw all sins into one pile. A man went with it—rope, hat, curse—all at once. The gourd lifted against Artemis's hands hard enough to numb bone. *Open,* the not-voice crooned. *You are drowning by inches. It will be simple. Seven is a door.*

"I won't pay you with my tongue, nor my friends," Artemis said—polite, exact. "I will name you this: a mirror. I will give you only what I point to."

"Then point," Tamsin said, wild grin flecked with salt. "Point at him."

The steamer crossed astern into the worst neighborhood of water. A breaker rose, forgot to be polite, and fell on the paddle as if paying off an old grudge. The wheel dove; the hull juddered. On the bow the emissary stood steady by force of disallowing physics. He looked across water and met Artemis's eyes exactly for the first time since the Ituxí. His mouth did not move. His gaze said: *Do it. Show me your bad idea.*

Clara's hand closed over Artemis's wrist like a cuff. "If the room wants blood," she said, matter-of-fact, "it can have mine. It has had enough of my work for free."

"No," Artemis said, too quickly, because grief had taught her to be stingy with all nouns that might be taken. "I will not trade you to it."

"You don't get to choose," Clara said, gentle. "We are already spent."

Another sea hit. Men who had been born in water spat theirs out and tried to decide between rope and love. The brig's longboat canted over their heads like a bad thought. Through the gap in tar and deck seam, a slice of horizon showed the steamer's stern climbing a hill of water it had no business on. Pistols cracked—pointless in rain. Lightning turned men into drawings of themselves.

"Artemis," Tamsin said, quieter than all the noise. "Make the numbers do their work. We didn't come this far to be eaten by weather that's bad at poetry."

Artemis salted the tin cup because ritual is the thing that will lift your hand when your will is water. One— two—three—four—five—six—seven. The spoon tapped at each number like a gallery of small hammers. She took the gourd in both hands, felt the hair bindings flex as if remembering a lover, and pressed her mouth to the blind Queen's paper eye.

"Listen," she told the thing. "You will open only where I name. You will bite only who I bless. You will take nothing from my house. You will not drink my people. You will not take our tongues. You will be a mirror and a mouth only for him."

She looked up through the slit of deck and storm and found the emissary again—still, poised, a man who believes the invoice will always arrive at the other party's address. "Take *him,*" she said to the gourd. "Take only him and whatever stoops to shield him."

It laughed in her hands. Not a sound; a *feel* like teeth choosing bread. The tiny bells along its neck thought about ringing and then behaved. The hair bindings lifted, one, two, three, like lashes after sleep. Artemis set the spoon along the seam in the wax, counted again because seven is a habit, and turned the knife just a little—Éloise's bone lent to violence.

The gourd opened.

It did not split like fruit; it sighed like a lock asked a password. A seam that had been tar gave up its history and let air have a taste. What came out first was old salt and women's combs. What came next had no smell and too much weight. The air around her skin dented. The deck above crooked its back. The world felt for a second like a bowl under a thumb.

On the steamer, the sea forgot the lecturer's lesson and remembered the auntie's. The water under the bow made a mouth and widened it. A hand whose fingers were river-teeth and women's ropes reached up and took hold of the hull where the paint lies about wood. The paddle dug at air. The sea said no.

The emissary did a new thing: he widened his eyes. He felt the ship stop in a way ships do not when engines make noise. He looked down and finally saw something that cost him insolence. The water around the bow thickened into hair-dark, salt-oil, green-chip glitter. A braid stretched from wave to keel and tightened with the gentle brutality of old women tying a knot over a child, saying *we do this so you do not run into the street again.*

"Christ," one of his men breathed, and made the sign wrong with the wrong hand on the wrong shoulder.

The emissary's cane met deck with a clack that belonged to floors. He raised his pistol to point—at Artemis, at the gourd, at the house of the world. Tamsin fired first. The ball didn't reach him. It hit the silver serpent's mouth again, out of stubbornness and poetry, and took the hinge. The head spun away into rain; the cane became a stick; the emissary remained a man reduced in his own hand.

"Take only him," Artemis told the gourd again, because doors like clear instructions. "You have no permission to learn another name today."

It obeyed with a relief that made her teeth hurt. The water made a throat. The throat made a sentence. A hand made of all the hair ever cut at an altar rose and closed around the emissary's calves tidy as a mother adjusting a boy's socks. He shot at it out of principle and scarred rain. The hand pulled.

He slipped. His hat went. His neat ear bandage peeled off like a lie. He went to his knees and then to honesty. Men reached for him—not love; pay. The water took their wrists and rearranged their minds about charity. He had time to look at Artemis once more over a ridge of water that had decided to stop being decorum and become teeth.

"You'll drown where money keeps," Tamsin called cheerfully over thunder, because she is a woman who does not permit the world to have the last joke.

He did not beg. He turned his face toward the sky like a saint discovering that canonization is not a thing you can buy. The hand pulled him off the bow quiet as thieving. He went into the mouth the water had made and did not trouble anyone ever again.

The steamer shuddered as if someone had leaned too hard on a table with a dead man under it. The paddle turned once, almost sadly. The men aboard made sounds that did not belong to hierarchies. The hull, relieved of the particular gravity of one man's intention, went where wood wants to go when nobody lectures it—sideways, down, wrong. She did not sink. She lay rocking with her shoulder dislocated, the storm patting her on the head with savage concern.

The gourd closed itself because Artemis lacked the hands to do it. The seam sealed with a little hiss like oil poured on iron. The bells went decorous. The hair lay. The not-voice stopped being honey and became silence that could be respected. Artemis lay with it against her ribs and shook once in all her bones as if a hand had been inside and had had to come out quickly.

The storm, deprived of spectacle, went about its work like any honest destroyer. The *Santa Dolores* rode it like a sinner who has received an indulgence he didn't trust. Men swore and spat and hauled. The captain took the wheel with both hands and muttered a promise to a woman he hadn't seen in ten years. Tamsin laughed like a woman who has kept a secret just long enough to enjoy telling it later.

Clara fell sideways and did not get up.

Not a dramatist's fall. Not the theater. A quiet failing of what had been too long employed: ribs bruised from the longboat, shins bitten by rope and gangway, a line of blood hidden under the wet that had kept time with her pulse too many hours and fallen out of step now. Artemis rolled to her in one crawl and put hands where Clara had taught her to put hands. The warmth was still there. The depth had decided to go somewhere it liked better.

"No," Artemis said, and learned again that the word is not a spell; it is only a word.

Clara smiled with one corner of her mouth—the one she used for jokes she intended as instructions. "You did it," she said. Her voice was a thread that did not insist on being rope. "You taught a door to behave."

"I wanted to keep you," Artemis said, messy, which would have offended Clara's surgical soul any other day.

"You kept the world," Clara answered. "That's a worse habit. Break it carefully." She put two fingertips to Artemis's throat, found the coin, pressed it until it hurt. "Spend this instead of me."

"I won't—"

"You will," Clara said, workaday and ruthless. "Because there is a woman with chalk under her nails and another behind her with a ledger and a third with a baby and a fourth with a knife and a fifth with a song. They don't need me. They need the girl who can tell gods *no* and men *not you* and not take *yes* for an answer." Her breath sawed once, twice. "Promise to burn what keeps them hungry."

"I promise," Artemis said, and will spend the rest of her life paying interest on that sentence.

Clara's hand slid off the coin as if it had been taken that one measure. She closed her eyes as if to get a better angle on resting. Tamsin's palm found the top of her head because that is how sailors say goodbye when they have no shores to bury you on. The storm wrote their grief down in slant lines and smudged it immediately like a kind, clumsy teacher.

They gave Clara to the Gulf at dusk in a lull that could be called ceremony if you were generous. Salt on brow. A strip of her kerchief tied to the longboat's thwart because wood loves old friends. No priest. Séverine would have been offended and proud. The dolphins came near and rolled and didn't make jokes; even happy animals can read a room. The gourd lay under canvas and did not ask to help. It had done enough.

By dawn the sea had scrubbed the sky white and made habit of breathing again. The *Santa Dolores* came up out of weather with most of her pride and all of her bad habits. The steamer had drifted off north-west toward slower water and men who would try to explain the shape of their fear to one another without using the word *hair*.

"Where to?" the captain asked, cap pulled hard over a haircut that never meets a comb. He didn't say *Havana,* though that was the arrangement. He had seen the way the tide toys with bargains.

"North-west," Tamsin said. "Catch the Loop, then west-by-north to the Mississippi delta, then upriver pretending we have regular sins."

"Customs?" the captain asked, wrinkling a decent nose at the idea of officers.

"Dead friends," Tamsin said. "They wave us through."

Artemis stood at the rail, the coin hot against new bruise, the spoon quiet as a kept promise, the gourd's weight a child she had not asked for and would not give away. The smell of wetlands came in paragraphs shorter than ocean: rot and grass and blackbird, oil of crushed things that make other things live. The Gulf turned brown under the keel's shadow; pelicans wrote their lazy holy letters across air.

Barataria gave them her ugly friendliness: bayous like faults in a drunk's story, the smell of men hiding and men hunting, cypress knees crowding up like small congregations. A pirogue slid by with two boys and a woman in it, the woman's mouth set to *don't,* the boys' eyes set to *yes.* Tamsin tipped two fingers. The woman did not tip back. Girls who live in swamps do not acknowledge ghosts, even polite ones.

They took the outer mouth because pilots are expensive and the captain liked his money. It cost them nothing—this time—except a scrape along a bar that made everyone on deck curse their mothers creatively and then forgive them. The delta opened like a hand: passes, bays, secrets. The *Santa Dolores* picked one and claimed it. The river took them back like a dog who will not admit it was looking for you after all.

By the second noon they smelled New Orleans: sugar and rot and God and music and sex and a little gunpowder. Masts shoulder to shoulder; steamboats pushing their weight around like men at a table; roofs sulking under weather; bells learning to be honest when it doesn't pay. Tamsin's shoulders dropped half an inch as if the city had put her coat on for her. Artemis felt her heart fling itself forward and be caught in a strange net—home, but with debts.

They tied up where men like their rope neat. The captain touched his hat brim as if it were a sentence he was proud of writing. "You got off cheap," he said, not unkind. "Try to make the next thing expensive to someone else."

"We will," Tamsin said, sincerity for once not a stranger in her mouth.

They carried the gourd through a city that pretends to be a story and is. Past the French Market where knives and onions are one poem. Past a drummer with his hand on skin and the other on his own need. Past a boy selling milk-water as lemonade and giggling like a conspiracy. Past Madame Léonie's quiet house where the courtyard had been swept and the dead had been spoken to pleasantly as if someone hoped to sell them something.

Léonie was waiting because women like her arrange rooms that way. White dress, chalk on fingers, eyes like water that has decided to keep the thing it reflects. Behind her, in the cool shadow, a woman who had never introduced herself sat and did not smile; her ledger was open but her mouth was not. The braid in

Artemis's oilskin twitched like a dog recognizing a door.

"You brought it," Léonie said, neither delighted nor surprised. "And it brought you back."

"You didn't say the price," Artemis replied.

"You would not have understood it until you spent it," Léonie said, without malice.

"Then say it now," Artemis said, because exhaustion makes honesty feel like hydration.

"You will open it where I ask, when I ask," Léonie answered. "And you will not open it for anyone else first."

"Wrong," Artemis said. Tamsin's hand was warm at her elbow; the city pricked up all its illegal ears. "I will open it for no one but the people the river owes. If you are among them, you'll have your drink. If not, you can go to market with the men who sell histories by the yard." She set the canvas on the table where Léonie had once set cups for weather and laid her palm on it as if it were a feverish child. "This is not your dog. It's a door. Doors open both ways. I name them now. Me and mine."

Léonie regarded her long enough to teach patience a little. "Your tongue has grown," she said mildly. "You paid."

"We all did," Tamsin said. "We canceled a man's account on the Gulf and stamped it paid in teeth."

Léonie's mouth curled one degree. "Good." She reached for the sheet as if to check a recipe. Artemis's hand met hers and didn't move. After a breath, Léonie removed her hand without loss of dignity and without humor. "You have questions you think are answers," she said. "Keep them. I have bread and names for the dead. Come back when you have weather." She tipped her chin toward the other woman, the one with a ledger for a face. "This is Dona Celestine. She keeps me honest. Say hello to the woman who will be your ash, if you don't learn to be your own."

"I plan to burn the right things," Artemis said.

"Then begin with your fear," Celestine said, voice like a match you haven't struck yet. "It burns quick and gives little smoke. After that, bring me a list."

Artemis gathered up the gourd. The bells did not ring. The hair lay. The Queen's blind face was not improved by travel.

On the way out, they passed a boy with a broom whose lip was split and watching the world with the precise courage of poverty. Artemis handed him a coin. It burned her palm and did not burn his. "For sweeping the weather where we can walk through it," she said. He nodded, as if that made sense.

In the doorway, the heat announced itself like a man who owes money. A trumpet two streets over put its mouth to the world and taught it to move again. Tamsin bumped Artemis's shoulder like a friend in a church. "Home," she said.

"Until it isn't," Artemis answered. She lifted the gourd a little in her arms, not to make it lighter but to make herself equal to it. "We have something to do."

"What," Tamsin asked, practical.

"Burn the right house," Artemis said. "Let the wrong doors be ash. Open the others. And make a list for Celestine that keeps poorer women alive next summer."

"And the man with no name now in the Gulf?" Tamsin asked, cheerful cruelty a habit that seasons grief.

"The Gulf keeps what it asks for," Artemis said. "I won't argue with a competent god."

They crossed the courtyard. The oak kept its manners. Somewhere, sisters of Carmo counted their dead and laughed anyway. The river slid by pretending not to watch. The city was theirs, on the condition they were willing to be scorched.

Artemis counted—not because she needed it to open a door, but because numbers are hands to hold when the floor is not obeying. One—herself. Two—Tamsin.

Two.

For now.

Epilogue — Ash & Renewal

"To rebuild, you must learn the use of fire and mercy at the same time."

Summer came, wearing yellow fever like a mask men kept pretending wasn't theirs. The city's breath shortened. The river widened her skirts and showed a little ankle to see if anyone remembered how to be charming.

Artemis worked. With Celestine's ledgers and Léonie's chalk—when Léonie allowed it—and Tamsin's dangerous smile at doors that wanted to be locked, the map of women's survival redrew itself. Salt caches under floorboards where poor hands could find them. Water boiled not when the priest said so but when the numbers did. A list posted at the market under the name of Saint Nobody: which houses to fear, which to enter, who would take a child with a cough without asking her mother for coin she did not have.

At night, in a courtyard salted and chalked so nothing uninvited learned why, Artemis set the gourd under a cloth and asked it nothing. Sometimes it answered anyway, like a friend with bad timing. *Open,* it would purl in her head between one breath and the next. *Open here. Open them.* She pressed her mouth to the Queen's blind eye and told it the weather. She told it *not yet* with the confidence of women who keep time while men keep ledgers.

Once, in late August, a steamer from Havana slipped into the bend below St. Peter. Men in neat coats came ashore with good boots and better knives. They asked for a woman who carried a little drum. They asked for a girl with a coin at her throat and a tongue more expensive than it should be. They asked politely, which is terrifying. The river, that day, rose half an inch, as if shrugging. When they left, they did not have all their hats.

Tamsin took to the levee at evening with the pistol she never admitted to owning and a habit of lighting a match, blowing it out, and smelling the sulfur as if learning its biography. "Ash," she said to Artemis, watching smoke remember it had once been wood. "Then what."

"Renewal," Artemis answered. "We are older women now. We get to choose what grows back through the cracks."

On a Sunday when drums courted the bones and rain behaved as if it had manners, Artemis carried the gourd to a house nobody claimed anymore—a brick ruin cooked hollow by last year's fire. The roof was a mouth. The floor was gone where rats had studied architecture. The chimney stood like a boast a man had forgotten to take home.

She drew a circle with salt. Another. A third. She laid the Queen of Cups on her knee and rubbed the wax until the face softened and felt like paper again. She put the spoon on her tongue and tasted Éloise's kitchen, which was a better liturgy than any incense. She said, not in numbers but in the sentence Clara had bought from her at the cost of being mortal: "I will burn what keeps women hungry."

The gourd was polite. It did not open. It let her set her cheek against it and breathe out once in gratitude.

On the way home she saw a girl with a red kerchief tied around her wrist, kitchen salt in her apron, a ledger of her own under her arm—a list of doors that could be opened without paying in bone. Old Carmo's bell rang thin out of the low sky. Artemis stopped under the Spanish moss and said Clara's name the way a doorframe remembers the first hand that touched it.

"Next," she told the city. "Next."

The river pressed her shoulder like a mother who has learned not to say *be careful* to daughters who have seen oceans.

Ash & Renewal had begun.

Printed in Dunstable, United Kingdom

67204556R00201